The Dotari Salvation

Terran Strike Marines Book 1

Richard Fox & Scott Moon

Copyright © 2018 Richard Fox
All rights reserved.
ISBN: 1985306263
ISBN-13: 978-1985306264

To my great grandmother, Emma Garrison, who always encouraged me to do something creative.
&
To Nathan James Fox, welcome to the world!

Chapter 1

Lieutenant Hoffman felt sweat run off his forehead and down the side of his face. Even with his body glove's coolant systems running at full power, the oppressive heat of New Bastion was worse than anything he'd felt in the hottest Phoenix summers or during survival training in the Australian outback.

He wafted air out of the rough cloth robes that the Shadoor aliens preferred to wear outdoors, wishing he could don the full helmet that would bring some respite from the environment once it locked into the rest of his suit, but he couldn't give the half-dozen screens bolted to the quick-crete walls of his hideout his full attention within the constricted view of the Shadoor-style helmet.

On one screen, Gunney King sat inside the cab of a delivery truck, his visor slid up onto his helmet, his face set and focused. The other screens showed Hoffman different angles on their target's location—a fenced-in building bordered by dirt streets filled with cloaked and hooded Shadoor working through the midday market.

A clock on the bottom of a screen flipped over to a new hour.

"Mobile, this is post," Hoffman said, his words picked up by his throat mic and shot out through infrared transmitters he and his team had hidden throughout this part of the city. "No activity."

"Mobile, acknowledged." King's hand touched a bulge on his chest where the Marine's gauss pistol was holstered, and he leaned forward and looked out of the alleyway where his truck idled.

The cab rocked slightly and a muffled cry carried from the sealed cargo pod. King shook his head as a sharp thump punctuated the air.

"Another one of the damn things got loose, Gunney," Corporal Garrison said over the IR system linking Hoffman's team.

"They're harmless, wuss," said Booker, the team's medic. *"And every time you kill a silverfish, it wrecks our cover as a silverfish delivery service. You know that, right?"*

"I swear you're letting them out on purpose. Do we even know if they're poisonous to humans? I do not want to go into anaphylactic shock—again—because someone forgot to do a gene screen against—"

Gunney King slammed an elbow against the back of the cab and the bickering ceased.

"Duke, what's your status?" Hoffman asked into the open line.

A screen showing the view through the scope of the team's sniper bobbed up and down. Duke's vantage point nearly ten stories up from within an unfinished building gave Hoffman's stomach fits, especially when New Bastion's winds sent a hot gust through the bare beams and struts.

In the distance, the wall surrounding the quarter formed a gentle arc. The crystal dome that would eventually cover the entire city stretched up from the top of the wall—but only a few hundred yards of the many miles it would have to cover to contain a more pleasant atmosphere and mitigate the heat and radiation pouring in from the system's twin suns. In the two weeks since Hoffman and his Strike Marine team had infiltrated the city, no progress had been made to the dome.

"It's a dry heat, sir," Duke said. *"Kind of wish I*

was on the hunt for whatever genius decided this was the place for the galaxy's spacefaring civilizations to work out their differences. It's like they picked a planet that everyone would agree to hate. Even those tardigrade-looking Orritans seem miserable, and their home world's hotter than this. Wasn't the old Bastion on a space station?"

"It will be again, once the committee works out the specifics of the new design. This will be, of course, a decision from the same committee that picked this planet and is in charge of building twenty-five different environmental domes for all the embassies," Hoffman said. "Temporary embassies."

"And I thought the bureaucrats on Earth were inept," King said. *"By the looks of things around here, I'm sure every race has their top men on that project. Top men."*

"From what I got from the Embassy Marines," Hoffman said, "every race with access to the Crucible gates realized if they didn't work out someplace to cooperate soon after the Ember War ended, there'd be a fight for every habitable planet out there. This shake-and-bake city was a quick answer. They did negotiate the Hale Treaty here."

"Embassy Marines," Garrison said. *"Bet they've*

got air-conditioning. Wonder if they'll accept a transfer…Ow! Why'd you kick me? What about my mic? Oh, is it—"

On his screen, Gunney King gripped his steering wheel so hard Hoffman worried he'd break it off.

"Got an air car coming in from the south," Duke said as a vid capture from his scope popped up in the center of the screens. The taper-nosed vessel flew on four repulsor lifts, and lights glinted off the silver exterior as it banked suddenly toward the target location, its engines ruffling the cloth roofs of the market stalls.

Icons for small laser guided missiles resting in Duke's sniper's perch came online and pulsed amber, ready to launch and home in on whatever target Duke had in his sights.

Hoffman's heart pounded in his chest and he swallowed hard.

"All stations stand by," he said. "Should be our guy."

King knocked twice against the back of the cab and eased the delivery truck forward onto the dirt road.

On the main screen, doors burst open from the building inside the compound and a pair of broad-shouldered Kroar aliens came out, both holding spiked mauls in their scaly hands. Their broad, flat reptilian heads hung low over their shoulders, and tufts of ochre-colored hair crept out from the edges of their loose sleeves and the collars on their leather coats that stretched down to their bare feet.

"These two are new," Duke said. *"Scale patterns don't match the other Kroar we've seen patrolling the perimeter."*

"Target's trusted bodyguard," Hoffman said. "Fits with the dossier intelligence gave us."

"Secret squirrels finally got something right?" Duke chuckled. "Will wonders never cease? I've got a clean shot on the door, sir…"

"Hold fire. Your rail rifle will set off every security sensor in the quarter and we'll get locked down in a heartbeat," Hoffman said.

"Moving into position," King said as he made liberal use of his truck's horn to hurry along a pair Shadoor idling in the middle of the road.

On the screen, a new alien emerged from the compound. Taller than the Kroar with midnight-black skin and gangly limbs, bony spikes ran down his forearms and jutted from either elbow. The Haesh wore a rebreather over his face, and a tube ran from it to a pair of air tanks on one hip.

Hoffman zoomed in and fed screen captures to the computer core beneath the desk. The computer analyzed the alien's biometric features and came back with a match to a series of photographs of the same alien taken in the rubble of a blasted cityscape.

"Got him," Hoffman said. "Fellerin, the Butcher of Galveston. Mobile, you have release authority."

King's response was lost as the air car rumbled over his truck and landed just outside the gates.

A Kroar bodyguard stepped between King's truck and the air car and pointed his club at King, then slowly waved the weapon toward the Shadoor walking along on the street. It didn't take much in the way of xeno communication skills to recognize "Stay back."

"Garrison, Booker, exit left side," King said as he made a Shadoor hand gesture toward the Kroar, indicating exactly what the bodyguard could do with his club.

The back door of the truck swung open with a clang and the Marines jumped out.

Hoffman mouthed a prayer as the two walked past the cab, carrying a wire cage between them inside of which metallic insects the size of the palm of his hand scrambled over each other. The silverfish grew more agitated as the wind blew smoke from a barbeque cooking insects over hot coals toward King's truck. A Shadoor rapped an empty skewer against his food stand and waved to the Marines.

Helmetless Shadoors tossed coins into a bowl on the cook's stand and gestured to the approaching cage. With their bright-red skin and yellow eyes, Hoffman could understand why the Marine embassy guards called the Shadoor "demons."

"Remember, everyone, act natural," Hoffman said.

"We look enough like the locals with the masks," Garrison said. *"Just don't talk to them."*

"Like you're doing now," Booker chided.

"Sir, we've got a complication," Duke said.

Hoffman snapped his gaze to the screen showing the compound. A Kroar came out of the center building leading a human woman, her blond hair a jumbled mess, her hands bound with silver wire. She wore a beat-up naval flight suit and was limping slightly.

Fellerin stopped at the gate and waited as the Kroar guard urged the woman forward with a blow to her shoulder.

Hoffman froze. Their mission brief said nothing about prisoners, human or otherwise. His entire plan, weeks of scouting and preparation, just fell through the floor.

"Continue mission," King said, a firm statement and not a suggestion. "No guarantee she'll get in the air car with the target."

"Stalling," Booker said, setting down her side of the silverfish cage and rubbing her carrying arm.

Hoffman froze, his mind dancing between options like someone falling out of a tree and grasping for branches on the way down.

"I want…Gunney, I need you to…" Hoffman pounded a fist against his desk in frustration.

"Eighteen thousand dead colonists on Galveston deserve justice." King drew his gauss pistol from beneath his robe and held it against the dash out of view of the Kroar guards. "I can take him as soon as he steps out of the compound."

"No! Mobile, deploy the limpet," Hoffman said.

Just as the compound gate rattled aside, Garrison "tripped" over his own two feet, sending the silverfish cage tumbling forward into the dirty street and the top bursting open. Silverfish scattered across the dusty street, veering away from the barbeque where their fellows were crisped into snacks.

Shadoor lurched into the street, grabbing at the loose creatures along with Garrison and Booker. Several silverfish broke for the shade beneath the waiting air car. The Kroar guards shouted in their own language and made exaggerated swings to keep the crowd away.

"Come on, come on," Hoffman said.

One Shadoor grabbed a slower silverfish and struggled to pick it up. The alien's head cocked to the side in confusion as he tested the heft on the creature.

Booker shoulder-checked the alien and sent him sprawling into the dirt. The silverfish he held bounced toward the air car, then skittered under the passenger compartment. An icon flashed on Hoffman's screens as the limpet mine he and his team had disguised as a silverfish magnetically locked itself to their target's vehicle.

Their plan called for the denethrite explosive charge to blow the Butcher of Galveston into hard-to-identify chunks once he took off. Hoffman picked up a detonator and rested his thumb against the trigger.

"Charge set," the lieutenant said. "Go for phase two."

Booker and Garrison picked up the broken cage and pushed their way through the scrum of aliens vying for a free lunch as the Shadoor cook waved his arms in the air, shouting over the ruckus. Hoffman had picked up a few words of the alien language since arriving on New Bastion and understood that the cook wasn't paying for this delivery.

"Civilian just got pushed into the target's vehicle," Duke said.

"Let me take him out, sir," King said, one hand on his door handle.

"Wait, the car might be for just the—" Hoffman cursed and looked at the main screen just in time to see Fellerin and two of his bodyguards climb into the air car.

King cursed and slammed a fist against his dashboard.

The air car rose in a billow of dust and slowly rose over the surrounding buildings.

Hoffman looked at the detonator in his hand and then back to his screens.

"Blow it, sir," King said. *"It took us months to track Fellerin down. Who knows where he'll go next. This could be our only shot!"*

"He has a prisoner, Gunney, a human prisoner," Hoffman said.

"You weren't there on Galveston, sir. I was. Do you know what he did to those colonists?"

"I know what he—" Hoffman shut his mouth when the air car turned toward the city's spaceport and accelerated. With one push of a button, he'd accomplish their mission...and murder another human being in the process.

"Duke, I need you to disable that air car," Hoffman said. "Get it on the ground. This is now a rescue mission."

"You want me to disable an air car...traveling eighty feet in the air at about thirty miles an hour that has a denethrite charge that'll probably explode if I hit the car with my rail rifle?" Duke asked.

"Can you do it or not?"

"Wait one, got an idea." Duke's scope feed angled up to the sky as the sniper moved away from the weapon.

Agonizing seconds ticked by, and a red icon flashed over Duke's position on Hoffman's map. One of Duke's laser-guided missiles zipped through the air toward the Haesh's air car.

"What're you doing? I told you to disable it, not—"

"Relax, sir. It's me. Besides, you ask for a miracle in thirty seconds or less, you shouldn't be choosy about how it's delivered. Now if I can just get it to..."

Hoffman looked on in dread as the missile closed on the air car. The missile icon disappeared, and he waited for the sound of a distant explosion to wash through his control room...but it didn't come. Instead, the air car veered to the side and descended.

"Ha! Smacked a seeker into a front repulsor engine. Like a bird getting sucked into a turbofan," Duke said. "Helps that I didn't pull the arming pin before launch. They're going down near the water treatment plant."

Hoffman panned the map to where Fellerin had gone down and double-tapped the roof of the plant to send a ping to his entire team. He then picked up a holstered gauss pistol and locked it onto his chest armor and ran for the door.

"Mobile, head for that location I just sent out. I'm taking Opal to the crash site," Hoffman said as he burst out of the room and took a staircase down two steps at a time.

"Max, can you read me?" Hoffman asked.

"Loud and clear," the last member of Hoffman's team said.

"We need an emergency extraction at the water plant. ETA?"

"Maybe…eight minutes. Just got a secure message from the embassy. Local first responders are spinning up. Guess that's us?"

"Correct. Pick Duke up first. Send the take-down order to the intelligence officer at the embassy if the police go airborne."

"I was just about to suggest that. Just another day in the Strike Marine Corps. See you soon."

Hoffman ran into the bottom floor of the incomplete building where another Marine stood against a wall next to the stairwell. The man was six and a half feet tall, broad-shouldered, and had hands the size of shovel blades. He wore the same Shadoor garb as the rest of the team, and his full-face helmet followed Hoffman as the lieutenant ran past him.

"Opal, follow me." Hoffman picked up a Shadoor helmet and slipped it over his head. Loosening a poncho tied to his shoulder, he let it flop over the gauss carbine locked onto his back, then vaulted through an empty window frame.

"All our stuff?" Opal asked, his voice low and gravelly.

"Doesn't matter!" Hoffman scanned the sky and saw a plume of smoke rising over buildings a few blocks away.

Hoffman ran toward the crash, Opal just behind him. The local Shadoor hurried indoors, and several watched as Hoffman and the other Marine—who was significantly larger than the aliens—went by. They came around a corner and found their target's air car canted atop a truck, smoke and sparks flowing from a damaged repulsor engine. The air car's roof had been bashed open. One Kroar bodyguard crawled out while the other stood nearby, club in hand, sneering and snapping at any Shadoor that loitered nearby.

Long black fingers curled over the edges of the bent roof as Fellerin emerged slowly from the air car. Bright-blue blood ran down a cut on the Haesh's forehead as he stepped onto the dirt street.

Hoffman bowed his head slightly and walked to the other side of the street, doing his best to appear like the other passersby that wanted nothing to do with the overly large and overly angry Kroar and their car trouble.

"Sir, bad one," Opal said as his mitt of a hand tapped Hoffman on the shoulder.

"Shh." Hoffman reached into his tunic and grasped the gauss pistol with his left hand, hiding the gesture from the Kroar with his body. The aliens were a massive, tough species, but a high-powered gauss bolt to the face would deal with them easily enough.

Hoffman pressed his thumb against the pistol's selector switch and a faint whine rose as it drew power into the capacitor. A few more steps and he'd have a clean shot at the target and both bodyguards.

Fellerin dropped onto his hands and knees, then cocked one oversized ear to the sky.

Hoffman felt a chill in his chest as the Butcher of Galveston looked straight at him.

"Damn it!" Hoffman drew the pistol and swung to face his target.

The blur of a thrown club flashed across Hoffman's vision and pain erupted in his hand as the spiked head struck his pistol and fingers, knocking the gun into the air.

The now unarmed Kroar lowered a shoulder and charged at Hoffman. Caught flat-footed, Hoffman realized he had his back against a wall and was about to be hit by a freight train made up of alien blood and bone.

"No hurt!" Opal tackled the charging Kroar and landed on top of him. The two rolled toward Hoffman and he jumped aside before they could steamroll him.

Hoffman, his hand throbbing, broken fingers refusing to bend, looked around for his pistol as Opal and the Kroar pounded on each other.

"Ee'di sha, kul!" Fellerin shouted, pointing at the Marine, and the other Kroar ran at him, club raised overhead with both hands.

Hoffman let off a war cry and charged forward. The Kroar slowed, evidently shocked that a smaller, weaker foe would have the guts to fight head to head. Hoffman jumped up and thrust his legs forward, kicking the alien in the chest with both heels. The blow barely rocked the bodyguard back and Hoffman landed in a puff of dirt.

The Kroar swung the club at the Marine's face. Hoffman rolled aside and felt the impact reverberate through the ground. The Kroar tugged at the club embedded in the dirt, then struck out at Hoffman again. Hoffman kept rolling until a massive hand grabbed him by the ankle.

The Kroar stomped a foot against Hoffman's chest and the alien leaned forward, squeezing the air out of Hoffman's lungs with his bulk. Saliva dripped from serrated teeth and onto Hoffman's visor.

"Dumb enough to be human," the Kroar said as he raised his club overhead.

Opal snatched the alien by the wrist. The Marine's helmet was gone, leaving his mottled skin exposed. Cuts and bruises marred the patches of brown, green, and black making up the surface of the bio-construct warrior's—the doughboy's—face.

"No. Hurt!" Opal wrenched the Kroar off Hoffman and drove a knee into the alien's side. He kicked the bodyguard to the ground, keeping a grip on the arm holding the club. Opal braced a foot against the alien's shoulder, then ripped its arm clean out of the socket with a wet pop. Opal tossed the limb aside and rained fists down on the still struggling Kroar's head.

"Opal…" Hoffman rolled onto his knees and elbows, trying to breathe through cracked ribs. "Opal…the other!"

The second bodyguard, his snout broken and one eye crushed, picked up his companion's club and cracked it against the back of Opal's head. The doughboy stumbled forward, one hand pressed against his skull.

A horn blared behind Hoffman, and King's truck rushed past him, missing him by inches and slamming into the club-armed Kroar, sending it under the wheels. The alien got caught in the axle and sent the truck out of control. It veered into a building and screeched to a halt, the windshield shattered and the front cab slightly compacted.

"Opal?" Hoffman reached out to the doughboy, who looked up at the lieutenant, pain writ across his face.

"Sorry, sir," Opal said.

Hoffman used Opal to haul himself up and saw Fellerin take off running.

"No! We can't let him—"

The snap of a high-powered gauss pistol shot echoed off the walls and Fellerin's chest exploded outward. His body pitched forward, carried by the momentum of a shot meant to pierce heavy armor, and slid to a stop, the Haesh's limbs spasming in death throws.

Hoffman looked over his shoulder. The blond woman stood a few yards away, the pistol braced in her hands. She spat in the dirt, then her head and the pistol snapped toward Hoffman.

"Wait—I'm human." Hoffman pulled his helmet off and tossed it away. "Terran Strike Marine Corps, we can…" He got to his feet and every injury screamed pain through his body. "We can get you out of here."

She stared at him with icy blue eyes, blood seeping down a gash on her temple. Her head shook from side to side.

"Cowards. Traitors!" she yelled before she turned and bolted.

Hoffman watched in disbelief as she ducked into an alleyway.

Garrison grabbed the lieutenant by the shoulders. "Sir, you all right?" He tapped his helmet. "Gunney's pinned against the wall. Not hurt too bad, but Booker can't get him out."

"Opal, go help." Hoffman looked up as the rumble of engines approached. A small Haesh shuttle swept overhead and hovered above the roof of a nearby building.

There was a groan of metal as Opal ripped open the truck's cab and wrenched the steering wheel off. He tossed it against the air car and pulled a struggling King out.

"Let go of me," King stammered. "I can walk just fine." He pushed away from Opal and stared at Fellerin's dead body.

"Rot in hell, you monster," King said.

"Team…let's get out of here." Hoffman winced as pain lanced through his chest. Garrison put Hoffman's good arm over his shoulders and helped him toward the waiting shuttle.

Chapter 2

Doctor Acorso walked through the deep shadow of a high-rise building as a green sun broke over the horizon. He adjusted his scarf against the biting air, wondering just how long this part of the Dotari Prime would lag through another cold spell.

The morning light glinted off soaring towers, casting small kaleidoscopes of color across the wide streets and frost-caked patches of grass growing in swirls within the sidewalks. Why the Dotari chose to incorporate so much detail into things that were mundane in his native Phoenix escaped Acorso's explanation. Asking any of the city's inhabitants now would be useless; over a thousand years had passed since the city was abandoned, preserved by the Xaros occupiers, then reoccupied by the Dotari after the Ember War's end.

The new residents had very little real connection to this city or the planet of their origin, a problem that vexed the doctor more the longer he was here. The Dotari that lived here were essentially squatters, long removed by a millennia spent in the stars traveling to a new world and scraping out an existence on Takeni. They'd reoccupied the city and the world like a poor family moving into a large estate willed to them by long forgotten relatives. .

What grated at the doctor more than anything was how empty the city was. The once bustling metropolis stretched for miles along the banks of a wide river flowing into the sea. Tens of millions had once lived here, but the Dotari had only a fraction of that to resettle the city and the rest of the planet.

Back on Earth, the capitol of Phoenix was alive with air cars and the constant hustle of the Terran Union's military and political complex in motion. While there were a few signs of life in the Dotari city—open stores, drones flitting about, a few aliens walking in the brisk air—the place felt like it was about to wake up…but just couldn't get out of bed.

Earth had an easier time repopulating, the doctor thought. *The Dotari are less and less each day.*

A pair of Dotari turned a corner and bowed their heads to him as they passed, the black quills on their heads rustling slightly in what passed for a Dotari salute. If one glanced at a Dotari quick enough, they could be mistaken for human. They were more slight of build and generally half a head shorter than most humans, but carried themselves with the same gait as most people. The loose quills in place of hair were thick as shoe laces on some, almost the size of dreadlocks on others. Their eyes and faces were nearly human, but the blunted beaks they had in place of nose, mouth and chin set them firmly apart from their human allies.

Acorso, his head of rapidly thinning hair covered in a black knit cap, nodded in reply to the pair of aliens.

He rarely saw anyone on his morning walk to the hospital as the few Dotari who lived in the city that once housed tens of millions preferred to stay far from the ill. After another few terribly cold minutes of walking, he arrived at his destination. The hospital's three tiers rested in a morning shadow, absent the sparkle the rest of the city enjoyed as a new day rose.

Black mesh incorporated into the fence around the hospital flapped against the chain links as a gust of wind assaulted the barrier. Sun-faded biohazard signs in English and Dotari swirls smacked against the metal wires in time with the wind as Acorso went to a gate.

"Mornings of good to you, Doctor," said a Dotari guard as he slid a partition aside and bowed his head as Acorso stepped through. "Please remove your outer garments and enter the containment shower."

"Hello, Vin'ci." The doctor followed the guard into a small room connected to the hospital by a plastic tunnel. Mercifully warm air washed over Acorso and he worked his hands together to bring back feeling in his fingers. "I've come here almost every day for the last six months. I am aware of the procedure."

Vin'ci let off a *tss-tss-tss* sound that constituted Dotari laughter as his beak clicked together.

"Every morning, the procedure is the same," Vin'ci said as he lifted a plastic bin onto a table.

"You missed your calling at the DMV, you know that?" Acorso shrugged off his jacket and tossed it into the bin with his gloves and scarf.

"I do not know this," the guard said. "I know that my wife made you candied *gar'udda* nuts to thank you for your hard work." He took a box wrapped in shiny paper and shook it quickly. Acorso's mouth watered as the gift rattled.

"I leave it here." The guard put it in the bin.

The doctor felt his stomach rumble. There was no way he could take the treat inside, not with the strict contamination protocols that he'd helped write.

"Thank you, Vin'ci, she is most kind." Acorso turned his head to the decontamination tank on the other side of the room and sighed. After thirty minutes of irradiation, sonic cleansing, and a shower in soap that stank of iodine, he could finally get to work.

"Your scrubs are inside, as always," Vin'ci said.

****

Acorso found his laboratory almost the way he left it. He set his tray of reconstituted food and a cup of steaming coffee on his desk and swiped his fingers over a screen, sending the latest batch of emails from Earth rolling down a holo projection. None of the sender names or subject lines caught his attention as being urgent.

He plopped into his chair and took a sip of the finest Kona coffee while he regarded the Dotari sleeping at her desk against the wall, her head buried in the crook of an arm, purring softly as she slept. She wore wide red strips of cloth, tightly wrapped around her body, which the aliens preferred as hospital garb.

Acorso tapped out a quick message and sent it.

The Dotari's workstation beeped and she popped awake with a snap of her beak, rubbing a hand against her eyes and blinking at Acorso.

"Doctor…you're here early." She picked up a data slate and tapped a finger against the screen several times.

"Are you here early, or did you stay late again, Bi'mal?" he asked.

"I was waiting for a gene sequence to come through…" Her eyes darted from side to side as she read. "The antihistamine trials from the lab in Gishara had a few variances I thought might…" Her hand gripped the slate hard and she slapped it against her desk, then shoved it away and crossed her arms over her chest.

"Who did we lose?"

"The hatchling in room fourteen," she said quietly. "He'd gone from phase two to three during evening rounds, then went into complete neural shutdown within hours. I would hate the phage less if only it would behave the same way in each patient. Instead, some suffer for years, others only days."

"Then let's do our rounds." He stood up and finished the last of his coffee. "See how the latest nano-regimen is working."

"Or not working." Bi'mal stood and straightened out her uniform. "No patient has made any improvements since your tiny machines started warring inside their bodies."

"But some of them stopped getting worse." Acorso picked up a large slate, slid an e-pen into his lab-coat pocket, and followed Bi'mal out into the hospital corridor where robots ran along the walls delivering food and fresh linen to all the rooms.

"The Dotari cannot survive like that," she said. "The nanos may stop the phage's progression in a few instances, but in the long-term, our immune systems will collapse completely if nanos interfere with our natural balance of—"

"You're going to end by saying the nanos are a treatment, not a cure," Acorso said.

"The Dotari once had the cure for the phage, one created in the laboratory of the interplay between the planet's ecology and our bodies." Her quills bristled slightly in anger. "Earlier generations did not suffer from this disease. We were in tune with the countless organisms and pollen that are all around us. Now, after so long traveling the void and living on Takeni, we return home and find that we are no longer suited to live here. You know there's talk of abandoning everything and returning to that wretched lump of rock and ice that you humans rescued us from? All that trouble to escape Takeni, fighting beside you on Earth, then resettling Dotari Prime just to give it all up…"

"The Dotari aren't quitters. I like that about you," Acorso said.

"But we may be overzealous fools. Every Dotari that's ever set foot on this world is at risk of their body going into system shock because we lack the immunity to our own environment. Did this ever happen on Earth?"

"It did. Native populations in the Americas suffered when explorers carrying measles and smallpox showed up to say hello. Those same explores didn't do well when it came time to deal with malaria."

"Tragic," she said.

"Tragedy implies there was no intention to spread the diseases, which wasn't always the case." Acorso looked over a data plate outside a room and pushed the door open with his hip. A spray of antiseptic mist washed over him.

Inside, a little Dotari girl sat on her hospital bed, clutching a teddy bear. She smiled at Acorso; the juvenile aliens didn't develop their beaks until just before puberty.

The alien children could almost pass for human, which made it harder to see them ill than Acorso liked to admit.

The girl's parents sat on a bench against the wall. Her mother wore black silk cuffs of morning; her father wore clothes that once fit a larger frame. Acorso suppressed a sigh. He'd hoped to visit this patient before her parents arrived; now he was in for another earful from her father, Lo'thar.

"Hello, Doctor." The girl held up the bear and swung it from side to side. "Look what Earth sent me! What is it?"

"Hello, Trin'a." Acorso flicked his right wrist to the side, then traced a circle around her face. Data fed into his data slate. "That is a teddy bear. We give them to all the sick boys and girls who are going to get better soon."

"Is it an animal?" She brought the doll's eye close to her own. "Perhaps I could have a real one as a pet once I go home. What do they eat?"

"Bears are not good pets. They eat…picnic baskets…and—squeeze my fingers, please," Acorso said, leveling a finger at her. She took one hand away from the stuffed animal, her fingers bent into a claw, and set her palm onto the human's finger. Icy-cold digits trembled against his skin as she tried to grip.

"It's hard," she whined.

Lo'thar leaned forward in his chair, his eyes wide.

"Look up. No peeking." Acorso held his data slate next to her feet, blocking her view, and squeezed a toe through the sheets. "Which foot am I touching?"

"You're not touching my feet, silly," she said.

Acorso looked at her father, then glanced at the door. He nodded quickly.

"Thank you, Trin'a," Acorso said. "Dr. Bi'mal will ask you a few questions? OK? I want to know what you named the bear when I come back, OK?"

"His name's Elias," she said. "Like from the story Papa tells me about Takeni."

"Elias…that's a good name. Excuse me." Acorso left the room and waited a moment for Lo'thar to join him.

Her father had the presence to wait for the door to close before blurting, "It's phase two, isn't it?"

"There are a few more clinical tests to run before we change the diagnosis—"

"You have to give her the latest generation of nanos that Earth sent us," Lo'thar said. "Just because her body rejected the last two regimens doesn't mean—"

"No." Acorso shook his head. "Her immune system would send her into shock fighting off another wave of nano-bots. That she's experiencing difficulty only with her extremities means she'll be in phase two for an extended period of time. The finest minds on Earth and Dotari are working on this problem, Lo'thar. You need to give it time."

"My daughter is dying, you pinky, soft-beaked…sorry." Lo'thar nuzzled his own shoulder.

"I've been called worse. We're doing everything we can."

"It is not enough!" Lo'thar's shout echoed down the hallway. "I've lost my brother-in-law and three flight mates from the war to the phage. All of them died waiting for you and your 'finest minds' to find an answer. What haven't you tried yet?"

"Lo'thar, your species lost their immunity to Dotari's ecosystem after your colony fleets left before the Xaros invasion. Trying to rebalance your bodies to the tens of thousands of microbes and viruses and everything else that's sending your autoimmune systems haywire is not something that can be done overnight."

"If only we could travel back in time to find Dotari with the right set of immunity and antibodies…" Lo'thar backed against the wall and sank onto his haunches. He crossed his arms over his knees and hung his head down.

"I delve in medicine, not fantasy," Acorso said. "Time travel isn't possible." He reached for Lo'thar but stopped short of touching him. The Dotari enjoyed close proximity to each other in social settings, but not while grieving.

Acorso went back into Trin'a's room.

Lo'thar wiped a tear against his sleeve, then looked up at a painting of the fleet that brought the Dotari colonists to Takeni. His head popped up as an idea struck him.

"We don't need to go back in time," he said. "We need Dotari *from* that time." Lo'thar pulled a cell phone from his pocket and made a call.

Chapter 3

Hoffman observed and cataloged details as he entered the office of Captain Bradford, noting pictures of him shaking hands with Colonel Hale and other heroes of the Ember War. Compared to the broom-closet workspaces he'd shared with his fellow lieutenants, the room threatened agoraphobia. Oak paneled walls, ten feet high if they were a foot, were covered with framed company guidons. The sight of fabric stretched tightly above brass plaques gleaming in the office light comforted Hoffman and helped him brace for what was coming. To the right of the standards were Bradford's graduation photos from the Academy, Force Recon, Strike Selection, and Basic School.

"Lieutenant Hoffman, reporting as ordered, sir," Hoffman said as he snapped a salute.

The captain remained behind his desk, working on

the controls to a large video screen. He didn't look up or return the salute for a painfully long time. When he did, it was perfunctory and clipped.

Hoffman remained at attention.

Hoffman's hand itched from the reconstructive surgery. Earth doctors were good, which was why they earned permanent assignments in Phoenix. He should feel grateful to be in one piece, but each time the itch flared up, he thought of the disaster at New Bastion and one important detail—his hesitation nearly got his team killed. Another item on the very long list of reasons why Hoffman stood before his company commander.

Bradford stood to face the video screen, chest heaving as he regained control of his breathing. Jaw clenched, he grunted each time the image of Hoffman appeared. Whoever filmed the New Bastion incident had flinched at the violence and screamed alien words Hoffman didn't know but thought he understood. Alien script bordered the edge of the screen, then cut to a Shadoor standing before a large screen who warbled words Hoffman didn't understand.

Hoffman suppressed the bile rising from his stomach. He hadn't been demoted yet. The company commander was a famous hard-ass—high-and-tight hair and perfectly bloused combat fatigues accenting his winged Strike Marine badge—but he hadn't killed anyone after a less-than-stellar performance. Yet.

Hoffman had been chewed out more than a few times. His father, so far as he recalled it, understood smoke and thunder to be more effective disciplinary tools than "please" and "thank you" and "let's work through your feelings." The Hoffman home had been…stern.

"Do you know how many members of the senior brass think I should rip your wings off and send you back to Fleet with that brute of yours?" Bradford asked.

Hoffman kept his eyes straight ahead. "Sir, the mission was a success."

"Your mission was to eliminate a single terrorist without showing the Terran government's hand in the operation, not carry out what looks like a cold-blooded murder in broad daylight. Do you know how close you came to causing a diplomatic shitstorm?"

Hoffman considered his options and chose silence.

Bradford slammed his hand on the desk, causing a half-full coffee cup to jump a quarter inch. "I've got military intelligence screaming for your head because they had to burn just about every asset we had on New Bastion to cover up the incident. Thankfully, the Shadoor can be bribed—and shamed—into compliance. That they let a known terrorist slip through their security is worse than a bunch of non-Shadoor bodies lying in the street."

Hoffman chewed the inside of his lip. This was to be a one-sided conversation until the captain intoned otherwise.

"What did I tell you to do if you didn't have a clean shot?"

"To abort, sir."

"And?"

Hoffman hesitated, unsure of the question.

"And what the hell happened?"

"The presence of a hostage altered the mission parameters."

Silence.

Hoffman saw a change in his C.O., an ominous clenching of his jaw. "You were rattled by the unexpected violence of the escape attempt, the local food, the color of the alien sky for all I care. Something made you think there was a human woman in danger."

"She was human, sir," Hoffman said with growing confidence. "Blonde hair, tattered naval flight suit…the Kroar had her hands bound with silver wire," Hoffman said, swallowing hard before his next question. "Sir, what I don't understand is why she didn't escape with us. Why the hell would she call me a traitor?"

"No, there was no woman."

"Sir, you have the statements from my team. She recovered my sidearm and took out the—"

"Officially, there was no woman in a naval flight suit. You didn't see her. She was never there."

"Sir?" Just when he thought he could ride out Bradford's tirade, he felt a cold stab of dread through his spine. "I don't understand."

"You don't have to. We all answer to someone, and when your after-action report went up the chain, I had a visit—civilian intelligence types and a full-bird army colonel. They said your report would be redacted, scrubbed from the archives and replaced with another, more acceptable version of events. They gave me no specifics, just your new report—already signed by you—and told me to follow the new script.

"You and your team will play along too. The mission is already black. If they breathe a word to anyone without clearance, I'll shit-can them anyway. Read your new report. Pass that to your team. Anyone ever says a word about the *maiden* in distress, they'll be peeling potatoes on Mars for the rest of their enlistments.

"Frankly, that's the only reason you're still in charge of your team and still a Strike Marine. Play along, and there will be no consequences from what happened on New Bastion. Decide to open your yap, you'll be thrown under the mother of all buses. Despite this, don't think I'll forget you had your first chance to shine and everything went wrong." Bradford shook his head and made a low sound of disappointment in his throat before continuing.

"New Bastion isn't exactly in our backyard. I have to trust you to make decisions in the field. Am I supposed to pop through the Crucible gate to check on you? Hold your hand? Wipe your…" Bradford exhaled theatrically. "How many of my other Strike Marine team leaders require this kind of maintenance? Don't answer that; it was rhetorical."

Hoffman's face burned. "I take full responsibility for what happened in New Bastion."

"Damn straight you do. The Strike Marines took a chance on you, Hoffman, you and that walking lump of muscle that's been following you around since the end of the war. You survive as an officer and a team leader by the skin of your teeth. Another screw up, we'll send you back to the fleet for garrison duty, promises from the spooks or not."

A hollow feeling, like holding his breath and getting an oxygen treatment at the same time, spread through Hoffman. It was like his first public-speaking class multiplied a thousand times. He needed to either calm down or start shouting. The internal tension in his core was intolerable.

Bradford's next words came slowly, barely loud enough to be heard. "There's an extended-duration mission available."

Hoffman stared straight ahead, realizing after several heartbeats that the captain was waiting for an answer. "Sir, my team and I would be glad for the opportunity."

Bradford's pause was shorter this time. "Good. Now get out of my sight."

Hoffman saluted, turned, and marched smartly from the office. He'd been prepared to dismiss Bradford as an overzealous ladder-climber whose most impressive accomplishment in the last five years was tightly rolling his sleeves to the perfect curve of his chin-up-enhanced biceps. But the truth hurt and he wished he could redo the mission and get it right. It had been his big chance to shine and prove his team wasn't a gaggle of talented misfits who would never gel into a cohesive team.

The captain wasn't wrong. Hoffman needed to do something to get his head straight—hit the gym or just run through the streets of Phoenix until he was too tired to keep reliving New Bastion in his head. Memories of the blonde prisoner shooting the alien crime boss replayed in his head when all he wanted was to forget she existed.

For the one-hundredth time, he reviewed the orders he'd been issued prior to the New Bastion deployment and looked for a hidden meaning. Black ops were part and parcel to Strike Marine duties. He understood direct-action missions and, despite Bradford's claim, had performed well until now. Having his report changed without his knowledge was confusing, something he'd never experienced before, suggesting a deeper level to the dark abyss of Special Operations than he thought possible.

Something was wrong with the mission before his team stepped foot on New Bastion. *Need-to-know* was an expected limitation of black ops, but this felt sinister.

What had he been thinking? Not only had he hesitated, he'd lost the respect of Gunney King, a competent NCO who knew what he was doing and had the intestinal fortitude to make hard decisions. What little control he had over his team was gone. He considered resigning but couldn't imagine life outside the Terran

Strike Marines. What was he supposed to do, go to bartender school and learn to make mojitos?

As the doors to the captain's office slid shut behind him, Hoffman heard something fly across the room and slam into the wall. His boss wasn't just putting on a show. Hoffman had never seen an officer so angry.

****

Hoffman moved steadily through the Mercy Convalescent Center, reminding himself there was no tactical emergency and no reason to visually scan three hundred sixty degrees for threats. The air was both too warm and too cool, the hallways too spacious and too closed in. He remained aware of his environment but dialed his combat readiness down a notch, which made him anxious for reasons he couldn't articulate.

Memories lurked under the surface of conscious thought. New Bastion wasn't the definition of his career, despite Captain Bradford's opinion. Things could go wrong during any mission. The residents of the medical center were the proof of that.

Down a hallway to his right, he saw an orderly moving a cart full of clean linen, her careful stride almost concealing the limp caused by her prosthetic lower leg.

"Good day, sir. Can I help you?"

"I know the way. Thanks."

Hoffman continued to the edge of a commons area, watching a dark-haired woman, a pilot he guessed, laughing with two ground-pounders. She spoke like an officer and a pilot and had that cocky stance unique to the profession. The men struggled to keep their language clean, sounding like grunts no matter how hard they tried to impress the woman. Her arm was in a cast while the two men had compression bandages and freshly grafted skin from recently repaired burns.

Others, in groups and individually, passed time in conversation or watching football on a video screen.

"Lieutenant Hoffman!" called a Marine missing both feet and one hand.

"How ya doing, Craig," Hoffman said, looking the man in his eyes instead of cataloging his temporary prosthetics.

"Winning, as always," Craig said.

"Then I'm glad I didn't bet against you like last time," Hoffman said.

The next section was dimly lit, cool, and very quiet. He'd spent his post-op time here re-growing his hand and sleeping. While the individual rooms were made for privacy, most of the slider doors stood open. He remembered listening for hours to the sounds of doctors, nurses, and other patients when they moved through the main hallway. Healing could be a lonely business.

 Pushing thoughts of his situation aside, he worried about Opal and hoped he wasn't causing problems, which his large, procedurally generated friend would never do intentionally. It was just that his size and direct nature didn't always mesh with day-to-day matters. With no enemy to fight, he was obsolete and directionless. Plus, a lot of people didn't like the mottled brown, green, and gray texture of his skin. It reminded them of what he was and how many like him had been sacrificed to save Earth.

 The third section of the convalescent center was more of an open floor plan where the patients interacted according to their current abilities. A spirited game of ping-pong entertained a group at one end of the room, televisions and checkerboards at the other. Soldiers tended to gather in groups according to their injuries, as though this was how squads might be assigned.

 For the second time this visit, he saw men and women with mismatched skin tones from burn grafts, and he rubbed his left arm, then the back of his neck. A nerve tingled in his regrown hand as a sharp memory of losing his hand during the boondoggle on New Bastion drove up his heart rate and sent images reeling inside his head. Sweat beaded on his forehead, but he resisted the urge to wipe it away, pretending it wasn't there and that the memories weren't real.

Across the room, a group was arguing over who had the better cyborg legs.

Hoffman drew a breath, held it, released it. The Ember War was over, but there were still conflicts across the galaxy. Hoffman would always have a job, even if it wasn't with the Strike Marines. If his last interaction with his commander was any indication, he'd probably be back at Camelback making coffee for some rear-echelon colonel.

Patients and medical staff greeted him as he moved on with his thoughts, and double doors to the next area opened with the thunk of magnetic locks disengaging.

He focused on the reason he was there.

"Good morning, Lieutenant," Dr. Lydia Nimms said. The woman always seemed to be the one to greet him. She stood like an officer, chin held high, everything about her appearance spotless and squared away, even though she wore only surgical scrubs and a simple lab jacket.

"Do you ever go home, Lydia?"

"I go home, Lieutenant. There is precious little rest for the wicked, and none for scientists." She offered her best institutional smile.

"Where's Opal?" Hoffman asked.

"Your bio-construct is in the garden. He's taken to assisting other patients who are trying to relax and center themselves," Dr. Nimms said.

"Is that a bad thing?"

The doctor clicked her tongue as she sought the correct words. "One of the other patients invited him but started the yoga drills by telling him to adopt a tactical posture and keep quiet."

Hoffman waited for the grim punchline.

"Your construct took a tactical position. Right after he ripped up the rose bushes and dug a foxhole with his bare hands."

Hoffman winced.

"Walk with me, Lieutenant," Dr. Nimms said.

"He takes orders seriously," Hoffman said as he fell in beside her. "It's part of his programming."

They stopped at a window overlooking the garden and watched yoga on an epic scale.

In the center of a dozen other patients, Opal held a wide, lunging stance to one side with his arms and hands stretched level to the ground. He stared intensely down the length of his right arm.

The instructor guided the group through breathing exercises. She spoke words Hoffman couldn't hear, then the group twisted at the waist and extended arms straight up.

The only thing that made Opal stand out in the group was his size. His yoga technique, to Hoffman's untrained eye, looked smooth and efficient despite his bulging muscles and serious expression.

"He seems to be doing fine now," Hoffman said.

Dr. Nimms pulled out her data slate and made notes, speaking without looking up. "Yes, Lieutenant. He is good at following instructions when clearly given."

"How is his neural activity? Any drops below the cognitive event threshold?"

She smiled skeptically, pushing her short dark hair back over one ear distractedly. "I didn't know neurology was a hobby of Strike Marine officers."

"I've been taking care of him for a long time, long before the rest of the doughboys…retired."

"You don't 'take care of him,' Lieutenant. He's encoded to you, responds to set commands like a well-trained dog. That he's managed to outlive the rest of his kind doesn't make him special," she said. "Not like you think, at any rate."

Hoffman pressed his teeth together to keep his jaw locked shut and regrettable words from escaping. A moment later, when his impulse to argue with a woman who wouldn't listen to him about Opal's true value was subdued, he selected a better question. "What about his MSE score?"

"Mental state evaluation scores are nominal. Ninety-nine percent of the doughboys that functioned during the war were removed from service within two years of V-Day. They weren't designed to last much longer than that. Opal 6-1-9 will succumb to the same fate, despite this unique persistence. As I stated, it would be foolish to view him as somehow special or immune to the science of his construction," Dr. Nimms said, firm but seeming to lose interest in Hoffman's argument.

"Yes, Doctor, I know he could…degrade at any time."

"I have colleagues who would be interested in studying it further, just in case the doughboy production facilities are ever restarted."

Hoffman didn't like where this conversation was going. "He's still in active service. By the Ember War

Recovery Act of—"

"Yes, I know it can't be taken away from you without your consent. But Ibarra put that clause into the act, and ever since he vanished on some *reconnaissance mission,* President Garret has been steadily removing every trace of Ibarra from the government."

Hoffman braced for the other shoe to drop.

"It's for the best, I say. Ibarra did his part for humanity. Now it's time for us to make the most of the sacrifices we all made to survive this long," Dr. Nimms said, waggling a finger near her face and pointing upward like she had handily won a debate. "The clause that keeps Opal in active service will be trimmed away once Congress revisits all the old legislation that Ibarra meddled with."

Hoffman took an involuntary step back and then inwardly cursed his reaction. "I haven't heard of this. Why wasn't I informed?" He looked through a tall, institutional window at Opal in the garden where a score of people performed the warrior, downward dog, and baby cobra poses.

A smile grew on his lips as two patient young women, combat Marines by the look of their scars, guided him into the tree pose.

"The government nationalized Ibarra Industries

while you were off world. Seems the president realized that with both Ibarra and his sole heir missing and presumed dead, there's no one to inherit the company. The government taking it over makes things easier. Could you imagine a probate court ruling slowing ship construction? But, as for Opal 6-1-9, I know you've some affinity for that unit, but let's be honest, Lieutenant, it is time to move forward."

"What are you talking about?"

Opal's yoga adventure ended and he wandered over to a female sailor in a wheelchair. Her mechanical arms and hands struggled to twist something Hoffman couldn't quite see.

"You changed your baseline features years ago. Why you would go to such lengths and still keep your bonded unit confuses me. You're a Strike Marine now; time to leave doughboy garrison duty behind," Dr. Nimms said.

"Opal is…never," Hoffman said, gathering his thoughts. "I promised him we'd stay together. I won't do anything to change that."

"You seem distracted," Dr. Nimms said.

Hoffman watched Opal thread flowers into a ring and place it on the head of the woman in the wheelchair.

When a bee spotted the arrangement and moved in, Opal chased the black-and-gold trespasser away with his huge hands and a determined look. The other people in the garden moved out of his way, avoiding the bull in the china shop, doing so easily, as though this wasn't the first time something like this had happened.

Hoffman laughed despite himself and it felt good.

"Cute," Dr. Nimms said. "And amazing. I doubt Ibarra expected doughboys to be such good companions. Like a big, goofy dog."

Hoffman clenched his jaw, avoiding looking at her. "He's neither an attack dog nor a companion dog."

"Oh, Hoffman. You're a good man. So generous. Doughboys were made to be attack dogs…guard dogs at the very least."

"You haven't spent as much time with him—or the others before they died—as I have," Hoffman said.

Dr. Nimms shook her head as though warming up for a lecture. "None of them died, Lieutenant. They would have had to have lived for that. Opal is a bio-computer."

In the garden, Opal carefully pushed the woman in the wheelchair around a fountain, earning smiles from his new friend despite her devastating injuries.

"He cares about people," Hoffman said.

"He was designed to care or, more accurately, protect us."

Hoffman exhaled, wondering if he needed to de-stress with a yoga session.

"Listen to me," Nimms said.

"I heard you." Hoffman turned his back on the doctor. "Thank you for the very enlightening conversation."

"Lieutenant," Dr. Nimms said, "think about what I said. My colleagues and I would treat him well."

Hoffman stared at the scene in the garden. "I'm sure." He hesitated. "You know they gave the doughboys only enough medical care during the war to keep them moving."

"Smart," the doctor said. "More economical to retire them and build another than repair such a complex biological system. That was then. This is now. I hope we have shown our good faith on this issue. Having him here at Mercy is most unusual."

The subtle hint, the roundabout attempt to intimidate him, wasn't lost on Hoffman. "I understand."

"Listen, Hoffman. He'd be no better off in the Dotari hospital on Hawaii," Nimms said. "I'm not the villain in this scenario."

Hoffman shrugged. "I know where he belongs and where he's going. Good day, Doctor."

"Lieutenant, the world is not the way you wish it to be," she said just before her phone rang. She answered it curtly and said, "Excuse me. I have to take this. Don't go anywhere."

Hoffman nodded absently toward the woman and went into the garden. "Opal."

"Sir!" The doughboy's eyes flashed wide. He ran to Hoffman, seized him in a bear hug, and lifted him off his feet. "Sir came back!"

"Yeah, big guy. I'm back. Now…can you put me down?"

Opal lowered him carefully to the ground. "Opal is glad Sir came back."

"Is he leaving?" asked the sailor in the wheelchair.

Hoffman didn't know what to say.

"Well, you better take care of my friend, boss," she said. The tears that accompanied her smile warmed Hoffman's heart.

"Good bye, Opal," the sailor said.

Opal trotted toward her, throwing his arms wide to grab her as he had seized Hoffman a moment earlier.

"Opal, no hugging!" Hoffman said.

Instantly, the heavily muscled giant snapped his arms down to his side, hesitated, then knelt before the woman in the wheelchair. "Goodbye, Petty Officer 1 Benckle, Susan D."

Her smile spread farther across her face as she looked him in the eyes. "You stay safe out there, Opie. I don't want to see you in the hospital ever again." She tried to touch him with her mechanical hands but struggled with the controls.

Opal pressed his forehead to hers, hands still obediently at his side.

"Time to go, Opal," Hoffman said.

"Sir," Opal said, rising immediately.

Hoffman and Opal walked out of the garden.

Up close, the size and strength of the doughboy still surprised Hoffman, and that was after leading a full platoon of them during the last Xaros attack on Earth.

Nimms slipped her phone back into her lab coat as she walked up to the pair.

"Opal 6-1-9," the doctor said, "why did you initiate skin-to-skin contact with that patient?"

"Petty Officer 1 can't hug goodbye. Acceptable responses limited. Sir cancelled all mouth-to-mouth contact," Opal said.

"Kissing, Opal. You're not allowed to kiss anything…or anyone." Hoffman faced the doctor. "There was a slight incident a few years ago."

"How far has he deviated from his base programming?" the doctor asked, her voice low and alarmed.

"He's been learning for years. He can adapt," Hoffman said, watching gears turn in the doctor's head he didn't like. None of the conversation had been reassuring, but this could make someone like the doctor take Opal away from him. "Opal, let's go."

"Sir," Opal said.

Hoffman headed toward the main exit, stopping only in the large foyer to pay his respects in front of a shrine to St. Kallen—fist to heart, then knuckles to lips. The statue evoked deep emotion. Situated on a marble foundation, the woman in the wheelchair sat with her hands folded in her lap. He wanted to look into her slightly downturned face but would have made a spectacle of himself, kneeling before the statue. Hoffman's reverence for the saint was complex. He felt love, fear, kinship, and hope at the same time as he wondered what it had been like for Kallen, Elias, and the other Armor soldiers inside the war machines.

"Sir?"

Welling in his chest was the need to pray, something he didn't feel often, but also something he didn't ignore. If he took the time to pray now, though, Opal would be confused and Hoffman was too tired from fencing with the doctor to explain.

"Let's go, Opal. No more hospitals for you."

"Like Petty Officer 1 Benckle, Susan D. said," Opal said.

****

Sergeant Madilyn Booker watched Eric Garrison eat. The young corporal gripped a shatterproof glass of whole milk in one hand as he shoveled bacon and scrambled eggs into his mouth with a fork in the other hand. Between bites, he drank milk and nodded to indicate he was tracking the conversation.

Corporal Kate Adams sat sidesaddle on the bench next to Booker, staring at Garrison. "How are you not five hundred pounds…what do you weigh?"

"One eighty-five, plus or minus," Garrison said as he chewed. "Keeping up with you ladies takes a lot of energy."

"I still say New Bastion was our last mission together," Booker said, glancing at the food line and deciding she wasn't hungry.

"Now pancakes?" Adams asked Garrison. Her own selection of food—only half-eaten—looked meager in comparison to the spectacle the unit's breacher was making.

"French toast," Garrison said. "Where's your sense of culture?" He set down the fork so he could pour syrup over the entire plate, including what remained of the eggs. "I set a PR for dead lifts yesterday…and ran this morning. Are you going to drink your milk?"

"You're a freak," Adams said. "I'm gaining weight just watching you."

Booker and Garrison laughed at that. Adams was tall and thin, looking about as athletic as a runway supermodel, despite being the exact opposite—a buzz-cut death-metal chick who spoke three languages and could drive anything with wheels or treads.

Adams gave Garrison the finger, then faced Booker. "Why do you keep talking like the lieutenant isn't coming back? You sound like Garrison."

"I heard he took a real ass chewing after we got back from New Bastion," Garrison said.

Booker nodded. "That goat fornication wasn't completely his fault."

"That's not what he'd say," Garrison said.

"Eat your pancakes," Booker said.

"French toast."

"Whatever. I have to admit everything went sideways, but no officer can control Murphy. Especially when there are a bunch of aliens in the mix," Booker said.

"Alien Murphys are the worst," Adams said, picking at what was left of her food.

"They train us to overcome and adapt, which is what the lieutenant did," Booker said.

Garrison sat straighter. "Right after we blew up the most expensive part of the city. Man, I loved that part. Boom!"

Adams slugged Garrison in the shoulder as he started to finish his milk.

"That's not what got our boss in trouble and you know it." Booker wanted to say more but held her tongue.

Adams laughed, watching Garrison choke on milk as she listened to Booker. "Blowing stuff up is what we do, but it probably wasn't good when Duke assassinated an alien in full view of a hundred witnesses."

"That guy can shoot," Garrison said, tears—or

possibly milk—filling his eyes.

"I'm not blaming Duke," Adams said. "Just to be clear."

"You're just blaming Lieutenant Hoffman," Booker said.

"Well, not exactly. Murphy happens, like you said." Adams shifted as though she might stand and leave, but rubbed the back of her neck instead.

None of them spoke as Garrison cleared his throat, then looked longingly at the cafeteria tray between his calloused hands.

"Officially, none of it happened," Booker said. "I shouldn't have brought it up."

"Yeah," Adams said, "that gives me goose bumps. It's my first time under a black ops gag order."

"Hush," Garrison said. "There could be listening devices everywhere. You're going to get jammed up for spreading rumors about Lieutenant Hoffman. And for assaulting an honest Marine while he's trying to eat."

"Shut up," Adams said.

Booker's head ached. Trying to have a serious conversation with these two was like playing checkers with her sister's kids. She scanned the room out of habit, cataloging the tables of Marines, sailors, and soldiers in their groups. A Marine from another platoon, commanded by Lieutenant Fallon, entered the room and scouted a table too close for her comfort, but she decided not to mention it to Adams and Garrison yet.

"We haven't been pulled from assignment rotation," Booker said.

"How do you still have security clearance?" Adams asked.

Booker chose not to answer.

Garrison leaned forward, lowering his voice. "I heard from a friend who may or may not have access to the NCO rumor train that Hoffman isn't coming back. This friend of this guy talked to a clerk in HQ who saw transfer paperwork with Hoffman's name all over it."

Gunnery Sergeant King walked into the mess hall, glanced briefly at the gathering of Fallon's team, then ignored them as he sat across from Booker.

"Gunney," she said.

He nodded once, then faced the food line as though making a tactical decision. A moment later, he looked Booker in the eyes. "What are we doing here?"

"You look like hell, Gunney," Adams said. "Have you slept this week?"

He didn't respond, keeping his attention on Booker.

"Our internal intelligence specialist here," Booker said, indicating Garrison, "has rock-solid information that Lieutenant Hoffman is being transferred."

King stared down Garrison, who started looking for something more to eat.

"You know how I feel about rumors," King said, the scar on his face adding severity to his already stern tone.

"Yes, sir," Garrison said.

"Aren't you going to eat, Booker?" King asked.

She shook her head.

"Remember the good times?" Garrison asked. "I miss running security for the Pathfinder Teams. Worst thing we had to worry about were the mosquitoes on Daursk."

"And the six-legged squirrel-things that weren't safe to eat," Booker said.

Garrison put down the crust of toast he'd stolen from Adams' leftovers and held his stomach. "They were not."

Adams laughed while Booker smiled appreciatively.

King watched Fallon's team dropping food trays on their table and sliding onto the benches, laughing and telling overlapping stories.

"If Hoffman did take a reassignment, would Opal go with him?" Booker asked.

King gave her the eye.

Garrison pushed aside his empty tray. "I don't understand the lieutenant and Opal. Why so loyal to a lost cause?"

"The lieutenant isn't a lost cause," Adams said.

"You know I meant Opal."

"You're the lost cause," Adams said.

"Say that again the next time you need a door breached." Garrison looked away from King, who sat like a god of silent disapproval. "Wouldn't Opal stay with us?"

"Now you care?" Adams said. "I thought you and the big lug didn't get along."

"I'm not a total jerk," Garrison said, pounding a burp from his chest with his fist.

"He's dumber than a bag of hammers, but nice to have around in a firefight," King said. "Hell of a lot bigger than Garrison, more sponge for the bullets than the pipe-cleaner here."

"I'm just trying to be lean and mean like you, Gunney," Garrison said.

"Careful, Corporal," King said, only half paying attention to the breacher as Lieutenant Fallon and the rest of his entourage quieted down at the nearby table.

"What's an officer doing here?" Adams said. "Their side of the mess hall is way over there."

Booker wondered the same thing but kept her mouth shut. She watched King instead and saw a vein twitch in the gunnery sergeant's neck. If it weren't for the chain of command and about a thousand rules and traditions, she thought there would be a brawl soon.

Booker, Garrison, Adams, and King watched Fallon's team. Blessed with nothing but good luck and a golden reputation, they were laughing and joking again. Their boss sat at the head of the table, quietly removed from the enlisted ranks yet present as a benevolent and much-loved overlord. Other Strike Marine teams nodded respectfully or saluted Fallon as they selected tables that wouldn't crowd his team.

"All hail the A team," Garrison murmured.

"Be thankful we don't work for that prima donna," King said, refocusing on Booker, Garrison, and Adams. "At least we have two extra weeks of leave. I'm heading to the armory. Some of our gear might qualify for replacement." He stood and walked away without another glance at his former boss.

"Awkward," Garrison said.

"You think?" Adams said, watching King exit the mess hall.

Booker wanted to get King alone and question him further. There was only so much the gunnery sergeant would say in front of the team. She didn't know the circumstances surrounding King and Fallon's relationship, only that King had requested a transfer and it hadn't gone over well.

Two tables away, Fallon stood and went for a walk with two captains and a major, crossing decisively over to officer's territory. Moments later, another pair of enlisted Strike Marines from Fallon's platoon approached Booker's table, ignoring her to accost Garrison and Adams.

"Where's your boss?" the instigator said.

"Bend over and I'll show you, Keith," Garrison said.

Booker was on the verge of pulling rank, hating the idea and pissed off Fallon wasn't minding his shop. For all she knew, the jack wagon had sent them over to push Garrison's buttons. The breacher had a bit of a discipline history for brawling before Hoffman calmed him down.

She stood.

Fallon's Strike Marines looked her up and down appreciatively.

"Sorry, ma'am," Keith said. "Garrison and I go way back. Wasn't trying to start trouble."

Adams popped to her feet. "Good, because she can't fix stupid. She's a sergeant and a medic, dumbass. Just because she won't throat-punch your rank and Garrison's on probation doesn't mean I wouldn't take you to the dance."

"I'd like that, Adams," Keith said.

"I guarantee you wouldn't," Adams said.

This was where Booker knew she should order Adams to stand down, but she let the moment draw out. "Is there anything we can do for you," she glanced at the man's name tape, "Corporal Landon?"

"No, ma'am. Just checking up on a buddy," Corporal Keith Landon said. He swiped a playful air punch at Garrison. "Did you eat three trays? You gotta have a tapeworm."

"Corporal," Booker said, tone hard.

"Ma'am," he said. "Sorry. Have a good day, Sergeant."

Fallon's Strike Marines retreated to their table where they were soon laughing too loudly.

Booker had barely sat down when Lieutenant Fallon ventured over from officer country. "Sergeant Booker, I must apologize for my men. They're spirited."

"Not a problem, sir," Booker said.

Fallon motioned for the three of them to sit. "I was talking to the captains. It's almost time for a new class of Strike Marines to arrive. That means we'll be considering internal transfers."

Booker said nothing.

"Again, Sergeant, I hope my men weren't a problem," Fallon said.

"No problem, sir," she said.

Fallon nodded and left the same way King had not long ago.

Booker stared after him.

"Are you serious?" Adams asked. "Did that just happen? He's trying to break apart our team."

"Sounded like he was recruiting us, me probably," Garrison said.

Adams gave him the finger, started to punch him, but pulled her fist back with a growl. Garrison laughed.

Adams ignored him in favor of Booker. "He's full of shit, right?"

"Who, Fallon or Garrison?" Booker asked, suddenly exhausted. "Are we done here or does Garrison need another fifteen million calories? Let's go before Gunney comes back and we've got to salute and execute on something."

Chapter 4

Valdar placed the palms of his hands on the desk and pressed down to stretch his back while sitting. In the age of omnium technology, paper had become a blessing and a curse. Stacks of the waterproof, flame-resistant stuff held down the left side of his desk. His mission since the end of the war had been to move these critical documents from left to right, sometimes reading and signing them during the process. To add insult to injury, all of it was duplicated on his data slate just to ensure humans never forgot the nexus between digital and analog tech.

He dropped his hands into his lap and stared. "Can we return to the digital age now that the Xaros are gone?"

The empty room offered no answers.

Leaning back, he took a moment to stare at the opposing wall where a picture hung of President Garret shaking his hand during his promotion to admiral. Another of a visit to the Dotari home world, and yet another of his nephew Ken Hale departing for New Terra, perhaps to find his brother Jared, perhaps to make something of his life with Gall—settle down and raise little Hales.

The strangest picture, the last group photo of the four Karigole, stared at him with disturbing force. Photogenic, they were not.

"My glory days," Valdar muttered defiantly, refusing to accept death by paperwork. Patton—that old warhorse of history—had it right, taking the old barracks song about fading away with a grain of salt. "Old goats don't fade away, they just butt out."

A chime sounded at his door.

"What?" he growled.

Egan, his executive officer, hurried into the office, a break from his normal decorum.

"Something on fire?" Valdar asked.

Egan shook his head quickly. "Worse, admiral. A Dotari VIP shuttle is on approach. No notice from Saturn command or Camelback."

Valdar pinched the bridge of his nose. The *Breitenfeld* was a popular site for alien dignitaries. Interest in the ship that delivered the death blow to the Xaros seemed to transcend species. No notice visits were a constant headache for the admiral and his ship.

"I cleared it to dock in Bay 19 as soon as it makes its way around the rings," Egan said. "You want me to get the dog and pony ready for the show?"

Valdar tossed the data slate aside as he stood. With one swipe of his hand to smooth his uniform, he moved toward the door. "Well, don't just stand there. We don't keep diplomatic envoys waiting on the *Breitenfeld*."

"Any paperwork I can take care of while you hobnob?" Egan asked, nodding toward the desk.

"Watch yourself, XO." With Egan at his side, he strode to the bridge. "You get too good at answering my mail and it'll become a permanent additional duty."

Valdar pulled up a sensor scan on his gauntlet screen. The approaching ship was small, even with enhanced optics. Valdar stared as though he could accelerate its progress across the panoramic space-scape on the main view screen.

The *Breitenfeld* orbited Saturn, gliding above rings of ice and rock. Colors shifted for thousands of kilometers on the flat surface. A faint image of the ship reflected like a ghost navigating in silence. Looming beyond the gas giant, the void joined forces with the shadow cast across the planet by the belt of debris. Cold, stunningly beautiful, and massive, the scene was daunting to a man who had spent most of his career in the blue-water navy prior to the Xaros invasion.

Admiral Valdar faced the view screen with his hands clasped behind his back. His crew, some old and some new, maintained the fresh silence. "We were on our way to establish this colony when it all started." His mouth felt dry and his voice sounded soft to his ears.

"We were," said Egan.

Valdar had preferred a career as a blue-water sailor. His sudden reassignment to the *Breitenfeld* on the eve of the Ember War had been unwelcome, but he'd excelled as a void ship commander. Something tightened around his chest and the corner of his eye twitched as memories came back. He'd been lucky enough to survive when the Xaros took Earth. His wife and children weren't. The original Saturn Colony, which Valdar thought would've been an assignment lasting a few months became a gambit to preserve the human race against an unstoppable enemy.

"Well, don't get all sentimental on me, XO. You have the bridge. I've got an old friend to greet in docking Bay 19."

Egan laughed under his breath. "Old friend? That doesn't narrow it down. Who is it this time?"

"A pilot. Someone the *Breitenfeld* picked up far

from home," Valdar said. He left the bridge, confident Egan could handle anything the Saturn Colony supply ships might do in the shipping lane they were monitoring.

As he walked the hallways and ducked through the lower bulkheads around reinforced areas, he paid special attention to structural details of his old ship, which hadn't seen action for a while. Stopping when no one was near, he patted a support beam. Drawing a breath and holding it with his eyes closed, he exhaled, growling softly. "You got us through Toth battle groups, Alliance treachery, and everything the Xaros could hurl at us, old girl. I cannot thank you enough. My crew thanks you."

Grav plates and ship ventilation purred at the edge of silence. He remembered warning klaxons and the sound of his voice ordering battle stations on the public-address system…rail guns hammering the enemy in space, Marines and sailors fighting Xaros drones and other nasty boarders, Eagle fighters making emergency landings after getting shot up.

Opening his eyes, he could scarcely believe the *Breitenfeld* had come through so much.

He walked taller and tried not to think about the past or the future.

A pair of junior officers snapped to attention as he

approached. He acknowledged them without saluting and continued to the docking bay. A petty officer gave him the all clear, then stood aside as the door opened. Out of habit, Valdar glanced at the emergency lockers where decompression and other safety gear were secured.

"You're doing good work here, Petty Officer Trentson."

"Sir," the petty officer said.

Valdar inspected the area, speaking briefly with each of the officers and senior noncoms running the docking bay.

"Admiral Valdar, I wasn't aware you would be visiting us today," a lieutenant said. He turned to give orders.

"As you were, Lieutenant. Let's keep this casual," Valdar said.

The bay was one of the largest open spaces in the *Breitenfeld*. A squadron of Eagles and their crews awaited his order to launch into action. "Always ready" was their motto, even on this dull assignment. On the other side, opposite the combat line, were maintenance ships and EVA stations for almost any peacetime contingency.

Lo'thar, one of the first Dotari to serve alongside humans, finished a conversation with the Marines guarding his recently docked shuttle and strode toward Valdar.

"Admiral Valdar! It is good to see you. I thought you would be in a special place befitting your rank," Lo'thar said after saluting in the way unique to Dotari.

"Lo'thar, it's been forever. I've got a bit of cabin fever. News of your arrival was most welcome," Valdar said.

"I was told desk work was such a noble pursuit that only the highest-ranking minds of the Terran Fleet could do it," Lo'thar said.

"Let's have a walk around my old girl and I'll show you my new toys," Valdar said. "The newer generation of Eagle fighters have a fair amount of automation in them now that the threat of Xaros hacking has gone away. And they're faster and carry more ordnance."

"And in one piece," Lo'thar said, moving close to one of the fighters when he'd received permission from the flight crew. "Easier to land with landing gears! Gall used to scream at me, 'Lo'thar, why are you trying to get us killed? Lo'thar, use the marked landing zone. Lo'thar, I swear you waited until I was getting shot before you blew up that drone. Lo'thar, Lo'thar, Lo'thar!' She was fun."

Valdar laughed but noticed how quickly the Dotari veteran abandoned his war stories. "Let me show you our new grav plates, then the armory."

"You are the admiral," Lo'thar said.

"An admiral with a single ship to worry about," Valdar said. "I spend most of my time training fleet commanders. They actually have to rise through the ranks now. We stopped minting tactical geniuses after the Hale Treaty."

"The Dotari were relieved—but surprised—when Earth signed the treaty. We thought the senior human named Ibarra would have protested more to the terms. The procedurals were his technology, yes?" Lo'thar asked.

Valdar stiffened slightly. "Ibarra protested enough."

"He is gone on a science expedition, yes? We have not seen him in Earth news for years."

"That he's gone is all that matters," Valdar said. "I never cared for him or his methods."

Valdar led the way to a platform facing a wall-sized view screen. The dramatic view of Saturn, which seemed closer than it was, still took his breath away.

The Dotari pilot seemed impressed but preoccupied.

"What brings you all the way to Saturn, Lo'thar?" Valdar asked.

Lo'thar produced a tablet and tapped until several pictures came into focus. Valdar raised an eyebrow at the image of an infant Dotari breaking free from an egg the size of a football. He wasn't sure if anyone had informed Lo'thar that humans—as a rule—did not share pictures of childbirth. Though the event for the Dotari was plainly less…messy.

"This is my daughter," Lo'thar said. He clicked his beak as he swiped through photos of the little alien who looked almost human but for her thick black quills in place of hair. Dotari infants suckled like human babies, developing their beaks later in life and changing their diet to hard shelled foods.

"She's adorable and I think fatherhood suits you. But I don't think you came this far out just to show me a photo album," Valdar said.

Lo'thar stared at the picture for several moments before putting the device away. "She is our joy."

The quills on his head drew into tight clusters and his beak locked tightly between words. With his feet set shoulder-width apart, he looked into Valdar's eyes as though he were a human negotiator rather than Dotari.

"We call it the phage, and it is killing us. Our home world is as we remember it, but over the many centuries since we fled the Xaros, the Dotari changed. We adapted to the long years in the generation ships. Adapted to the barren rock that was Takeni. And when Dotari was freed after the Ember War, we rushed home…far too quickly. Our immune systems weren't ready to fight the old diseases on Dotari and now we're dying.

"I came to you because you saved us from the Xaros on Takeni. You saved us from a threat we could shoot, that we could run away from. The phage is a different enemy, but one that can still be beaten with your help," Lo'thar said.

"I'm a ship driver, not a doctor," Valdar said.

"My ancestors made it to Takeni, and from there, our separation from our home world and our doom began…but there were other fleets," Lo'thar said, "like the one the Xaros twisted and used to attack us on Takeni."

"I don't follow," Valdar said, playing dumb as wheels began turning inside his head, all leading to one conclusion.

"The Golden Fleets that left Dotari before my ancestors departed with the best technology. They were not generation ships, but sleeper ships. The passengers on those earlier ships walked on Dotari. Grew up on Dotari. Their blood carries the immunities we need to survive," Lo'thar said.

"You found such a fleet?" Valdar asked.

"Yes, yes, we have," Lo'thar said. "But there are a number of complications."

"You know more than you're telling me, Lo'thar."

The Dotari veteran shifted, adjusting the distance between them. A tremble went through his quills and he looked embarrassed.

"Tell me all of it, or we're done here," Valdar said.

"The fleet we found is in interstellar space. It will reach its intended destination in another three hundred twenty-five years—Chosun's Star, you call it. There is a Crucible gate there."

Valdar's lip twitched. He had an inkling where this was going.

"That's a long time," Valdar said. "Can the Dotari survive that long without a cure to the phage?"

"Some of us might. There are protocols moving into place. The Dotari serving in your Armor Corps, pilots and support teams on the carriers, our small base on Hawaii; all will be cut off from the home world soon. A seed for future generations. But this does nothing for those on Dotari, for everyone with the phage. To do nothing is a death sentence for so many of us. My daughter especially." Lo'thar ended his words with a low trill. Valdar wasn't sure how to interpret the new sound.

"And how do I work into this?" Valdar asked.

"You can take us to the Golden Fleet," the Dotari said, his eyes sparkling. "You can help us bring back a cure."

"Lo'thar, old friend," Valdar said, holding up a hand as a chill shook him. Lying was part and parcel of protecting classified information. There was a potential solution to Lo'thar and the Dotari's problem, one they shouldn't know about. "That isn't possible. Knowing where the Golden Fleet is doesn't do us any good. The Crucibles can send us one way. A fleet goes out, it's stuck in deep space with that Dotari fleet too. We'd have to wait until it reaches the next star hundreds of years later."

Lo'thar didn't respond.

"Sorry, Lo'thar, it doesn't do us any good to find a cure we can't bring back."

"But there is a way," Lo'thar said, taking a step forward with renewed energy and determination.

Standing tall, staring Valdar in the eyes, Lo'thar made a Dotari sound in his throat that might have been a word. His eyes glowed with an intensity he had lacked while touring the flight deck. The quills like thick hair braids on his head moved with each deep breath and his stance looked both relaxed and ready.

"And what…exactly is that?" Valdar asked, feeling as though a stone was balancing on his chest, needing only to be shoved aside.

"Let's talk somewhere private, Admiral Valdar," Lo'thar said.

"No one will pay attention to us here. I selected this observation deck for privacy. There is…ambient noise in the system here. One of my secrets."

Lo'thar nodded, then began as though his life depended on what he said next. "We know about the portable Crucible program. Our leaders thought we'd be told, and there are many of us unhappy that it has been kept secret, but we know it must be complete by now. In the—how do you say it—the testing phase by now."

Valdar controlled his surprise, but the Dotari father didn't wait for him to get his balance.

"I just need you to champion our cause," Lo'thar said.

"How could you know about the Grinder—the program?" Valdar winced at his major gaff, admitting he knew exactly what Lo'thar was talking about. Keeping secrets was not his forte; Earth had spies for that.

As Lo'thar laughed without much humor, his quills fluttered on his head. "The Mutual Defense Treaty allows us access to the omnium reactor on Mercury. Think about it, Valdar. How could we not figure this out? We are not *ga'amon'an*, sitting around with our heads ducked beneath our wings. For the last year and a half, an exceptionally large amount of mass was transmuted that was not listed on the production schedule."

Valdar clenched his jaw. The Dotari had his facts down pat and had clearly been practicing his delivery.

"All of this was shipped away within hours of creation on the same navy ship that kept changing its transponder identification. It left the Mercury base on the same course every single time, out to Sedna. Given the mass that was transmuted, the hull size of the ship, and the amount of strain her engines exhibited each time she pulled away from the factory, we—"

"Deduced what it was carrying," Valdar interrupted.

"Yes. Material the same volume and density as a Crucible gate," Lo'thar finished. "If you—I mean, they—hadn't tried so hard to hide what they were doing, we might not have noticed."

Valdar frowned. "Very clever, Lo'thar. But if what you're saying is true, and I can't say that it is, why do you think I can acquire it for our—your—purpose?"

Lo'thar laughed, finally rolling aside the imaginary

stone on Valdar's chest.

"Admiral Valdar, the *Breitenfeld* could jump to the lost Dotari fleet, construct the mini-Crucible on site, then we can all be home in no time. We can cure the phage if we but have the courage to go and grab it!"

"That doesn't answer my question, Lo'thar."

"It does!"

"Calm down, friend. I am neither confirming nor denying anything we've talked about."

Lo'thar stepped back, expanding his chest and drawing his hair quills back slightly. "You are offering me bovine leavings!"

Valdar looked down just long enough to avoid making an open challenge to the prickly Dotari code of honor. A second later, he met his friend's level gaze.

"The Dotari diplomatic corps will make an official request to the Terran government in a few hours to utilize the Grinder program. If you, Valdar of the *Breitenfeld*, of the motion picture *Last Stand on Takeni,* takes an interest and volunteers for the mission, it should go easy with President Garret. Yes?"

"My volunteering is no guarantee," Valdar said.

"Also," a rustle went through Lo'thar's quills, "we will release a press statement on New Bastion making our request public to the rest of the—"

"Stop," Valdar said. "You'd tell the rest of the galaxy about our top-secret project. A tool of great strategic value."

"Our survival is at stake. If our plea is not enough, then perhaps the rest of New Bastion could compensate the Terran Union for the great costs incurred," Lo'thar said.

"Bovine leavings, Lo'thar. Bovine leavings."

"But if the Terran Union agrees to do so right away, then there would be no need for a press release."

"And I thought the Dotari were poor negotiators," Valdar said. "What makes you think we'd say no?"

"You kept the Grinder development hidden from us. We would've helped."

"I made that case to the brass at Camelback," Valdar said.

"But if you, hero of Takeni, commander of the final assault on the Xaros, receiver of the Medal of Honor, and—"

"I'll do it," Valdar said. "You think I want to sit around resting on my laurels? Attend staff functions, make small talk, and drink crap coffee? This sort of mission is too important for me to leave to anyone else."

Lo'thar lunged forward and hugged Valdar, pinning

his arms to his side.

"I…forgot your Dotari attitudes about personal space," he said.

Lo'thar stepped back. "I forgot you are an important desk worker now," the Dotari said, eyes dancing with excitement and quills puffing up slightly. "I knew I was right to come to you."

"Lucky me," Valdar said, squaring his shoulders to the Dotari and smoothing his uniform.

"You have—how do you say it—clout. Wasta. Influence. Grand Poo Bah. You are the big man on campus. Huge swinging—"

"I get it," Valdar said.

"All I need from you, Admiral, is to make public statements about helping the Dotari. We will get tons of support. Like the movie!"

"No public statements and don't remind me about the movie," Valdar said, looking past his old friend to watch the rings of Saturn on the oversized wall screen. He considered everything he'd learned and studied Lo'thar's expressive behavior. "One message to President Garret should be all it takes. How bad is it, Lo'thar? What's our timeline? I'm not a fan of rushing to failure. There remains testing to be done, strategy and politics to contend with."

Lo'thar looked down. The quills on his head drooped. When he raised his eyes to Valdar, they were damp with restrained tears. "Is there time for my people and my home world?" He shrugged unconvincingly. "Maybe there is time, maybe not. More die every day. All I know is there is not time enough for my daughter. She has months if she is lucky."

Valdar felt as though someone had stabbed him in the gut.

"We have our objectives," Valdar said. "Get to the Golden Fleet. Find a Dotari with the immunities you need, build the Grinder and jump back to your home world. Too easy. Unless the Grinder fails and we're stuck in deep space until we die of old age."

"The *Breitenfeld* is the blessed ship, is it not? This is where the human magic happens."

Valdar patted Lo'thar on the shoulder. "You served on this ship during the war. Did it feel like things were 'magical'?"

"No. It felt like we were lucky to survive by the skin of our beaks," Lo'thar said.

"Nothing's changed. But the old girl needs to stretch her legs. Thanks for the chance."

Chapter 5

Corporal Max dropped to a squat and kicked his feet back, situating him in the much-loved position commonly referred to in the Corps as the top of a push-up. Did he hold it? No, that would suggest he was near the end of the lesson. Gunnery Sergeant King would never shortchange him with an easy lesson. Many, many times he had promised to make Max push the floor until he died.

This was one such occasion.

Max yanked his feet back under him and jumped into the air. "Thirty-seven!"

"Keep it tight, Marine! Stop swinging my gear around! You gonna pay for that armor when you break it?" King shouted.

Max dropped, kicked back, tucked in, jumped into the air. "Thirty-eight." His unpowered Strike Marine armor felt unsecure, sliding this way and that with each change of direction as though it were too big for him.

"Thirty-nine!" He snarled the number like a curse as the loose armor reminded him of being the fat kid in high school football practice.

"Forty!" He screamed the words, not wanting to remember being the coach's kid who was slinging around an extra fifty pounds.

"Were those burpees or interpretive dance?" King grunted. "I thought you were a hot-shit Strike Marine. Peter, Paul, and Mary, will you look at that."

Sucking air into his lungs, he avoided looking at the team on the Terran Strike Marine virtual range. Holographic projectors gave the place the feel of an outdoor firing lane, complete with a wind sock on the berm and a safety tower at the east end of the line. Max wished it was just an underground bunker. Reality could be nice…if the hardest-assed squad boss in military history hadn't just busted you.

Standing at attention, sweat running down his back…and front…and everywhere to pool in the unpowered armor, Max waited for King to get creative—maybe tell him to start over or something clever like that.

As his chest rose and fell and he waited for the

force of nature that was Gunney King to decide his fate, Max watched Booker and Duke. Sergeant Booker was outstanding, the best medic Max had ever worked with. She lay prone, facing the virtual firing range with her feet spread wider than her shoulders, a sniper rifle pulled in hard against her shoulder. In this position, she was compact, stable, and made the smallest target possible for counter snipers to aim at…or hopefully not aim at.

Duke, the team sniper, lay next to her, serving as her spotter and holding the position like he was born to it. Max could believe he was. Duke had three basic skill sets—killing things, chasing tail, and brutal honesty only a salty grunt could manage.

Booker and Duke glanced at him from the firing lane. She smiled and shook her head before returning to her rifle. Duke stared a moment longer.

Max thought the man must be refining his plan to kill everyone in the room, although the scary old bastard was good to have in a fight. Everyone treated him like a living legend, but he creeped Max out.

King paced back and forth between Max and the firing line. He was thinking, deciding, and muttering under his breath.

Max waited.

"Give me ten more, Marine," King said levelly.

"Don't count 'em. Just remember why we're here."

Max sprang into the air at the top of each burpee as fire burned through his legs. Oxygen and all that other stuff that made Earth's atmosphere so nice to breathe whistled in and out of his lungs. Sweat soaked the body-glove uniform between his skin and the unpowered armor.

"Family," he grunted inside his helmet.

Another rep.

"Corps."

Another rep.

"God."

Maybe that was the wrong order, maybe not.

"You about done over there?" Booker said as she logged a shot in her book.

"You want to join him?" King asked.

****

Sergeant Madilyn Booker adjusted her firing position, trying to find the sweet spot between stability and comfort when firing a weapon with the kick of a gauss sniper rifle. She pulled the weapon firmly into her shoulder and exhaled as she looked through the scope at a VR target downrange. "I could have been a sniper. This is easy."

"Focus, Doc," Duke said.

She felt his presence like a bad day about to happen, which strangely reassured her. Duke was Duke, even if he was one of those guys who never really seemed to accept women in the armed forces. He didn't say it, but a girl could tell.

"I'm about to kill this 1500-meter shot," she said. The legendary sniper was prone next to her, his rifle tucked up close to him like a girlfriend.

She fired. The virtual round kicked up virtual dust next to the itty-bitty target in the distance.

"Clear miss," Duke said.

She dropped her forehead against her rifle.

"Your breath control is off," Duke said as he slipped a tin of chewing tobacco into his back pocket.

"Whatever."

"This is simple stuff, Booker. Did you skip basic marksmanship training or something? Is that what medics do these days?"

"I drew this rifle straight from the arms room. It isn't zeroed," she said.

"It is."

"No, Duke, it isn't. How could it be zeroed?"

He exhaled, looking down the scope of his rifle as though bored with this conversation. "This is a VR range. They come zeroed."

"You trust the arms room?"

"Your problem," he said, "is your breath control."

She looked at his rifle, noting scrapes and scuffs that had been buffed over then refinished for proper camouflage. Blood, sweat, and tears seemed embedded in the stock and fore grip…not that the omnium-crafted weapon could absorb such trivial fluids. "I could drill it with your rifle."

He slapped the back of her hand hard, striking right where the bony part was the most sensitive. "Were you about to touch Buffy?"

She pulled her hand back. "Sorry."

"Don't you ever touch my Buffy without asking! In fact, never touch her. Don't even look at her like you're going to touch her."

Booker pulled her hand back and looked down the firing lane, smiling as soon as she peered into her scope. "Sorry, Duke. Didn't know you were the jealous type. But you know it's not my breath control. This thing from the arms room is crap."

"Try again," he said.

She aimed, pulled the weapon into her shoulder, and exhaled. Everything looked good through her optics. The computer-assisted reticule promised a solid hit. She pulled the trigger.

"Miss."

"What the hell?"

"Try again."

Repeating the procedure with extra attention to hold her breath after she exhaled, she squeezed the trigger with the exact same amount of pressure she'd used on the previous shot.

"Well, look at that, another miss."

"This weapon. Is not. Zeroed properly," she said. "I don't have the luxury of carrying the same weapon since sniper school—which I never went to, FYI."

Duke took Booker's generic weapon, standing and emptying his lungs on the way up. Booker knew how to fire during the low point of the breathing cycle. She was less certain how Duke thought he was going to achieve this delicate moment without lying prone. Each joint of his body below the weapon—ankles, knees, hip, spine, shoulders—was instability waiting to happen.

Duke pulled the trigger three times in quick succession. The electromagnetic snap of the weapon's retort thundered through the range.

Booker peered through the spotting scope and witnessed three virtual holes lined up across the bull's-eye in a one-inch group.

"Oh," Booker said, her face turning red.

"It's your breath control."

****

Gunney King crossed his arms and watched his team. Good Marines, good people, but in need of discipline. Duke was one of the best snipers he'd ever met, and generally, he didn't push back. That was good. King respected experience. He saw right away, however, that Duke was focused on Booker.

King spotted a more immediate problem—one that would lend itself to today's lesson about professionalism and discipline. Striding forward, he stopped next to Max, who was bent over at the waist and breathing hard after his calisthenics.

"Corporal Max, recover."

As Max stood, turning to face King a bit more slowly than normal, one of his hands trailed from a utility pouch on his thigh rig.

King narrowed his eyes. "Missing something?"

Max stood up, straining against the weight of his unpowered armor. With the pseudo-muscle layer beneath his ballistic plates disabled, moving felt like wearing thick clothes soaked in water. Strike Marines trained to keep fighting after a catastrophic loss of armor function, but working in unpowered armor was one of the more miserable things any Marine did outside getting shot at.

King touched a button on Max's gauntlet and his armor reengaged and tightened, pressure squeezing some of his excess moisture out one-way filters. Nearly inaudible, the coolant system hissed to life.

Max breathed a little easier.

"Corporal Max, what is the Strike Marine standard operating procedure regarding use of personal electronic devices while on a firing range, virtual or otherwise?" King asked.

"They're forbidden, Gunney."

"Then why did I catch you tap, tap, tapping away on this?" King pulled a scuffed-up Ubi slate from a pouch on his belt.

"No excuse, Gunney."

King handed Max the Ubi. "You're a Strike Marine, Max, not some recruit at basic who doesn't know better.

There something you need to tell me?"

Max hesitated, then started to grind his teeth.

King kept his face impassive, with an edge of affected hardness. He wanted the younger Marine to show contrition but not kiss ass.

"My girls, Shelly and Sam…Samantha, they're excited to have me home. About to drive my old lady crazy with stuff they want to do as soon as I get there. They were fighting about going to the R&R resort in Cuba or the rebuilt park in Anaheim. Hard to parent on one side of a screen, you know?"

"I don't. We were dark for the last month. You can make it another day before working out vacation plans. Don't let me catch you distracted on the range again," King said.

"Yes, Gunney."

King jerked his head toward an empty firing position, knowing hard silence was safer. No need to explain further. Max was a solid Marine. King's job was to keep him that way.

He moved down the firing line, pleased to see Adams and Garrison had successfully zeroed in their weapons and were kneeling behind virtual cover killing virtual Toth warriors in one of the more challenging training programs.

"I'm watching you, Adams," he said.

"Everyone is, Gunney," she said.

King let it pass and took a firing position. The first thing he learned in NCO school was to remain tactically proficient. No one followed a team leader who couldn't shoot straight. He cycled power into his gauss rifle and keyed up a mobile target sequence.

Holographic drones the size of small plates hovered down his firing lane as a timer ticked down. He readied his rifle when a haptic feedback sensor on King's wrist vibrated, warning him just before Lieutenant Hoffman entered the room.

"Officer on deck," King said, frowning as he saw Private Opal following Hoffman like an extremely large, extremely well-trained service dog.

"As you were," Hoffman said as he walked into the range, his stern expression driving a spike of dread into King's gut.

"Hey, Opie! You're back and bigger than ever," Adams said, her weapon still pointed downrange despite the way she twisted to face the new arrivals.

King opened a keypad on his harness and thumbed a button to kill the range. "Render your weapons safe and leave them at your positions." He remained in his firing lane, methodically removing his rifle magazine, then the internal grenades from the launcher slung under the main barrel. Virtual ranges were treated with the same cautions and procedures as live-fire exercises. It kept people focused…except when they were video chatting with a nagging wife back home.

Hoffman walked to King's position as the other Marines fell in line facing them.

King decided not to mention Max's range violation to the lieutenant.

"Let's see it, Opie," Adams said.

Without hesitation, the doughboy lifted his shirt to show a raw, pink scar.

King said nothing, staring at the mass of older scars that nearly concealed Private Opal's most recent acquisition.

"Other one," Opal said, hooking his thumbs into his belt to drop his pants.

"At ease, Opal," King said. Once he was certain the doughboy heard him, he stared daggers at Adams.

Her eyes went wide, her face a picture of innocence, while Opal proceeded to stand with better military bearing than any of the other soldiers.

Hoffman nodded once to King, then faced the team. "You all performed admirably on New Bastion, above and beyond my expectations of Strike Marines. Any…friction…on the way to accomplishing that mission is my responsibility and no one else's."

No one moved or spoke and King felt the silence like it had physical weight. Ventilation and climate control units suddenly sounded like the launch platform of a cruiser.

"We have…" Hoffman looked at Opal as he trailed off. "Block leave has been postponed."

King thought he could feel Max seize up.

"We are now tasked to join a highly sensitive mission on the *Breitenfeld*, under command of Admiral Valdar. More details will be released when we are on board and under commo lockdown."

"This is just some kind of Saturn run, right, sir? Do a drop on Titan for some civvie bigwigs, then we're home in another week?" Max said.

King locked his jaw as Lieutenant Hoffman cleared his throat. "The assignment is of indefinite duration."

King looked at the wall and swallowed a mouthful of hot profanity. He'd just lit a fire under Max's ass about family time. The only married member of the team was going to have a rough time when his wife found out about this.

"Given our recent off-planet assignment, I was able to secure a forty-eight-hour pass for you all starting tomorrow morning. Your forms are signed and with the company admin section. Gunnery Sergeant King has release authority. I don't have any other information to share. Gunney?"

King snapped his hand up in a salute and Hoffman returned the gesture, then left the VR range. Opal remained behind.

"Hold it together a moment longer, team," King said as he counted to nine and a half.

"This is some bullshit!" Max said.

"At ease yourself, Corporal."

"We were dark for three months. I missed my son's second birthday and now I'm gonna miss the twins' birthday if we're gone more than six weeks. You know what the old lady's gonna do when she hears this?" Max snapped his knees together.

King leveled a knife hand at Max's sternum, then lost the words he needed. He wanted to swear but didn't trust his mouth, so he clenched his jaw until his eye started twitching.

Max resumed the parade-rest position, chest rising and falling angrily but eyes straight ahead.

Booker broke the tension, moving closer to King. "You seem just as surprised as the rest of us, Gunney."

King resisted the urge to confirm her suspicion with profanity and declarations of innocence. There was almost nothing worse than getting blindsided with something like this.

"The only thing that matters are the orders our lieutenant just gave us. Let me tell you jarheads something right now. Not a damn one of you will see anything but the faded paint of these walls until you've qualified expert on your assigned weapon and every piece of equipment we drew is cleaned and returned to the armory."

Booker, Max, and Adams turned around and walked toward their downed weapons, shaking heads and muttering but not loud enough to be heard. Duke and the others stared at him.

"Wait. I will say this one time only. Any of you show up back from pass with a mosquito fart of alcohol in your system, you can kiss your block leave—when we finally get it—goodbye," King said.

All eyes turned toward Duke, who looked at the clock, then at his watch, and pulled a small plastic bottle from near his shooting mat. He unscrewed the lid and spit into it. "Challenge accepted. Anyone know if the titty bar on Black Canyon Highway is still off-limits?"

Garrison stretched his back and rotated his shoulders. "Another place opened on East Washington."

Duke put forward a fist and Garrison bumped it with his.

"You want to keep jaw-jacking or you want to finish this range?" King asked.

Silence.

"Back to your weapons," King said. "Opal, come here."

The doughboy presented himself with alacrity—best damn Marine in the Strike Marines if the ability to snap to attention could win wars.

"Unit Opal 6-1-9, report status," King said. The infantryman loomed large. King marveled at how easy it was to forget not only the mass of the doughboy, but the aura of raw strength.

Opal's eyes focused on something far away, or on nothing. King could never decide which it was. He knew, however, the unit was shifting into base programming. "Unit operating at suboptimal condition. Residual pain from damage will degrade focus and mobility for nineteen hours."

A shiver wormed up King's spine. Talking to the biological computer within Opal's brain never felt right. He didn't go in for weirdness or new-age spiritual stuff. Just when he grew accustomed to the doughboy's steady, dependable mental plodding, this clinical analysis came from his mouth.

"Synapse function?"

"Unit's function is aberrant."

King wasn't sure what to make of that. These bio diagnostics usually reported normal or degraded if Opal was recovering from a serious injury. He kicked some ideas around with less-than-scientific reasoning and wondered if "aberrant" could be a by-product of some new treatment.

Maybe the doughboy was degrading permanently. King wasn't sure how to feel about that possibility. "Exit diagnostics."

Opal's face softened and he looked around like he wasn't sure where he was.

"Opal, how is the lieutenant?"

"Sir is quiet and sad."

King shook his head. This day was feeling long, and tension gripped the back of his neck like a vise. Hoffman was hiding something, he knew it. How far should he press the doughboy to find out? Popping his neck with a short twist, he addressed Opal. "Go to firing point three and qualify on your assigned weapons."

"Yes, Gunney."

King watched Opal run to comply. "Garrison, watch out. You've got incoming."

Garrison snatched the rifle from the shooting bench out of reflex.

"Opal qualify."

"Okay, buddy. Not with this one. I'm using it," Garrison said.

"I told him to go to firing point three. You're on four. Why is your rifle sitting on three?"

Garrison shrugged, possibly feeling chastised but more likely embarrassed for being caught in the middle of a lazy, sloppy habit. "Sorry, Gunney."

"You're on my list, Garrison. Get it together. What do I have to do to keep you sharp, toss you into a firefight?"

"Pretty much," Garrison said. He handed the doughboy the correct training weapon and stepped back.

"Opal qualify," Opal said as he aimed his first shot.

"Do your worst, big guy," Garrison said.

"Don't tell him things like that," Booker said.

King faced away from the banter, fists clenched as he stared at the door where Hoffman made his exit.

****

Hoffman walked through the ship in a kind of daze he hadn't felt since his first days in command of a doughboy platoon. He'd been on other ships of the same class and seen videos on his Ubi…but this was the *Breitenfeld*. Every step toward the conference room felt important.

Gunney King walked beside him, silent as the walls. More so, perhaps.

"This way, gentlemen." A sailor standing against the bulkhead pointed down a passageway where the mingling of military civilian parties had already cause a bottleneck. The lieutenant and his team sergeant shuffled inside.

The conference room felt small when he stepped through the doorway and looked around. Navy and Marine officers gathered near their seats speaking in low voices. A Dotari delegation clustered around one of their own wearing a sash bedecked with medals.

"I never thought I'd be here," Hoffman said. "You

know who's been in this room? What was set in motion here?" On the upper walls were armor unit patches carved in wood. Iron Hearts. Templars. Hussars. Each bore a black cloth tied around the middle. He'd gone to Memorial Square in Phoenix and seen the marble statues of the armor's last stand. That was one thing. Standing in the room where those same martyrs had once been was another.

Hoffman looked over the seats, wondering where legends like Hale and Carius would've sat.

A moment of silence radiated ahead of Gunney King's words. "I lived through the Ember War. The *Breit* was the first ship to return to Earth after the…event. She found herself in every major battle during the war and took the fight to the Xaros Masters. Won the war. Some say she's blessed, unless you were aboard her. Then it might've felt more like a curse."

"Plenty who'd say it's blessed. Especially those that keep to Saint Kallen," Hoffman said.

King didn't respond. He seemed to be in his poker-face mood today.

"Let's get out of the way," Hoffman said, pointing to lower rows near the stage. Although the *Breitenfeld* was a carrier, he didn't see any pilots with fighter wings, but he did note plenty of engineers and Dotari.

"There's Captain Bradford," King said.

Hoffman looked across the room, not liking King's tone but not blaming him for his resentment. Things had been rough since the New Bastion incident. He wondered how much the gunnery sergeant knew about their situation…just how close the captain was to cannibalizing the unit for his pet projects elsewhere.

Bradford stood near the presentation screen talking to Lieutenant Fallon and the other company officers. That they all must have accompanied the commander and Hoffman had arrived by himself was not a good sign to the lieutenant.

"This ship's been off the line since the end of the war," King said. "Hasn't left the solar system except for that time it went for Ambassador Pa'lon's funeral. Wonder why we're aboard now."

"I heard rumors they wanted to turn the ship into a museum, but Valdar wouldn't allow it. Guess war heroes have veto power where it counts," Hoffman said. The lights flickered and a hush fell over the room as people made their way to vacant seats. Hoffman stood in front of a seat near the captain.

The room snapped to attention as Admiral Valdar

walked onto the stage, looking older than Hoffman expected. He knew the admiral's face from the media frenzy at the end of the Ember War—some years ago—and the movie *Last Stand of Takeni*, which was of dubious historical value.

"Seats," Valdar said.

A holo wall appeared in the middle of the stage, but the main light stayed on Valdar.

"This briefing is classified," Valdar said. "The ship will remain in a commo blackout until the mission is complete and all personnel have been debriefed."

Tension rippled silently through the room. A few civilians murmured softly enough they probably didn't realize they might as well be shouting. Hoffman resisted the urge to dress them down for their lack of respect and discipline and looked instead at the Dotari delegation. A classified human-alien mission was a rarity in his experience.

He thought he could hear King's teeth grinding.

"As you may or may not know, the Dotari are suffering from a plague of concerning proportions. Think of the way the North and South American indigenous peoples died off after Europeans brought a whole host of diseases that those populations had never been exposed to.

The Dotari's home world is toxic to them. The best doctors and scientists in our multi-race alliance have been hard at work on a cure, work that's yielded little progress. In the meantime, a probable cure has been found," Valdar said.

Hoffman wondered if the Dotari plague could pass on to humans.

Valdar continued. "We've recently discovered a lost Dotari fleet in deep space, part of the diaspora that left their home world prior to the arrival of the Xaros. In that fleet will be Dotari with immunities and antibodies that our allies need to survive on their home world. While we could reach the lost Dotari fleet via a wormhole jump, coming back would be nearly impossible. Any ship we send to rendezvous will be stuck on the same journey as the Dotari colony fleet for…about 350 years."

As the audience rumbled, Hoffman forgot to be annoyed and stared at Admiral Valdar, hanging on every word.

King leaned toward Hoffman and spoke quietly. "Is this what they mean by an 'indefinite duration' mission?"

"The *Breitenfeld* will jump to the fleet's location through the Crucible gate, wake up the crew, and return the Dotari to their home world with the cure to the phage. There isn't a Crucible in deep space, so we will bring our own—the Grinder," Valdar said. "Think of it as a mini-Crucible we will build on-site when we rendezvous with the Dotari ships. The *Breitenfeld* already has the component parts stored on the flight deck. Because of this, our fighter wing and most of our support ships will stay behind. We have one corvette—the *Barca*—lampreyed to the hull for ship-to-ship duties. It will take some time to assemble and power up the Grinder. As of now, the entire operation should take eight weeks."

Hoffman didn't need to see their faces; he could feel the audience's incredulity.

Valdar continued in his rough, no-nonsense voice. "The Grinder is a leap forward in gate technology. It's the product of years of work and intelligence gathered by our Pathfinder teams on artifact worlds. This *is* the reason this mission is classified." Valdar paused to make eye contact with several people in the room. "Once the technology is perfected, it will give the Terran fleet a significant operational and strategic advantage. You all know as well as I do that it skirts the authorized use of Crucible gates laid out in the Hale Treaty. Relations are bad enough with the Vishrakath and the fight we've got going on Cygnus II."

King flinched at the mention of the Vishrakath and Hoffman saw him tighten up. No one hated the Vish more than King.

"The Dotari ships will reawaken their crews once the codes are transmitted to them. Should that fail or function below standards set forth by the science team, we will use Strike Marines and Dotari advisors to board the ships and reboot key systems. Walk in the park. Flip some switches and try again with the codes. No problem." Valdar paused. "The Dotari need us. They are dying. This ship and her crew saved them once before, and they repaid that debt by fighting and dying beside us during the Ember War. They've remained our closest allies ever since. They have given us their all." He looked up at the Iron Heart crest, and Hoffman remembered that two Dotari armor soldiers were lost in the final confrontation with the Xaros.

"This sounds like fun," King said dryly.

Hoffman had kept his mouth shut as long as he could. "We're a side show on this one, Gunney. We won't do much but keep our gear clean and qualify at the holo range between briefings."

King nodded, still staring at the admiral. "I thought this was a chance to prove ourselves, get back on top. Now it looks like more punishment duty," King said. "The team won't be happy."

Hoffman shook his head and forced a smile. "Don't

jump to conclusions. Bradford and his golden child, Fallon, are here. He wouldn't have volunteered the company unless there was a real chance to do something."

Valdar continued. "The Dotari know they have no better friend than Earth. Every hour we spend here is another hour for the phage to claim Dotari lives. Failure is not an option. Not for the *Breitenfeld*. Not for her crew. We will make the jump through the Crucible to the rendezvous location in twelve hours. We remain on commo blackout until the mission is complete, and will remain on blackout after we return until the ship's intelligence officers have nondisclosure agreements signed by every crewmember, sailor and otherwise. Questions?"

Hoffman felt the moment like it was a physical thing. His mission might be a backup plan or, at best, a side show, but the moment felt historic.

No one said a word as Valdar looked around the room, then nodded slightly to himself. "Got Mitt Uns."

Everyone stood as the admiral left.

Hoffman looked at King, who was staring back at him. "What do you think, sir?" King asked.

"Never a dull moment on the *Breitenfeld*."

Other members of the briefing consulted with one another and began to file out.

"When was the last time our Marines got certified on boarding operations?" Hoffman asked.

"The team's individual certifications are up-to-date, but we've never trained this together," King said as Hoffman watched the wheels turn in the senior NCO's head.

"Anyone on the team trained in Dotari tech?" Hoffman asked.

"Negative, sir."

"We've got eleven hours before we have to secure for the jump…lot to do," Hoffman said. "Heads up, Gunney."

Captain Bradford strode forward with Lo'thar in tow. "Lieutenant Hoffman. Gunney."

"Sir."

"Meet your new technical specialist." Bradford jerked a thumb at Lo'thar. "Don't embarrass me by asking for his autograph."

Hoffman and Gunney gave the Dotari veteran a respectful but noncommittal nod.

"How long have you been a technology specialist?" Hoffman asked, squirming as the Dotari stood close enough to smell his breath.

"I am Lo'thar, pilot by trade and your technology

specialist by recent good fortune. I fought in a squadron commanded by Lieutenant Durand during the days of hay of the *Breitenfeld*." He reached his arms around Hoffman, hugging him and gripping his hands together, burying his face in Hoffman's shoulder.

"Uhh…" Hoffman gave him a quick pat on the back.

Lo'thar stepped back. "That is how it is done? Correct?"

"Sure," Hoffman said.

"I'll leave you gentlemen to it, then," Bradford said and walked away.

"Why does he insist on calling us that? What is the meaning of men gentle?" Lo'thar asked. "Lieutenant Durand preferred a wide variety of expletives from several human languages."

King stared at Lo'thar. "Lost in translation, I guess."

"Are you angry with me, Gunney?"

King shook his head about a millimeter and a half in each direction.

"My experience with gunnery sergeants is that they are always angry. Forget I asked."

Hoffman put his hand on Lo'thar's shoulder and

guided him a step back from King. "Do you have much EVA experience, Lo'thar?"

"EVA?"

"Extra vehicle activity…space walking…ship boarding," Hoffman said.

"I trained to eject from my fighter and survive in the void," Lo'thar said. "How much more is there?"

King muttered under his breath.

Chapter 6

Admiral Valdar felt the deck move ever so slightly as he looked into the holo tank on the *Breitenfeld*'s bridge and watched as his ship stopped in the center of the giant gate. He cleared his throat to get the attention of Ensign James Lancer, his navigation officer.

"Sir, the *Breitenfeld* has come to a complete stop within the Crucible," Lancer said.

"XO, status report," he said to Egan, standing to his right.

"Yes, of course, Admiral. Right away." Egan's hands flew across his control panel. The view screen showed only one part of the Crucible and the *Barca*, a recently refitted corvette now attached to the *Breitenfeld*'s hull, blocked a corner of this particular camera view. "The *Barca* sends that she's secure against the hull."

A small fleet of escort ships sped away from the Crucible. The timing of this jump would send the *Breitenfeld* into deep space while the gate orbited on the far side of Ceres, blocking line of sight from Earth and Luna. So far as the solar system knew, Valdar's ship was still somewhere around Saturn on maneuvers. The mission was still largely a secret.

"We'll miss the Terra Nova mission," Egan said. "Just occurred to me."

"Such is our duty," Valdar said. "I had the chance to see Hale and his family a few days ago and say my goodbyes."

"You told him about this?" the XO asked.

"He still has his clearance. And who's he going to tell in the Canis Major dwarf galaxy? He gets to lead a lucky group of colonists to some untouched garden world beyond the reach of all the problems in the Milky Way. But if there's anyone on Earth that deserves such a break, it's him," Valdar said.

"You could have gone with him," Egan said.

"And who would take care of the *Breitenfeld?* Speaking of, double-check the atmo seals on deck nineteen. They've been sending bad readings for weeks."

"Admiral Valdar," said Ensign Nichols, the

communications officer, "we have a confirmed IR link for President Garret's message."

"Very good, Ensign Nichols. Send the transmission to my tank."

The president of the Terran Union came up on a screen in the holo tank, looking healthier and a bit more robust than during the final years of the Ember War. "Valdar, nice to see you back in action," Garret said. "Couldn't risk you or your ship on the front lines after the war ended. But this mission suits you."

"It's been some time since we made a jump. The engineers swear the enormous amount of mass we're carrying on the flight decks won't affect our transit, but we'll maneuver like a barge with a fishing boat's engine until we can unload the Grinder. Bad enough I had to leave my fighters behind to make the thing fit in the hull. I've been training officers for years, and I would never teach them to jump into an unknown situation like this."

"The Dotari will be tickled pink to see you," Garret said, "or your Dotari advisors at any rate. This is a milk run, Valdar. Don't overcomplicate it. Besides, Earth needs the good press after the fight on Cygnus."

"Yes, Mr. President," Valdar said.

"See you soon." Garret cut the transmission.

Valdar returned to his command chair and the bridge but did not sit down. He felt the eyes of his crew as he looked out the windows to the massive basalt-colored spikes that made up the jump gate. It had been a long time since he and his ship had made a journey like this. Memories of Takeni—where the *Breitenfeld* had jumped into the planet's upper atmosphere and right into a battle—grasped at the edge of his mind.

I may be too old for this, he thought.

"Admiral, Keeper sends the gate is ready," Egan said.

Valdar nodded slowly.

"All stations make ready for jump." Valdar buckled himself into his seat and donned his helmet. Doubts were for him alone. He would never let his crew see him waver.

"Once more unto the breach, dear friend." Valdar tapped his armrest and watched as the Crucible's spikes shifted against each other and a field of white light engulfed his ship.

****

"That was a rough one," Ensign Lancer said as his hands moved across two control panels and his eyes tracked data from a holo screen. "My apologies, Admiral."

Valdar massaged the back of his neck as he got out of his seat a bit slower than usual and went to the holo tank. "No need, Conn. I'm still a blue-navy man at heart, but I have it on good authority that not even veteran spacers get used to the feeling."

Smiling despite the sour taste in his mouth, nodding despite the transitional vertigo, he maintained the air of authority while ignoring the gut-wrenching feeling that lingered after every wormhole jump. The years since his last experience with quantum wormholes had not made the experience any more pleasant.

"Initial scans confirm we're in deep space," Ensign Lancer said. "Would you look at that? We're a hundred light years from the nearest star with a Crucible gate."

"Right on target, then," Valdar said.

Polite laughter rippled through the bridge crew.

"We're pulling the pulsar feed now," Ensign Lancer said.

"Go hot on all sensors. We're not here to be subtle. Find the Dotari fleet. Spare me the science tour of the void. If we're in the right place—and it'll be a long day if we're not—those ships should be the only thing out here that are remotely interesting," Valdar said. He pulled data feeds up on his control panels and brought them into the holo tank with a swipe of his fingers.

"XO? Report."

Egan cleared his throat as he called up various readouts on his holo workstation. "She took a fair amount of stress coming through. We're carrying a high amount of mass in addition to the corvette, and if we'd made that jump anywhere near a gravity well, the hull might have sheared apart. We really did jump a long way."

"How bad?" Valdar asked.

"Some buckling to the frame around the flight decks…damage-control teams are looking it over, but it looks like the ship can handle some acceleration. Say half ahead with all engines. We push any faster, something could buckle."

"Weapons?"

"Rail cannons are online. We need to run some simulations against the stress a broadside would put against the ship. I don't recommend getting into a fight just yet," Egan said.

Elevator doors opened and the Dotari ambassador, Bol'gan, moved awkwardly onto the bridge. Valdar could spot someone unused to vac suits easily enough, even if they weren't human.

"Didn't I tell you to keep him off my bridge?" Valdar signed at Egan.

"Diplomatic immunity." Egan shrugged.

Bol'gan came up to Valdar and pressed the side of his body against the admiral's. Of all the cultural quirks he'd encountered with the Dotari, it was their concept of personal space—or lack thereof—that bothered him. The ambassador spoke rapidly, his words muffled by his helmet. Valdar removed his helmet and the Dotari's eyes widened. The ambassador struggled with his helmet for a moment before Valdar unlatched it from the neck ring for him.

"My apologies to your security soldiers, Admiral. They kept nagging me about remaining in my seat until you called for me. I may have used a few untranslatable euphemisms as I made my way past them. As if I'd miss this glorious event. A Golden Fleet! One of the first to leave Dotari and I simply must be here to speak with them. I've been brushing up on the old higher-caste dialects…where is the fleet?" Bol'gan reached into the holo tank and began moving data feeds around. Valdar grabbed him by the wrist and put his hand onto the edge of the tank.

"We're still doing the initial sensor intake," Valdar said through gritted teeth, regretting that he couldn't have the ambassador thrown off his bridge nor break his fingers for fooling with the displays. "That's why I wanted you to wait before coming onto the bridge. My bridge."

"Admiral," Ensign Lancer said. "We've got something. Putting it on the main holo now."

Bol'gan let off a high trill that made Valdar wince. In the tank, tiny green icons came up. A dozen ships appeared...then almost twenty more. Valdar frowned. The Dotari said the Golden Fleets numbered barely ten ships.

"How fast are the contacts moving?" Valdar asked.

"So many ships!" Bol'gan's quills jumped up like the hair on the back of a startled cat. He smoothed them down with a swipe of his hand and tapped on the control panel with the other. One icon grew larger, forming into a wire diagram of a vessel of Dotari design. "Many more than our records promised. That...that ship is larger than the *Canticle of Reason*! There must be hundreds of thousands of Dotari. Many times more than on the home world. This is a glorious and welcome surprise!"

"I've never had a surprise I liked during a mission," Valdar said. "XO, get the Grinder lead engineer up here now."

"Aye aye." Egan ran fingertips down a panel and put his other hand to an earpiece.

The elevator opened again and a contingent of Dotari hustled onto the bridge. They spoke to each other in their native language, which struck Valdar as birdsong mixed with lizard hisses. They crowded around Valdar and patted him on the back, shaking his arms in happiness.

"Gentlemen…" Valdar elbowed the Dotari away, but they pressed in closer. "Gentle—son of a bitch." He pulled one hand up, clamped it onto Bol'gan's shoulder, and looked into the ambassador's eyes.

"Get. Them. Away from me," Valdar said.

Bol'gan nodded quickly and made a quick trill. The rest of the Dotari lined up on the bulkhead.

Valdar kept his grip on the alien and looked at Egan.

"How fast are they moving, XO?"

"Calculating the velocity now," Egan said. "Fast. Almost three kilometers a second relative to us. We're close to their projected course and could make intercept in…now the math gets tricky."

"Hail them," Valdar said. "Use the frequencies the Dotari gave us and first-contact protocols as well."

"My apologies, Admiral," Bol'gan said, bowing his head slightly. He faced the team of scientists and Dotari VIPs. "What we've found is beyond our wildest expectations. Imagine if you came across an island full of humans that survived the Xaros occupation of Earth. This is an incredible moment."

"There were no survivors," Valdar said. "And on Earth, we advise not to count chickens before they've hatched. If we can't get those ships to stop, we'll never get them back to Dotari."

"My greatest apologies, Admiral Valdar," Bol'gan said. He rattled off stern Dotari words until the others looked chastened.

"Conn, set us on course to merge with the fleet, best speed as the ship's frame can handle," Valdar said.

"Aye aye. It'll take three days before they're within visual range," Ensign Lancer said.

"XO, give me an update," Valdar said.

"The Dotari fleet is not responding to our hails," Egan said.

Silence gripped the humans and Dotari. The only sounds for several seconds were the mechanical whispering of the Breitenfeld's computers, grav plates, and atmosphere regulators.

Bol'gan shifted restlessly, then spread his hands before talking. "The crew and passengers are in stasis. The ship's computers should awaken an emergency response team to anything that could affect the fleet."

"I assume getting hailed by a warship in the middle of deep space qualifies," Valdar said.

"Being hailed by an alien fleet certainly meets the criteria." Bol'gan held Valdar's gaze almost defensively, as though he didn't want to make eye contact with his own team. "It may take them some time to respond."

"Egan, prep the corvette. Maybe the Dotari will stop hitting the snooze button before the *Barca* is ready. Maybe they won't," Valdar said.

As Bol'gan looked at the other Dotari and chattered with them, Valdar picked up the word "snooze" being bandied back and forth, but he pretended not to hear.

He faced Egan and the other officers of the *Breitenfeld*. "We still have lots of work to do. First priority is to make contact."

Chapter 7

Hoffman led the way into the access tube connecting the *Breitenfeld* to the corvette. His team was silent—everyone gazing through the small portals at the exterior of the carrier as they left her. Few ships had seen more action or earned greater honors, though none of the battle scars remained.

The *Barca* looked much worse for wear. Scuttlebutt was that the ship had come off the line from fighting around Cygnus, given quick repairs in orbit around Ceres, then attached to the rescue mission before the weary crew could enjoy shore leave after a combat deployment. Hoffman and his Marines could relate.

His team followed him through the final coupling and into the wonky gravity of the corvette. The lighting felt grim and the paint had a gray texture of antiquity. Hoffman shrugged as the straps of his pack pressed against his shoulder. He and his team carried a fair amount of gear, as there was no way to tell what exactly they'd need once the *Barca* left the *Breitenfeld*.

Hoffman felt his stomach twist and decided he needed to relax. He and his team were made for this, he thought, as the details of Bradford's quick briefing a few hours ago still ran through his mind. The *Breitenfeld* would merge with the unresponsive Dotari fleet in a few days. In the meantime, the *Barca* would cross the gap, burning hard to catch the silent derelicts and board the largest vessel to make contact with the crew.

King had been riding the team hard. Every spare moment was filled with ship-boarding drills, close-quarters tactics, and constant equipment checks. Hoffman had heard his Marines grumble that they were looking forward to the acceleration chairs; at least then they could finally sleep. For the first time since New Bastion, Hoffman detected signs of unit cohesion. Misery had that effect on Marines.

Just a stride or two behind him, the grumbling started. He performed one of a platoon leader's greatest magic tricks…watching and listening without appearing to watch or listen. Hoffman led the team into the cargo bay of the *Barca*, which was full of acceleration chairs arrayed around a hatch in the middle of the deck, affectionately known as the hellhole.

"I always liked the idea of corvettes," Adams said, not quite smacking her gum as she talked. "Just big enough to get out into space and get lost."

Garrison grunted. "I told you I don't like the ship-to-ship stuff."

"Dude, you never tell a fellow Marine your deepest, darkest fears." Max moved around each seat in the infantry deployment bay of the corvette conducting a safety check on harness, digital readouts, and general wear and tear. "This bucket of bolts should've been retired years ago." He held up a strap. "Gunney, does this look frayed to you?"

King grunted and shook his head. "Put Opal or Garrison in that one."

"Opal hold Garrison inside," Opal said.

"Forget about that," Garrison said. "I'm more worried about that ugly-looking hatch. Don't lie and say you're not."

Adams sauntered closer to the heavily armored hatch. "Just a hellhole. Like one on an air-assault-configured Mule. Don't you like to fast-rope into hot landing zones?"

Hoffman shuddered at the memory of his last grav-cushioned landing. He felt King look at him even though he was facing away from the gunnery sergeant.

"Fast-rope into an LZ, you've got something to stop your fall. Screw the pooch on a void assault, you're floating in nothing, contemplating your poor life decisions until your air runs out. You keep floating after that. Then maybe aliens find your body millions of years later and they wonder what kind of a dumbass decided to go for a walk in space," Garrison said, needlessly checking his gear for the tenth time.

"You think too much," Adams said.

"That's never occurred to you?" Garrison asked.

"Not until now. Asshole."

Other Strike Marine teams moved into the bay, checking seats and equipment with about the same amount of foul language and nervous banter.

Hoffman continued into a cramped hallway that connected the habitable compartments of the *Barca*, pausing until the door shut behind him.

"Welcome to hell in a tin can," he muttered.

Reinforced bulkheads should have offered comfort; instead, they emphasized the deadly consequences of a hull breach. Rows of insulated, armored pipes lined the corners near the floor and ceiling. Scuffed paint designated this four-meter-long hallway the "blue corridor," which connected to the "green corridor."

Everything led to the tactical command center just behind the cockpit and engineering center/engine room.

As Captain Bradford and the other three platoon leaders—Fallon, Camp, and Eisenbeis—waited impatiently, sweat beaded on Bradford's forehead. The aristocratic powerhouse held Hoffman's gaze for a time, his mouth a perpetual frown that meant he was addressing his least favorite officer in the Terran Strike Marines. "Your team is taking this mission seriously, I hope?"

"They're Marines," Hoffman responded.

"That's arguable," Fallon said.

Captain Bradford snorted.

Eisenbeis remained stoically neutral. As far as Hoffman could tell, the captain neither loved nor hated them. It was an easy arrangement, since all the crap jobs on this deployment went to Hoffman and his team by default.

Hoffman watched the other officers and catalogued every detail of the room.

"Problem?" Eisenbeis asked Camp.

"I'd feel better in a *Breitenfeld* acceleration seat for the first high-G burn," Camp said.

"Can that ship pull g's that high? That may be an

option for you, but wait for the briefing. I'm not going through this twice if I can help it. The *Barca* has plenty of crash seats…" Eisenbeis said.

Standing next to Bradford was a short Dotari, the captain's high-ranking aide, who shuddered in relief, his quills rippling like a wave. "Why are they called 'crash seats'? Crash seats do not seem fortuitous." His gear was new and meticulously set up. "I am both nervous and excited to be part of this historic mission, especially since good fortune has assigned me to you, Captain Bradford."

Hoffman politely ignored the captain's Dotari aide and focused on his fellow team leaders. He didn't disagree with Camp—or Garrison, for that matter—on this one. Corvettes were big enough to run missions on their own and often got left behind to take care of this or that. Strike Marines often hitched a ride on the small ships.

Getting back to the *Breitenfeld* would be the problem…if there was a problem.

Bradford ran through administrative details and Hoffman pretended to listen.

"One more time for the doughboy babysitter over there," Bradford said. "It's been six hours with no response from the Dotari fleet. Their ships are operating under minimal power. No damage that we can see from out here.

Valdar is sending us to the biggest ship, which he tells me is named *Kid'ran's Gift*."

Eisenbeis snorted. "What's a Kid'ran?"

Bradford gave him the eye normally reserved for Hoffman. "Some mythic hero. Doesn't matter. What does matter is that our Dotari advisors know where we need to land and make contact."

A haptic feedback alert vibrated in Hoffman's gauntlet screen as a diagram of the alien ship glowed to life. He studied the details he'd already all but memorized from the initial briefing in the ready room and the mission download packet.

"I've selected three breach points. I land with Fallon's team at site alpha and make our way into the bridge. Eisenbeis to the secondary bridge at site B. Hoffman, you get the engine room. Might have to hit the brakes on these ships one at a time if there are…issues. Camp, you're staying on the *Barca* as reserve."

Lieutenant Camp's expression went into the freezer, but he kept his mouth shut.

One of Hoffman's eyebrows perked up. Who did the captain have less faith in? Hoffman, for sending him to secure the engine room, or Camp, to remain in reserve? If he was in charge, he wouldn't have his worst leader in reserve and responsible for pulling someone's ass out of a fire.

"Enjoy those cozy acceleration seats," Fallon said.

"Cool it, boys," Bradford said.

"What about defenses?" Hoffman asked.

"These aren't warships. No weapon systems, no counter-boarding systems. I doubt we we'll run into any awake Dotari. They would've answered us. If you do, let your advisor do the talking. Doubt they'd react well bumping into a Devil Dog, even ones as good-looking as we are."

Hoffman chuckled along with the others. Bradford wasn't a total prick. It only felt that way lately.

"Run IR relays to your breach point," Bradford continued. "*Barca* will be our commo nexus back to the *Breitenfeld*. Questions? All right, get to your teams and prep them for a high-G burn to overtake the Dotari fleet, then everyone's favorite deployment tradition…"

"Hellholes," Hoffman and the others said in unison.

"Get to it, gentlemen," Bradford said.

Hoffman moved through the cramped hallway to blue bay where the boarding teams waited. "Strap in and get ready. We're a go."

Lo'thar ran forward wearing half a Dotari void suit,

causing Hoffman to look around for Fallon and Eisenbeis. Fallon laughed and chin-pointed at Hoffman, saying something that caused Eisenbeis to shrug noncommittally.

Hoffman focused on his Dotari advisor.

"Is this armor? It doesn't feel like armor. I miss the cockpit of my fighter. These new suits are so complicated," Lo'thar said.

Hoffman resisted the impulse to admit he wasn't an expert in Dotari equipment, or Dotari for that matter. "Let me have a look. Stand up straight."

"This is nothing like my old flight suit. They said it would be just the same," Lo'thar said.

Hoffman tightened the sleeves, wincing at the idea of his tech advisor losing air. "Where's your weapon?"

"What?" Lo'thar asked. "Why would I need that?"

"Better to have it and not need it than need it and not have it."

Lo'thar looked around blue bay. "I must have left it in the ready room." He turned to leave.

"You *left* your weapon unsecure—"

Hoffman spotted a small pistol strapped to the small of Lo'thar's back and pulled it out of the holster.

Lo'thar spun around. "If it were a snake, it would've laid eggs in my quills. I much prefer void superiority fighters. Easier to keep track of."

Fallon shouted from the other side of the deployment bay. "Do you need a hand there, Hoffman?"

Hoffman turned his back on Fallon, then drilled his gaze into Lo'thar. "You forgetting anything else?"

Lo'thar slapped the pouches on his chest and thighs. "I've got my kit."

Hoffman looked him in the eyes.

"Which I'll go through one last time."

Red warning lights flashed.

Hoffman dragged Lo'thar toward the acceleration chairs. Each of the protective units looked like a mold a passenger could be poured into—deep and shaped like a humanoid. The chairs weren't soft, but rigid and tough with two padded straps for each limb and three to hold the body in place. He tightened the restraints until Lo'thar resembled a package ready to be shipped at high velocity.

"Booker," Gunney King said. "Double-check everyone. Strap them into their acceleration seats about three notches tighter than comfortable."

Booker nodded. Despite her stature, the years of mixed martial arts and jiu-jitsu training she'd done as a teenager to annoy her mother had strengthened her grip. Hoffman and most of the others had been choked out by her during combatives training.

She stepped to Garrison's seat and clamped him down with a violent tug to each of his restraint bands.

"Damn, Booker. I think I need a medic after that unnecessary assault," Garrison said.

"I am the medic."

"I know."

Adams, Max, and Opal laughed.

Hoffman looked at the doughboy. He hadn't seen the big guy crack a smile for weeks.

"What's the chance the *Barca* breaks free and flies against the hull?" Garrison asked.

"Name one time that has ever happened," King said. "Cancel that. Try shutting your mouth until I need you to break something."

"Shutting my mouth, Gunney." Garrison leaned closer to Adams, stage whispering, "Just imagine the silence of floating in the void. Tumbling end over end until—"

Adams smacked Garrison's chest plate.

For about five seconds, the high-G burn felt good. Hoffman braced in his acceleration seat and ignored the mission details in his HUD that he'd already read a dozen times forward and backward. This was nothing compared to the rough ride the *Barca* would make for the next eight hours away from the *Breit*.

"Oh, here comes the real gravity," Adams said. "You okay, Garrison?"

"Sure thing, little sister."

"That's enough," King said. "Focus."

"Ten minutes," Hoffman said. "Then the *Barca* will undock from the *Breit*."

"Then it's time to kick ass. Board a defenseless ship. Full of sleeping Dotari. Run some sensors! Oorah!" Garrison said. "After eight hours with our thumbs up our butts and nothing but empty space for a million klicks in every direction."

"What the hell did you put in his omelet this morning, Gunney?" Hoffman asked.

"Two scoops of stupid," King said.

"Good. I thought it might have been three."

****

Hoffman swallowed a sour taste and blinked three times as gravity faded away and the *Barca* moved closer to *Kid'ran's Gift*. "I'm gonna miss this bucket of bolts," he said to King.

"That's funny, LT. I was just thinking the same thing." The gunnery sergeant's voice was rough from the prolonged silence.

There had been no contact with the Dotari fleet since the *Barca* left the *Breitenfeld*. Deceleration warnings popped up on each of the team leader's screens, then for the rest of the team.

"Brace for deceleration," the pilot announced. "Thank you for flying *Breitenfeld* Spacelines. Please make sure that all personal effects are properly secured and remain seat belted until the ship reaches a relative stop. Lance Corporal Eric Garrison, you still owe me twenty dollars and two cigars. That number you gave me to your sister went to a certain admiral's voice mail."

Hoffman and the rest of his team faced Garrison.

"What? I'm a bad gambler." Turning his eyes to his work, Garrison diligently checked his acceleration-deceleration chair restraints.

Hoffman looked at Lo'thar. "Your suit doesn't have the compression system of your void superiority fighter craft. Don't want you to pass out. Again."

"Rather embarrassing," Lo'thar muttered. "You get so used to the suit doing the work for you."

"Stand by for breaking maneuver," the pilot said

over the intercom. "Sergeant Robert Duke, you also have an open tab, so please watch your ass in there."

"That smart-mouthed punk. I bet he was cheating." Duke yawned. How the old veteran had managed to sleep during the entire transit while under acceleration was a trick Hoffman needed to learn.

The crash seats turned around and Hoffman felt the press of heavy gravity against his body as the ship slowed. He tightened his core muscles as though performing a deadlift or resisting one of Booker's jiu-jitsu submission attempts. Fighting to keep the blood in his head was nearly as challenging as having the small woman kick his butt.

When the g-forces subsided, Hoffman looked around to check his team. "Opal, are you okay?"

The doughboy turned in his seat, which should have been nearly impossible regardless of strength or flexibility. "Sir need help?"

Hoffman continued his visual inspection.

Lo'thar gave a thumbs-up.

King released an exasperated sigh. "We have a winner. Adams is unconscious."

Hoffman tapped his gauntlet screen and Adams' armor puffed a whiff of smelling salts into her helmet.

"I wasn't sleeping, Drill Sergeant!"

Things started to happen before King could dress down Adams or her team could harangue her.

Bradford and Fallon's team unstrapped with practiced efficiency, did a quick buddy check, and ran to the hellhole. They looked down for a quick inspection of the landing zone, then jumped in an orderly sequence. Fallon's team and their Dotari specialist followed with no gaps in the deployment rhythm.

The hellhole closed.

Eisenbeis and his team moved faster than alpha team, leaving their acceleration-deceleration seats in near-perfect synchronization.

"Get ready," King said, calm as a sunrise. "This isn't a race. Move with violent intensity."

Hoffman watched Eisenbeis' team and waited for an update on his radio and infrared commo link.

"Alpha team on the LZ," Bradford announced. "I want regular updates. Eisenbeis and Hoffman, acknowledge."

"Heard," Eisenbeis said.

"Lima-Charlie," Hoffman said as he pulled up the camera feed and looked over the target ship's outer hull. For a moment, he forgot politics, personal doubt, and pre-deployment fear. The exterior of the Dotari vessel gleamed darkly with a deep-blue hue, nothing like other Dotari ships he'd seen.

"Looks more advanced," King said quietly.

"Agreed," Hoffman said, still staring at the ship.

Eisenbeis and his team jumped through the hellhole, the last member of the team whacking his armored head hard on the way out.

Everyone stared at the hole.

"He'll be fine. That's why you kids wear helmets," King said roughly.

"Yeah, Gunney, but it's bad luck," Adams said.

"So is passing out in your deceleration chair. Focus, team. We have a mission and it's a go," King said.

Hoffman stepped forward. "All right, team, we've rehearsed this so many times, we're dropping on easy street. Let's go in there and see who wants to say hello."

Booker looked up and down the line, checking each team member for two seconds, then she checked her deceleration-seat neighbors. Opal was on her right and Lo'thar on her left. "Dotari are friends, right, Opal?"

"Why does he need to be reminded?" Lo'thar asked.

"There've been issues in the past with doughboys encountering aliens not white-listed on their targeting protocols. Opal hasn't crushed your head out of reflex, so you're okay. Rest of the Dotari look like you, right?"

"Certainly." Lo'thar swallowed noticeably and looked around the deployment bay. "If this was going to be an issue, I think we should have addressed it earlier."

Hoffman watched the byplay, then ordered his team to release as he removed his safety harness and ran to the hellhole as it opened. The hull looked just as alien and strange as it did on the camera feed but felt bigger to his eyes. He glimpsed a swath of blackened hull plating and exposed decks as the *Barca* glided above the centerline of the sleeping vessel.

"Lo'thar, what was that?" he asked.

"Checking the video footage," Lo'thar said, cool and professional as a veteran combat pilot now. "I can't find it. Can you be more specific?"

Hoffman hailed the *Barca* captain. "Captain, send that data I just witnessed back to the *Breit*."

"Of course, Lieutenant. God's speed," the corvette captain said. "My pilot informs me that we have arrived at your insertion point."

He considered adding a verbal description of what he'd seen, but the words failed him. Other damage on the exterior of the ship appeared random, obvious products of space debris encountered during a long voyage. The now-sleeping counter-asteroid batteries had obviously destroyed large meteors, leaving the smaller debris to spatter against the hull. What he was looking at now was a line. For a split second, he thought he saw a right angle cut into the anti-meteor plating.

Hoffman spotted the outline of access doors in a wide trench running along the edge of the ship. During the briefing, he'd thought back to holographs of the *Canticle of Reason* he'd seen during mission research and movies. The last of the Dotari had been rescued on the *Canticle*. Such a massive ship was hard to take in all at once. The *Kid'ran's Gift* was bigger…and darker. The endless presence of the ship was high-jacking his imagination.

"There we go," Lo'thar said.

Hoffman grabbed the rim of the hellhole and went out face-first, pushing off with the anti-grav liners in his boots. He flew toward the Dotari ship, looking back once to see his team right behind him.

Opal's performance was as textbook as ever. The only thing that made him stand out in the formation was his size.

Hoffman twisted at the last second and grabbed the edge of the trench with his boots. He'd known they would work, but feeling them grab hold always felt like a huge milestone during any boarding operation.

His team formed a perimeter, weapons facing out to protect the desired landing zone of their principal.

Lo'thar came in too fast and missed the edge of the metal canyon.

Hoffman grabbed him by the ankle, struggling to slow him. "Cut your thrusters!"

Lo'thar smacked against the side of the trench when he complied, hanging downward in the lack of gravity. He kicked his legs and slammed his heavy gloves on the vertical surface until he locked on with his grav liners. "I'm okay. Linings are tricky. The access door looks just fine."

Hoffman released the pilot and stepped over the side. Pushing with his legs, he flew toward the door, grabbing Lo'thar by the wrist and landing on the hull beside his inverted form.

The door curved at the top and stood twenty feet tall.

"IR relay set up," Max said.

Hoffman repositioned Lo'thar.

"Thank you, Lieutenant. This is a much more dignified orientation."

The *Barca* floated overhead. Hoffman stared past them at the other Dotari ships—dozens more than mission planners had expected—ships that seemed far away to a man standing on the exterior of a strange ship in the middle of deep space. Light from distant stars barely reflected from their strange surfaces. He gave a hand signal to King, instructing him to get ready to follow with the rest of the team into the canyon-like trench Lo'thar had fallen into.

Disorientation was part of every EVA deployment. The worst had come as the icy grip of the void and the complete lack of gravity warped his armor and his senses during the jump. Blood pressure changed. He saw spots in his vision. The sound of his respirator amplified. All of it was strange.

Planting his feet on a vessel the size of the *Kid'ran's Gift* turned his already tortured disorientation sideways. Now there was a metal landscape and a horizon. Radio towers, sensor platforms, counter-meteor batteries, service trenches, and thousands of other Dotari-fabricated outcroppings gave the surface texture. The lack of light made everything a shadow on top of a shadow. His optics enhanced his vision only to make the scene appear haunted and dangerous.

The *Barca* looked like an insect gliding overhead.

"We're like ants on this thing," Booker said.

"All the world's a stage and we be but players,"

Garrison said, doing his best to ruin Shakespeare with his best grunt-Marine voice.

"Do your thing, Lo'thar," Hoffman said.

The Dotari pilot moved to the access panel.

"Is he tiptoeing?" Adams asked.

"It takes a while to get the feel for this," Booker said. "How long was your training?"

"About a million years, felt like," Adams said. She turned in a circle to observe the surface of the Dotari ship. "Got to say I'm impressed, actually."

Lo'thar opened an access panel and attached something from his Dotari technology kit while King and the rest of the team jumped down and set a new, smaller perimeter in the limited space of the metal service canyon.

"There's a problem," Lo'thar said. "The door has power but won't open. Overrides aren't working."

"The other teams didn't have this problem," Hoffman said.

"This is perplexing. Likely an issue that we're trying to access an engineering space, not a command area like the other teams," Lo'thar said.

Hoffman attempted to get Bradford on the IR relay, then glanced at his comms specialist.

Max shook his head after the second attempt. "Out

of line of sight. Won't hear anything from them until the corvette relocates."

Hoffman turned to Garrison. "Get it open."

"Thought you'd never ask," Garrison said, breaking out his breacher kit. With slick professionalism, he pulled out a roll of burn cord and searched for hinges or other weak points. He stopped and looked around at his feet.

"What the hell are you doing now?" Duke asked.

Garrison shrugged. "Access points are a good place to look for loose bolts, ball bearings, and other junk. Sometimes you can even find tools left by careless maintenance workers."

"Why would you need cast-off tools?" Duke asked.

"You ever seen what an IED made from wrenches and ball bearings can do to an enemy?"

Duke stared at him.

"Me neither," Garrison said. He faced the door again and held up a clump of denethrite next to a hinge.

"This ship is an important relic to my people. You can't just break it," Lo'thar said.

Garrison looked over his shoulder. "You haven't been around Marines much, have you? Killing people and breaking things is most of what we do."

Lo'thar frowned inside his helmet. "What is the

rest?"

"Not getting annoyed with useless questions." Garrison tapped his fist against the doors. "She pressurized?"

"Shouldn't be," Lo'thar grumbled. "But there must necessarily be some baseline atmosphere."

Garrison removed a compact device from his pack. "This here is a hydraulic spreader. Some call it the 'jaws of life.' I like to think of it as an eviction notice. Should barely tear up this relic. Maybe a little."

Grav liners on his boots gripped on each side of the centerline. The nose of what looked like two steel chisel tips pushed slowly into the seam where the doors met.

Hoffman felt an increasing vibration as the door spreader pushed deeper and deeper.

Garrison grunted as he leaned on the device. "Oh, I'm getting in this…"

"Language," Adams said from her position on the tight perimeter.

"What was he going to say about my people's ship?" Lo'thar asked.

"Breachers have lots of technical terms," Hoffman said, not waiting for a response as he studied Garrison's work.

Garrison pulled his weight off the door spreader, then slowly leaned on it again. His effort this time was more controlled. "I'm trying to pop it open so we can shut it after we're through. You can all thank…" he grunted with such force his voice gave out, "…me later."

The door popped open a finger's width and air escaped in a rush for a split second. "There we are. Another job done to perfection."

Hoffman tensed.

"That wasn't so bad," Garrison said as he widened the opening. "I mean…if there wasn't an inner air lock and the whole ship was pressurized, I could have been blasted halfway to the *Breitenfeld*. But I'm a professional."

"Was that a lot of air?" Lo'thar asked.

Garrison shrugged. "Consistent with an air lock. Glad the Dotari have some sensible ship construction."

Hoffman stepped forward and stuck the muzzle of his gauss rifle into the door as Garrison stepped aside. When the camera on his primary weapon revealed an empty air lock, he went in smooth and fast. Once the team and Lo'thar were inside, he directed the Dotari to what looked like a control panel.

Max ran IR strips, bending the thin material expertly into place. Made to be unobtrusive, the strips looked like thin, flexible film that allowed IR transmissions to relay around corners and bypass closed doors.

Lo'thar nodded several times and muttered something in Dotari under his breath. "The inner door is working correctly. Please close the outer air-lock door before I open this one."

Hoffman looked at Max.

"Comms are set. Close it or leave it open. Doesn't matter to me," Max said.

Hoffman smiled nervously. "I'd rather not have air rushing out. Suffocating our hosts isn't a good way to make a first impression."

Hoffman pointed to Garrison and Adams, then at the door.

With Adams standing overwatch, Garrison slipped a metal wedge into the base of one side of the double exterior doors he had opened, retrieved his device, and hopped sideways a step as the door slammed halfway closed. Once he folded the spreader and repacked it in his kit, he pulled the wedge and slid it into a utility pouch on his leg armor as the second half of the door boomed shut. Adams took a small spray can off her belt and ran the tip along the door seams. Foam filled the cracks and expanded for a moment before hardening. Garrison ran a second line on top of

Adams', then rapped his knuckles against the door.

"Glued tighter than Duke's budget before payday," Garrison said.

"Very subtle," Duke said into the total darkness of their new environment.

"Too dark," Opal said. "Don't like."

Emergency ship lighting—equally unsatisfying in all ships, Hoffman thought—came on.

Lo'thar opened the inner door and air rushed around them.

Hoffman moved in with Garrison and Adams, practically at the same time, and the junior team members went through the room-clearance drill automatically. Booker came next, despite his aversion to placing the medic too far forward in the stack. King and the rest of the team brought Lo'thar in. Duke held the rear.

The dimly lit passageway gave them plenty of room to set up. "Don't overextend," Hoffman said. "Booker, how's the atmo?"

"Breathable. Little light on pressure. Suggest a breath of O2 every half hour until we acclimatize," she said.

"Adams," King said. "Pop your visor."

Adams complied and drew a quick breath, then

exhaled as she spoke. Fog blew out with her words. "How long do I have to remain the new guy?"

The team watched her for a few seconds.

"It's like watching the Super Bowl," Garrison said.

"Why? Because it's something you bet on? Will she die? Will she live? Will her face melt with alien space poison?" Adams asked. "Jerk." She gave Hoffman a thumbs-up. "Smells like team spirit."

"All right, team. Go on shipboard atmo. Save the drain on our batteries and tanks." Hoffman lifted his visor and felt a chill bite his exposed skin. The air smelled stale, laden with ozone. "Pleasant."

"Smells like home," Lo'thar said.

"Give me a link, Max," Hoffman said.

"You got it. Ready to transmit to the *Barca*," Max said.

"Hoffman to *Barca* actual, we're in. No contact."

"Acknowledged," came the scratchy reply. "We're moving to relay position."

Lo'thar stared at the control panel. "I have no contact with the *Kid'ran's Gift's* systems. Got through controls integral to the air lock, not the rest of the ship."

"Someone forgot to pay the bills," said Duke.

"Is this normal?" Hoffman asked the Dotari.

"These are sleeper ships," Lo'thar said. "My ancestors traveled on generation ships. The systems would be different. But an air-lock entry would get attention from one of my ancestor's ships. A lot of attention. Atmosphere containment was a major concern, naturally."

"Some welcome." Hoffman peered down the dead corridors where a light rime of frost clung to exposed metal. The Dotari architecture favored more angles than Terran ships, enough to give him a sense of being out of place.

Hoffman looked down the corridor, studied the layout for a moment, then signaled his team to move forward.

****

Vibrations groaned through the floor, walls, and ceiling, creating a sound right at the edge of Hoffman's hearing. He felt more than heard it. Fresh from an intense deceleration burn and a grav-boot insertion to the alien ship, his mind was playing tricks with his perception. He understood the hallway was not twisting but couldn't get the thought out of his head. Uncertain lighting forced his optics to adjust. A thin patina of frost—nearly invisible in the gloom—covered everything.

Adams whispered through her helmet comms. "Boooooo…hahahaha…We're the ghouls of the *Kid'ran's Gift*."

"Unnecessary!" Booker said. "The whispering, I mean."

"What is a ghoul? Is that a great honor to my people and their ship?" Lo'thar asked, looking around nervously. "What is that horrible sound?"

Adams continued in her whispering stage voice. "Loooo'thaaaar…It's your soul slipping into the darkness…"

"I wish you wouldn't do that," Lo'thar said, the ends of his quills twitching visibly inside his helmet visor.

Adams started again, but her voice lost conviction as she peered into a dark side hallway.

"Watch your zones," Hoffman said, bracing for an attack from the frigid darkness until the moment passed. "Max, do your thing."

"Watch my back, Lo'thar," Max said as he kneeled to apply IR strips to the bulkhead the team had just passed.

"Your back?" Lo'thar asked.

"Protect him. Watch for threats," King snapped a second before Hoffman could do the same thing.

"Sorry. 'Watch your six.' That's what Gall taught us to say. This is different from void combat. You have nothing to fear from my people. Just let me do the talking." Lo'thar crowded Max, who muttered as he finished his work.

"Team move." Hoffman signaled his team forward just as the ship shuddered again.

"I didn't like that," Adams said.

"Keep moving and watch your zone," King said on the IR comlink. "Maybe next mission, you'll think twice before making ghoul jokes."

Garrison and Adams slipped forward to a rounded bulkhead and stopped, each taking a knee to aim their weapons. Their grav boots left footprints in the frost-covered decking.

Adams adjusted her position a few inches out from the wall to get a better angle on her zone—a reverse wedge shape that included the area immediately in front of Garrison and the hallway beyond. "Set."

Garrison cross-covered anything that might pop up immediately in front of Adams just as she was doing for him. None of them could see what might be around the lip of the bulkhead—an unseen door or passage or an alien pod creature hanging in the shadows that wasn't mentioned in the briefing. "Set." Garrison's voice rumbled low and gravelly.

"Report," Hoffman said.

"Nothing seen," Garrison said.

Duke, situated near the back of the formation, covered the long hallway and said nothing. Max and Lo'thar brought up the rear.

King came to his feet and glided forward, knees slightly bent, shooting platform perfect despite his fast pace. "Moving."

Booker moved a half second later, slightly behind him and to his left, covering his non-shooting side and looking for doors or other openings that weren't obvious from where they had been stopped before the bounding overwatch. On this team, she was a medic and an operator first, then a sergeant. By doctrine, everyone on the team was cross-trained to do each other's duties, but no one could replace Booker's medical expertise. She was the last person any of them wanted to see injured.

Hoffman glanced at the metal tracks on the ceiling, then checked the exact location of each Strike Marine. The long silence of the ship made him long for the nervous shit talk from his Marines. That was the difference between training and actually clearing a ghost ship. With such a small team, it seemed paranoid to do regular headcounts, except now it seemed more important than ever.

"Lo'thar, what are those rails on the ceiling?"

Lo'thar's fists shook like a child's about to open a Christmas present. Hoffman wondered if it was nerves or some sort of psychological defense mechanism for the bad vibe every member of the team seemed to be getting.

"Those are cargo rails. Very useful in zero gravity. Dotari never developed the miniaturized grav plating Terrans utilize. My ancestors didn't want heavy cargo drifting around smashing people, did they?"

"Your ancestors sound brilliant," King muttered.

"Has anyone else considered the importance of this?" Lo'thar asked.

"Trying not to, Lo'thar old buddy," Adams said.

"I am meeting my ancestors. These Dotari walked on our world over a thousand years ago. They built the Golden Fleets that saved our species. It's like meeting your Moses or Napoleon the pig."

"Napoleon?" Duke asked.

"The leader from your children's book about animals on a farm. The leader that took his people to a great place," Lo'thar said.

"I don't think you got the right message from

Orwell," Duke said.

Lo'thar clacked his beak. "I bet the crew of this ship will be excited about the technological improvements we will bring to them. Grav plating is a good example. Our new ships are much improved..."

"Do you always talk this much?" Duke asked.

Hoffman checked his team. When he came back to Lo'thar and Max, the Dotari fighter pilot was standing in the middle of the hallway, holding his weapon in a relaxed position as he talked.

"Lo'thar," he said. "Keep your eyes open for a computer node. You don't need to talk while you're doing that. Team move."

King acknowledged the order, then gave hand signals as needed and made eye contact with Hoffman every five or ten meters.

"Let's hold here," Hoffman said.

"Ooo, look at that!" Lo'thar rushed ahead of Garrison and Adams, who watched in stunned horror as he passed in front of their weapons.

"Damn it, get back in the stack!" King shouted.

"Lo'thar, stay close to your partner," Hoffman said.

Opal growled.

"What the hell was that sound?" Duke asked.

"He's frustrated. Watch the long angle. I don't want anyone getting sniped from an opening farther down the hallway."

"No shit," Duke muttered.

"King, I'm taking charge of our principal for a minute. You have the team. Opal, stay with Gunney," Hoffman said as he advanced, weapon ready, to Lo'thar's side. When he was there, he turned in a tight circle, gun tight to his body and pointed down but ready to swing up for a shot without drawing his sights across any of his divided team.

Lo'thar wiped frost off a panel that was slightly raised from a bulkhead.

Hoffman grabbed the collar of his suit and yanked him back, shoved him into the crevasse on the friendly side of the bulkhead, and stood between him and anything that might attack. He quick-peeked the corner high, then dropped to one knee to do the same thing from a different position. Sticking his rifle barrel around the corner to use the camera was an option, but that risked an unseen enemy just around the corner snatching his rifle away.

Satisfied for the moment, he stood to keep Lo'thar trapped in the bulkhead corner. "All right, Gunney."

"Team move," King said with a corresponding hand

signal.

The rest of the Strike Marines executed a perfect, if accelerated, bounding overwatch to secure the area around Lo'thar and Hoffman.

"What the hell are you doing?" Hoffman asked.

"It's a deck marker." Lo'thar seemed embarrassed as he watched the Strike Marines guarding him. "An original deck marker. All the ones on Takeni were worn away during the transit from Dotari. It's like we're in a museum."

"If that deck marker can tell us where we are, now's the time to read it. In the future, don't get ahead of the team."

"He's clear to come up," King said.

"Don't sound so enthused," Adams said.

King made an unhappy sound low in his throat. "Watch your zone."

Hoffman tapped Max on the shoulder as the communications specialist rejoined Lo'thar.

"Sorry, boss."

"You may have to clip on to his utility gear to hold him back at some point," Hoffman said and went back to his position in the stack, reminding himself Lo'thar was a hero of the Ember War who had destroyed more Xaros drones than most.

Lo'thar ran his hands down the side of the marker until a glass panel flickered to reveal Dotari writing. The exotic script looked three-dimensional but wasn't. Max moved closer and peeked over Lo'thar's shoulder.

"Do you read our language?"

The Dotari script flickered and changed, then blinked several times on the faux holo panel.

"I taught myself a little back when I thought it might help me get selected for the Strike Marines." He squinted as he considered the writing, mouthing the words as though sounding them out. "These words don't make sense."

Near enough to hear the exchange, Hoffman listened as he checked his zones, then looked back at the Dotari marker.

Lo'thar pressed his fingertips against the screen, then twisted his hands in a deliberate pattern. The movement looked like it had meaning, perhaps an unconscious Dotari ritual. The screen filled with text.

"The language is off," Lo'thar said. "Syntax issues…"

"Your language would have changed a bit in the thousand years since you left Dotari," Hoffman said.

"The code base from our ships never changed. They should all be the same." He crowded the panel so that Hoffman couldn't see what he was doing. "I sent a reboot command that should clear it up."

Max gave a short laugh. "Turn it off and turn it back on again to make it work. Glad some tech tips are universal."

The screen snapped off. Deathly silence held the ship.

Hoffman swept his eyes over the situation. As each member of his team held their positions, he felt their impatience and respected their discipline to resist it.

King cleared his throat.

Lo'thar and Max stared at the blank screen, oblivious to anything else around them. Lo'thar slammed the heel of his hand against the bulkhead. Hoffman gritted his teeth. The entire team flinched at the poor noise discipline.

"It appears to be broken," Lo'thar said. "But I did see the marker's metadata code. If this ship follows the same layout as the *Canticle of Reason*—and it should, we built these ships on an assembly line—there's a communication nexus two air locks that way." He pointed down the hall. "And one level up."

"And if that's corrupted?"

Lo'thar held Hoffman's gaze. "Engineering isn't far away."

Hoffman nodded, checking his team and his weapon as he stepped away from the marker. "Let's go."

Max put IR tape on the bulkhead under the marker.

"You are getting much faster at that," Lo'thar said.

Chapter 8

"How does our guide want us to get to the next level? We are at what looks like a closed elevator shaft," Garrison said. "I can open it, if Lo'thar's okay with me scratching the paint."

"Get it open." Hoffman advanced the team to set up a security perimeter around Garrison as he worked the hydraulic spreader.

"If that thing breaks, we're screwed," Adams said.

"Oh, little sister, I have other tricks." He paused, looking down near his feet. "Well, look at that. A loose nail—screw, actually—but very nice." He slipped it into one of his pouches.

"What is wrong with you?" Adams asked.

"Nothing's wrong with me," he said. "What's wrong with you, little sister?"

"Call me that again and I'm going to throat punch you."

"Promises, promises." Garrison stepped back as dust blew out onto the corridor and he repacked his tools, admiring his work. "I've gotta say, Lo'thar, your ancestors built a pretty clean ship. Design-wise, I mean. The lifts operate on tracks rather than cables. Almost abates my paralyzing fear of riding on elevators."

"I love elevators," Adams said. She leaned into the opening, looking up and down through the sights of her weapon. "Looks like they could move some big stuff by the size of this shaft."

"Adams, lead the way," Hoffman said. He looked at Opal. "Good?"

"Don't like the dark," Opal said.

"The dummy has optics like the rest of us," Duke said.

"It *is* creepy," Garrison said, peering after Adams as she climbed the elevator shaft with grav boots and gauntlets. "I'm coming up."

"About time," she said.

Hoffman waited at the bottom with Opal. His point team was a pair of shadows penetrating darker shadows at the top.

"Set," Adams said.

A second later, Garrison reached his position. "Set."

"Follow me, Opal," Hoffman said.

"Opal first. Keep Sir safe from dark places."

The team navigated the shaft in pairs. Duke came last after Max and Lo'thar.

"We're at a pair of double doors," Adams said. "Garrison wants to blow them up."

"I see you. We're going to tighten up a bit," Hoffman said. "We're making progress."

"Agreed," King said.

"My IR scan shows a temperature change beyond the doors," Adams said. "Colder, if that's even possible."

Hoffman signaled Lo'thar to the double doors. "Is that normal?"

Lo'thar moved his head in a gesture Hoffman had always wondered about but only now interpreted. The Dotari was twitching his quills inside the helmet where no one could see his nervousness.

"Stacks should be cooled, but not frozen. Perhaps this is why the marker was malfunctioning," Lo'thar said as he tried the door panel.

Something electronic threw a spark and popped. Lo'thar jerked back his hands. He paused, staring at the panel, then carefully forced it open. "I can…hot-wire…the doorway, but it'll take time."

Hoffman felt tired and ready to be at the objective. "Garrison."

The breacher stepped forward, hydraulic spreader already prepped, and slammed it into the seam between the doors. He paused, checked the positioning, then opened the doors a crack.

Icy fog filled the hallway. For a moment, it looked like it was starting to snow. Garrison wrenched the doors open wide enough for an armored Marine to slip through.

"Moving," Hoffman said, leading the way inside with Opal as Garrison folded the spreader and jammed it into a leg pouch.

King and Booker came next, then Max and Lo'thar, with Adams and Garrison last.

"Team, reposition. Garrison and Adams back on point. Look sharp, people," Hoffman said as he studied the enormous, V-shaped cryo chamber. Scaffolding went up and down the sides of each tier-like stadium seating under construction, and pipes ran beneath the floor grating several levels down.

Water had been condensing or leaking from someplace and formed bizarre ice patterns more reminiscent of a glacier than the interior of a starship. He couldn't see through the glass on the horizontal cryo pods that lined the walls. "Anyone bring an ice scraper?"

"There's a word for this type of cold and it is *yuck*," Adams said.

"*Yuck* is bad word," Opal said.

Hoffman and the team burst out laughing.

"I don't get it," Lo'thar said.

"Nothing to get. Just a little pent-up tension," Hoffman said.

"*Yuck* not bad word?" Opal looked around in confusion.

"Don't ever change, Opie," Booker said.

Max placed IR tape across the threshold of the doorway. "Need some help here."

"Garrison," Hoffman said.

The breacher moved back to the doorway. "Garrison, open the door. Garrison, close the door. An honest man's work is never done." He passed Hoffman and Lo'thar on the way back to his position near Adams.

Lo'thar pressed the sides of his helmet with his hands as he stared in dismay. "This is not the computer node."

"No kidding," Hoffman said. "You care to explain

what's going on?"

"Obviously, things have been rearranged. The colony fleet that settled Takeni didn't have cryo sleep. So that means…"

King cursed. "You don't know the layout."

Lo'thar dropped his hands and faced King, who ignored him to watch his zone. The Dotari hero spoke louder than necessary to emphasize his point, talking with his hands and pacing the floor between Max and Hoffman, who corralled him.

"Do human ships do repairs while underway? I think they do, Gunney King. Such things happen in deep space. Why, I remember many times on the *Breitenfeld*…"

"Lo'thar," Hoffman said.

"Lieutenant?"

"Focus on the mission." He turned to the nearest cryo pod, wiping frost from the glass. "I bet whoever's in here will know their way around." He scraped ice away, activated a small light on the side of his glove, and looked inside. Nothing.

Lo'thar pressed his head against the cleared section, then pulled back in surprise.

"It's empty," Lo'thar said, as though he'd been punched in the gut.

Hoffman leaned closer. "There's a depression in the cushions. A Dotari was in here, but whoever it was is long gone." He signaled his team.

King was the first to act. He wiped another pod and then another. The rest of the team checked pods with one hand and held weapons ready with the other.

King cursed. "Empty."

Hoffman faced Lo'thar and stared into his eyes. The Dotari's face flushed a slightly darker color as he opened and closed his beak without saying more.

Shaking his head, Hoffman strode to a better position to see all his team.

"Got a temperature variance on IR," Adams said as she slipped her rifle sling around to her back. She jumped up to the next level of the scaffolding and performed what sadistic basic-training instructors called a muscle-up—a pull-up that immediately turned into a vertical push-up. Done twenty or thirty times, it was a physical trainer's wet dream and every recruit's worst nightmare—unless the recruit was as lean and strong as Adams. With the assistance of the pseudo-muscle layer beneath the armor plates, doing the maneuver was almost too easy.

"I'm covering her," Duke said as he aimed his rifle and sidestepped for the best angle.

Hoffman and the rest of the team watched her every move.

"You need me up there, little sister?" Garrison asked.

"You couldn't get up here."

"That's some bullshit." Garrison jumped onto and climbed up the scaffolding a second later. "Ha!"

Meanwhile, Adams jogged to a pod, pulled her rifle around front, and scraped the glass with her non-shooting hand. She froze.

Hoffman held his breath.

Gripping her rifle with both hands, she said, "Sir, you want to see this."

Hoffman jumped up, did the chin-up then the press-up, and moved quickly to her side. Garrison aimed his rifle into dark areas Duke and the others couldn't see from their lower position.

Hoffman traded positions with Adams and scraped away more of the ice, his mind rebelling at what he saw before he realized what it was. As a Strike Marine, he'd seen plenty of dead bodies—many of them mangled by explosions or sliced apart by Xaros energy beams. He was less familiar with decay and corruption of flesh.

Inside was a long-dead alien. Sections of the

Dotari's face were stretched tight while other parts had sluffed away from the yellowed skull. Veins and scraps of tissue clung to bone. One eye was open, literally frozen wide. The other had been replaced with black metal and frosted over lenses. A thin frame of wires wove through his quills like a frame and his bottom jaw was covered in metal, so heavy that it hung slack. Whatever happened to him looked like it killed him.

Staring at the decayed body inside the non-functioning cryo pod, Hoffman became aware that Max was making a lot of noise behind him as he helped Lo'thar up to the second level.

"I don't like the mechanical parts," Adams whispered. "And the glass has some kind of moldy ice crust around the edges."

"Lo'thar won't like it either," Hoffman said. He'd never seen a Dotari with advanced prosthetics.

"What is this?" Lo'thar said in breathless dismay. He warbled something in his own language and brushed his sleeves energetically.

"What happened to him?" Hoffman asked. "I've never seen a cyborged Dotari before."

Lo'thar warbled words again, then composed himself with visible effort. "Cybernetics were never something we embraced. Pa'lon and the Qa'Resh warned us against augmentation. It became anathema after centuries of being outlawed. He must have been badly injured before he was put in the cryo pod."

"Gunney, scope the rest of the pods. See if any others are full," Hoffman ordered.

Garrison and the rest of the team started doing the same thing. "Where'd they all go? All the pods I can see from here are a uniform temperature."

"I hate ghost ships," Max said. "Have since the old vids of the *Midway* salvage. Gave me nightmares for years." He gave Opal a nudge. "IR sweep, big guy. No need to be scared."

"Opal 6-1-9 not scared. You don't be scared. Opal keep you safe."

Hoffman watched the interaction between Max and Opal from above.

"I never said I was scared," Max said, then whispered loudly, "I'm able to not like this without being scared, right? Don't project on me. Doughboys get scared all the time."

Opal hefted his oversized rifle up with one hand and looked through the scope as he put his other hand on Max's shoulders. Max tried to wiggle away.

Opal pulled him close, then patted him on the head. "Don't be scared. Opal will kill enemies."

"Got a hot spot," Duke said, then pointed toward the bottom few rows of cryo pods.

Booker pointed toward a larger concentration in the upper corner. "Which way, sir?"

Hoffman pointed to the lower, closer location. "Form up. Move out. Look sharp."

"We're going down," Garrison said.

"You wish," Adams said. She dropped from level to level, taking a knee and sweeping the area with her rifle as Garrison followed and did the same thing. Booker and King followed him.

Hoffman controlled his breathing and checked everyone. He had a bad premonition but was finally feeling the mission groove. This was where he and his team belonged, for better or worse. From his early days as an officer, he'd practiced mission review as a calming technique. Now, with images of the rotted, mutilated corpse of the Dotari in the pod filling his imagination, he searched for anything in the briefing that had suggested this was even a remote possibility. All he could do was press forward and maintain control of his team. If they saw him hesitate, they'd doubt him, the mission, and themselves.

The six pods King had spotted through his scope were on the bottom level.

Hoffman moved toward King and Lo'thar, who were at the first pod. King brushed it off, then paused. Lo'thar stood nervously beside him, wiping his arms and twitching his quills inside his helmet.

"Well?" Booker asked. "You're killing me, Gunney."

"I sure as hell don't want to look," Max said. "Commo guys don't do haunted ghosts ships."

"Keep team safe," Opal said.

King made eye contact with Hoffman, then considered the warm cryo pod. Hoffman could see only a portion of the scene over the gunnery sergeant's shoulder.

Cybernetic attachments covered the definitely not decayed Dotari body inside. Muscles and surgical scars crisscrossed its body. Unlike the corpse, this Dotari's body carried an increased amount of dense muscle—enough to support heavy armor. He couldn't be sure, but it seemed too tall to fit in the pod, as though it had a growth spurt while in stasis —impossible and illogical. Most of all, the creature radiated the potential for berserker violence.

"It can't be," Lo'thar said. "No, no, no…it can't be!"

"Can't be what?" Hoffman asked.

Lo'thar reached to the small of his back, pulled out his pistol, and pointed it at the cryo pod. Hoffman grabbed him by the wrist and jerked his arm toward the ceiling.

"What the hell are you doing?" Hoffman asked.

"They are *noorla*!" Lo'thar yelled and tried to pull his hand free from Hoffman. The alien word sounded familiar to Hoffman, but he couldn't place it.

In the pod, the cyborged Dotari's chest rose and fell slowly, then a bit quicker.

"Sir, I have a heat-signature bloom. And it's growing rapidly…pod bays levels three through twelve," Booker said.

It hit him. The word *noorla* was from the movie *Last Stand on Takeni*, a dramatization of the *Breitenfeld*'s rescue of the Dotari from the Xaros. The Xaros and Dotari they'd twisted into slaves. Violent, berserker slaves called *noorla*. The Marines and sailors on the *Breitenfeld* called them banshees.

"Max," Hoffman said as ice filled his veins, "signal the *Barca* and Admiral Valdar. This mission—"

Inside the cryo pod, the Dotari's eyes snapped open, focusing with the split-second precision of a killing machine. Glass exploded outward as the creature punched through the pod cover and grabbed King by the throat.

A deafening howl cut through the air.

Hoffman popped his Ka-Bar knife from his armor sleeve and chopped through the modified Dotari arm. He sawed the blade back and forth, scratching the surface of the armor and drawing a thin line of blood as it bit down. He wrenched the knife free and thrust the blade into the banshee's mouth. He locked his arm out, pushing with the aid of his armor, and the Ka-Bar broke through the back of the banshee's skull. The alien went slack and released the team sergeant.

King stumbled backward, bumping Lo'thar.

"Fuck!" Max, Booker, and Garrison yelled at the same time.

Opal boomed a warning, "Sir, look out!

Five banshees broke out of their nearby pods, moving like someone had flipped a kill-everyone switch.

Duke dropped two with precision head shots before they could get out of their pods. "Get clear. Move, move, move!"

"Busy fighting!" Garrison said as he pressed the barrel of his rifle to the forehead of the next attacking creature and pulled the trigger. "Little close!"

"Garrison, move left!" Adams leaned around his

right shoulder and shot the next attacker before the first fell away from Garrison's barrel.

Lo'thar stepped in front of Hoffman, fumbling with his pistol. Hoffman shoved him aside.

Max, Booker, and the other Strike Marines opened fire on the remaining two as they charged like drug-crazed mutants. Hoffman added several quick rounds to the lead beast. Both Dotari monsters were flung onto their backs despite their size and forward momentum.

"Let's call our shots if we can. Conserve ammunition when we can," Hoffman said as he scanned his zones and hand-signaled his team into a better defensive formation. Breathing hard, he focused on not sounding like he was breathing hard.

"Screw that!" Max said.

Lo'thar warbled in Dotari, weapon pointed here and there without rhyme or reason. "How can there be banshees on *Kid'ran's Gift*? This isn't possible…"

"This is only going to get worse," Duke said, his voice so level it gave Hoffman chills.

Banshees smashed free of the cryo-pod chambers on the upper level and swarmed down the scaffolding. Howls filled the big room as their bodies crashed down level by level.

"Duke, you mind?" Hoffman asked.

The sniper took three head shots before aiming at the rapidly moving, very large torsos of the creatures.

"Lo'thar!" The lieutenant grabbed the Dotari by the shoulder and gave him a quick shake. "We need a way out of here!"

"The...water access," Lo'thar mumbled, then his head perked up. "Yes, coolant pipes run below the deck." He pointed to a metal hatch at the bottom of the room in the space between the two angled levels of cryo pods. "There! There!" Lo'thar jabbed a finger at the hatch.

"Booker, Max, and King, secure the exit," Hoffman ordered. "Rest of us will cover you." Hoffman lined up a careful shot and pulled the trigger, but instead of hitting the chest of a banshee, he blew off the creature's hand—or thought he did.

A long howl reverberated through the chamber as more banshees broke out of their pods.

"They've got armor. And claws. Shit, they look mean," Adams said, firing in an excruciatingly slow cadence to conserve her ammunition. "I'm bumping my mags." She dropped her current magazine into a leg pouch and slammed a magazine she knew was full into her gun.

"Covering you, litter sister," Garrison said, firing

once, twice, and a third time.

"You're so sweet," Adams said.

"You love me."

"I'm still going to throat punch you when we get out of this."

"It's a date."

"It's not a date. It's me kicking your ass."

Lo'thar got to the hatch to the coolant access and kicked ice off a control panel. Booker and Max crowded around him, using their bodies to shield the Dotari while he worked.

Hoffman and the rest of the team dropped to the next lower level. He saw a shadow move inside a pod and a banshee punched through the glass. It wrapped a massive hand around Hoffman's forearms and looked at him with yellow, insane eyes. Hoffman tried to break free, but the creature's grip was stronger than his armor.

"No hurt!" Opal shouted and his massive fist shot past Hoffman's face and into the banshee's temple. There was a crack of bone, and blood splattered against the broken cryo pod. Hoffman pulled free from the dead alien.

"I can't open it," Lo'thar said, his English deteriorating slightly under stress.

"Opal!" Hoffman pointed at the plate.

"Save team!" Opal jumped over the railing and landed hard next to Lo'thar. He grabbed the lip of the hatch, lifted it up with a grunt and accompanying snap of freezing cold metal, and raised the hatch up on its hinges.

Stench flushed out as the team retreated and formed a perimeter around their inevitable destination.

Banshees bounded down the levels, heedless of the casualties the Marines inflicted with their gauss rifles.

"Oh, God, that's bad," Booker said. "And I worked in a morgue one semester in college."

"Coolant systems shouldn't smell like this," Lo'thar said.

"Flashbangs," Hoffman said, slapping his visor shut as his team followed suit in rapid succession.

King and Booker pulled bangs from their tactical gear and tossed them into the air. "Bangs out," King said.

"What are we doing?" Lo'thar shook his head in confusion just before Opal grabbed the Dotari pilot and threw him into the pipe opening.

Hoffman looked away from the flashbangs as they went off. The sharp concussion of their deflagration popped against his armor, the concussion drowning out the screams of the banshees for a moment. The aliens advance had stopped as they tried to recover from the assault of light and sound from the flashbangs.

The team had bought some time.

"Team move." Hoffman waved toward the opening and Marines dropped into the hatch. He waited for Garrison before jumping into the darkness.

"Last man," Garrison called.

Hoffman jumped into the dark hole and braced himself against the wall, feet spread for stability as he grabbed what he could. Frozen mold cracked against his touch.

Garrison, one hand on a handle on the bottom of the hatch, swung down and closed the heavy metal disc. He stood on Hoffman's legs, using his lieutenant as support, then yanked a welding tool off his belt. Garrison ignited the star-hot flame and welded the hatch shut along the interior line.

Hoffman's legs quivered under the strain. The pseudo-muscles were only so strong, serving to enhance his strength, not replace it.

"You done?" Hoffman asked as banshees screamed and pounded on the other side of the manhole cover.

"Good as it gets," Garrison said.

Hoffman released his hold on the wall and the two Marines fell into the abyss.

****

Hoffman slid feet first into the tube until he struck a corner hard enough to rattle him inside his armor. The more he bumped against the walls of the sewer, the more he questioned his decision, even though the other alternative was a last stand against dozens of bloodthirsty banshees.

Thick muck sloshed over him and he found himself suddenly airborne, tumbling head over heels, until he landed in muddy water. He struggled to pull his head up, but whatever he landed in had the consistency of wet cement.

Turning on the lights mounted to his helmet, he saw brown chunks floating in front of his visor. He wouldn't drown so long as his armor maintained its integrity, but being stuck in god-knew-what was not a good place to be if banshees caught up to him.

Something grabbed the carry handle on his back and he grasped for his rifle mag-locked to his back. He came out of the muck with a wet pop and saw a hulking silhouette through the grime covering his visor. A massive hand slapped against his helmet and wiped the muck away.

Opal looked at him, then grinned. Teeth like ivory

grindstones shone out from the doughboy's mottled, filthy skin.

Hoffman tried to activate his IR transmitter and got an error buzzer. He tapped Opal on the wrist twice and the doughboy dropped him. Hoffman sank to his ankles in the muck and took a deep breath before he popped his helmet off. The air smelled of rot and earth.

"Sir hurt?" Opal asked.

"Bruises," Hoffman said. "Where's the rest of the team?"

Opal grabbed him under one arm and dragged him onto a muddy island behind the doughboy, where the rest of the team formed a perimeter beneath the opening for a massive pipe. He glanced at raised walkways on either side of the blessedly horizontal passage. Most of the recessed maintenance lights were broken or flickering.

"Sir safe," Opal said, dropping him on the sandbar that wasn't a sandbar.

Hoffman did a head count as he spat and coughed. "Where's Duke?"

The veteran Strike Marine crawled out of the water, sniper rifle held over his head. He removed his helmet, sat cross-legged, and started cleaning his rifle.

Hoffman watched the man with a mixture of respect

and annoyance. Other members of the team wiped off gear and commented on the smell.

"Lieutenant." Booker stood up and waved. "Good news, we ended up in the soil re-processors system. This isn't the sludge room."

"How do you know?" Hoffman looked around for a written sign.

"The smell," Booker said, nodding quickly. "And my bio-contamination sensors aren't going berserk."

"It's just mud," Garrison said. "Thank God for small favors. Can't imagine telling the grandkids about the time I was covered in alien dooky."

Hoffman ran his tongue around his teeth, gathered everything he could from the lining of his mouth, and spat it out. "Guess it could be worse." He cleaned gunk out of the IR antenna on his helmet.

Booker laughed. "Right there with ya, boss."

King knelt by Lo'thar, who was curled into a ball on the dubiously gritty beach. "What the hell were those things?"

Lo'thar pulled his knees to his chest, hands pressing the sides of his head as he chattered in Dotari.

King grabbed him. "Lo'thar!"

"They can't be!" Lo'thar wailed. "The Xaros are

gone, their drones destroyed. How can there be *noorla* here?"

Max moved closer. "You mean banshees? The Dotari the Xaros changed into their foot soldiers, the ones that attacked the colony on Takeni?"

Booker's eyes went wide. "The Xaros are here?"

Hoffman took a deep breath, held it, then let it out and stepped across the squishy island. "It makes sense. The Xaros found a Dotari fleet in deep space and sent it to attack Takeni. They must have found this one too."

King shook his head. "How can Xaros drones be here? I thought they self-destructed after the war."

"They were reprogrammed to fly into the nearest star…and that order came out of the Crucible gates at the speed of light."

Max snorted unhappily. "We're fifty light-years from the nearest jump gate. Guess this fleet hasn't got the message yet."

"We're on an ark ship full of banshees and Xaros?" Garrison said. "What the hell are we going to do?"

Everyone stared at the breacher as his voice climbed half an octave.

"Stow it, Marine," King said.

"Yes, sir. Right away, Gunney." Garrison snapped

the words like a curse and started raking his fingers through the muck in the lowest part of the pipe, picking up random bolts and bits of scrap that had been slowly migrating through the sewer for years.

Booker ignored the exchange. "There can't be that many banshees aboard. This ship must hold a half million Dotari. It doesn't make sense to change all the sleepers into banshees right now. They're centuries away from another planet and those banshees got to eat, right? This is a cold sleep ship, not meant to move with crews and passengers. All the banshees active now will get old and die before they get to the next star."

"So why'd we run into any banshees?" King asked. "If the Xaros control this ship and the others…Lo'thar, tell us something."

Lo'thar looked up and worked his jaw from side to side. "We recovered nothing from the Golden Fleet ships the Xaros used to attack Takeni. At the beginning of that fight, before the *Breitenfeld* arrived, the ships were dead silent when we detected them at the edge of the system. There were drones in the ships, but the *noorla* landed in escape pods. We captured one *noorla* alive, but it died when its link to the Xaros was severed. The ones we fought on Takeni had more armor, more augmentation. The ones we just escaped from were…less changed."

"The Xaros must have activated the banshees when we came aboard," Hoffman said.

"The ones that came through the doors looked ready for a fight," King said. "Better equipped."

"We don't know how long it takes the Xaros to fully change the Dotari," Hoffman said. "But the longer we sit here, the more time they have to get ready for the next round. If there are Xaros drones…we don't have a single quadrium shell to hit them with."

"Been a long time since I trained to fight a drone," King said. "Duke?"

"I was on Luna when the Xaros smashed it." The sniper snapped his rifle back together and looked down the sights.

"Opal and I fought them in Utah," Hoffman said. "Opal? Xaros."

Opal smashed a fist into his palm.

"High-power gauss shots on drones," King said to the team. "Only way to crack their shells. Don't stop shooting until they disintegrate."

Hoffman's mouth went dry as he remembered battles against the drones. Days of constant battle, his doughboys disintegrated by the Xaros' weapons. The skies dark as the enemy descended from orbit…

He banished the thoughts and checked his team. Looking around, he put on the mask of command.

"The mission…the mission is to contact the crew and get the fleet back to Dotari. We're aborting as of now. We need to get word to Captain Bradford and Admiral Valdar on the *Breitenfeld*."

Lo'thar fought to get to his feet. "No! We can't leave without a viable blood sample. The phage! My daughter needs—"

"We can get a sample off one of these creatures if we run across them. Maybe," Hoffman said.

Lo'thar rushed forward and grabbed Hoffman by his breastplate. "We can't give up, not when we're so close. She'll die if I don't do something. Hale wouldn't run away from—"

Hoffman grabbed the Dotari by the neck and gripped it so hard the color on Lo'thar's face changed.

"I am not Hale." The lieutenant let Lo'thar go. "This isn't the same as Takeni. If the *Breitenfeld* doesn't know about this threat, the Xaros could capture the ship. Capture the Grinder. The Xaros can change humans too. Hale fought coopted humans on Pluto during the war. What would happen if the Xaros got Valdar's ship?"

Lo'thar rubbed his neck. "The Xaros drones can replicate themselves if they have the matter to do it with. If the drone gets the Grinder…it could jump to a world with a Crucible. Vanish in the network."

"It would be the Ember War all over again," King said. "Countless drones unleashed on the galaxy."

"But the self-destruct order…" Adams said.

"One-time event," Hoffman said. "Spread from the Crucible gates at the speed of light. The drone jumps behind the line and it's like it never happened. The laws of physics aren't on our side."

"Valdar would never let that happen," Duke said. "He'd blow the *Breitenfeld* up before the Xaros could take over."

"Which is why the ship needs to know about the Xaros and the banshees right now," Hoffman said. "We're aborting this mission."

"There's still a way," Lo'thar said. "There has to be."

Hoffman shook his head. "There are half a million Dotari on this ship that could have been turned into screaming monsters dead set on killing us all. I have six Strike Marines. We're tough, we're trained, but we didn't bring enough of us to retake this ship. Even if we link up with Bradford…" He looked up and down the long tunnel around their muddy island and contemplated his next move.

"Weapons check," Gunney King ordered.

Opal hefted his big gun, pulled the magazine free, and watched mud plop out. "Dotari poop bad." He wiped the magazine clean, then dropped it into a leg pouch. With quick, efficient movements, he reloaded from a backpack.

The rest of the team sounded off.

"Good to go, LT," King said, switching his glance from Hoffman to the sniper. "Except for our prima donna here."

Duke blew something from one of his tungsten-clad bullets.

"You're not going to need that in these hallways," King said.

Duke's eyes focused with unusual intensity as he used "the tone" to correct the team NCO. "She's dirty. And I need a dip." Moments later, he folded the sniper rifle in half and slammed it onto his back. Without wasted motion, he pulled his carbine and thumbed the power on.

King made the rounds, quickly checking each team member. He patted Booker on the shoulder. One by one, he refocused them on the revised mission.

Hoffman went to Lo'thar, put a hand on his

shoulder, and spoke quietly. "I need you to take this one step at a time."

Lo'thar nodded. "The wastewater systems connect to most everything. If the ship has the same base structure as the ship I grew up on, then there's a maintenance tunnel farther along the tunnel." He pointed downstream.

Garrison's head perked up. "Hey, Dotty, there any kind of weird fertilizer in this sludge?"

Max moved between the breacher and the Dotari pilot. "Shut up, Garrison."

"I got some of it in my mouth," Garrison squeaked.

Booker slapped him on the back of the head.

Hoffman and Lo'thar led the team up a ladder onto the nearest walkway.

Chapter 9

Hoffman and King kept the team on the move, approaching every intersection as though it might be a life-and-death battle.

"Adams, Garrison. Watch that next intersection. My infrared optic is showing a slight elevation in temperature," King said.

"On it," Adams said as she moved and aimed her gauss rifle at the same time. Garrison, searching through his sights, adjusted the length of his stride to move in perfect unison with Adams.

"Looks good. We're pushing through," Adams said.

Seconds later, King and Booker followed as Max ushered Lo'thar behind them.

"Opal, let's go," Hoffman said.

Duke brought up the rear without comment.

They repeated the procedure over and over.

"This ship feels like it's the size of downtown Phoenix," Adams said.

"Stay sharp," Hoffman said to the team. "Head on a swivel. We don't need any more surprises." He made eye contact with King, who replied with a nod.

Lo'thar muttered and looked at his feet as he traversed the metal walkway. The Dotari pilot seemed detached after the recent events. Hoffman didn't know what it was like to have a sick daughter, but assumed it would influence his judgment. He moved to the pilot's side.

"You OK, Lo'thar?"

The Dotari looked up, eyes unfocused. "What if I fail?"

Hoffman struggled for words. "Lots of ships in the fleet. Others may be different than this one. Admiral Valdar's not the type to give up quick or easy."

Lo'thar nodded with grim determination. "This way."

Hoffman and Lo'thar arrived at a door. Garrison and Adams each gave the Dotari a dirty look as they hustled to set up security around the door.

"There is a hydroponic farm through here," Lo'thar said as the rest of the team caught up.

"I'm not trying to rain on your parade, buddy, but this is an odd place for a hydroponic facility," Garrison said.

Lo'thar wiped frost away from a panel on the doorframe to reveal Dotari script. "It says Hydroponics Bay 99."

"We're burning daylight," King said. "If I don't see a little sense of urgency, I'm going to light a real fire under your asses."

"On it, Gunney," Garrison said as he pulled his multitool from his kit. One end was a two-pronged pry tool like an industrial-strength chisel. At the other end was a sledgehammer on one side and a spike on the other. Garrison hit the spiked end against the door frame and cursed as his strike proved too weak to puncture the metal. Garrison hefted the tool back like a club and swung it with all the might his suit could muster as Lo'thar protested.

Ignoring the lock and the door handle, he aimed at the hinges one after another. The door fell partially inward, hanging from the locking mechanism, which wasn't designed to hold the entire weight of the door. He stepped back and launched a front kick that sent it spinning into the room.

King and Booker went in first, followed by

Hoffman, Max, and Lo'thar. The rest of the team fed off their movements and filled the gaps until they were all inside.

Mist swirled around them as warm air met cold air from the sewer tunnel. The clouds dispersed quickly in the large room. Hoffman thought the tangle of trees and vines before him had once been orderly and well-maintained. Unlike the rest of the ship, this area was well-lit with high-powered grow lamps. Irrigation tubes sprinkled water onto trees and plants.

He moved forward beside Lo'thar, who was reaching for a bunch of nuts hanging on a tree branch like grapes.

"Visibility is crap in here," Duke said.

"Remember when I said you wouldn't need that sniper rifle?" King asked. "Watch your zone and look for work."

"These are *gar'udda* nut trees," Lo'thar said. He twisted one off and nibbled on it. "Almost ripe. These branches have been trimmed recently."

"Hungry," Opal said as he grabbed a fistful of the nuts and tossed the cluster stems and all into his mouth. After two more handfuls, he handed some to Hoffman.

"Not hungry," Hoffman said.

Duke sniffled and rubbed his eyes with one hand.

Booker shined a small light in his eyes. "Allergic reaction?"

"Little bit," Duke said.

Hoffman tried not to have his own sympathetic reaction. The sniper looked miserable. He faced Lo'thar. "You said we're close to a hangar bay?"

"Certainly. Just on the other side," Lo'thar said.

"We get to the hull, we can send a message to the *Breitenfeld*," Hoffman said. "Call in the *Barca* for evac. Everyone get that?"

The team nodded and Duke clicked his tongue into the open IR channel.

Booker froze, then held up a fist next to her helmet. She put one hand over the Dotari's beak and pulled him into the shrubberies. In the distance, trees and bushes rustled.

"Good job, Booker," King whispered as the Strike Marines crouched low and went silent.

Heard more than seen, banshees entered through a door on the far side of the room. Branches moved. A small animal darted away from the approaching monsters about twenty meters from the team.

Hoffman typed out a text message on his arm panel

and sent it to each member of the team. "Watch your zones. Stealth mode." The words popped up in the projected HUD that worked regardless of whether the visor was up or down.

The first banshee continued forward until it was uncomfortably close to the team. The creature lacked most of the armor Hoffman had seen on the first wave of banshee attackers. It had no eyes or ears but picked nuts with machine-like efficiency, dropping the produce into a filthy apron with unerring accuracy. Others joined the harvest.

"Is it injured?" King messaged Hoffman.

Hoffman typed on his arm panel without taking his eyes off the pathetic banshee. "Unknown."

Booker's message crawled rapidly up Hoffman's and the rest of the team's HUDs. "Don't you do it, Duke!"

Hoffman looked at the sniper, who was stifling a sneeze.

A second message popped up, this one labeled with Garrison's online tag of "Legendary Badass": "What kind of sniper are you?"

King killed the message board.

The banshees froze, then turned their eyeless, earless heads. Moments later, they slowly converged on

Duke's position.

Hoffman slid his Ka-Bar from his armor and adjusted his grip.

The banshees moved closer.

Another of the small, rat-like creatures scurried out of a tree and ran between the lead banshee's legs. It half-turned to look for the rodent, then snapped its arm into the trees and grabbed King by the throat.

Opal lashed out with his armored fist, smashing the banshee's head.

Worker banshees hissed.

"So much for stealth." Garrison snatched the breaching hammer from his pack, swinging it around and down on another as it charged, the force of the blow driving its head between its knees. Bits of bone and brains sprayed the ground.

Adams dashed forward. "On your right, Garrison! I'm on your right!" She jumped into the air, executing a flying kick that collapsed the banshee's chin.

"Gotcha, little sister," Garrison said, redirecting his next swing to avoid her.

Booker, Max, and Hoffman rushed past King, who was still struggling to his feet. All three stabbed banshee throats with their Ka-Bars.

"Nice work." Hoffman wiped off his knife on the side of a gar'udda nut tree. "Time to get out of here."

"Wait." Lo'thar went to one of the bodies. "I need a sample."

The entire team watched in stunned silence as Lo'thar removed a bundle from his pack and spread out a roll of vials and syringes.

"Help him, Booker." Hoffman pulled King to his feet with one hand.

"Have you ever done this before?" Booker asked the Dotari.

Lo'thar picked up a metal syringe. "I used to draw my daughter's blood, though the implement I used was less frightening than this…and we could get what we wanted from her veins. Dotari immunity factors are in our bone marrow. Bit less pleasant to collect."

Booker kicked the dead banshee.

"He's not going to mind," she said.

King checked his gear and then the bodies of the banshee farmers.

The sound of hydraulic doors opening carried through the trees. Hoffman looked at Lo'thar and Booker, who were moving far too slow.

"Opal, get a sample."

The doughboy bumped Lo'thar and Booker out of the way, then grabbed the banshee by its bicep and forearm. He twisted, then pulled it apart at the elbow. Tendons slipped free, slick with gore and connective tissue that tore like wet sheets. One of the joints popped and blood spattered Lo'thar's gear.

Without a word, Lo'thar held a plastic medical bag up and watched Opal drop the severed limb inside.

"More samples?" Opal asked.

Lo'thar shook his head vigorously. "This is not what I trained for. At all."

Hoffman grabbed his shoulder, forcing the Dotari pilot to look him in the eyes. "Which way?"

Lo'thar pointed to the right but seemed preoccupied as he stuffed the bagged banshee hand and forearm into his backpack. Two-thirds of the macabre body part poked out. He made two attempts to put it in his backpack, turning and reaching around himself with limited success.

A heavy door banged open and closed, then bright-white energy blasts cut through the room, slicing through gar'udda trunks and exploding them into razor-sharp splinters that pelted Hoffman's visor. He aimed his rifle and blind-fired toward the source of the attacks as he moved toward the cover of a tree reduced to blackened shards.

"On your right, Garrison!" Adams said as she cranked off three-round bursts at banshees.

"King. Bounding overwatch," Hoffman said. "Assault through."

Watery foam sprayed down from the ceiling as fire alarms went off.

"Booker, with me." King and Booker raced forward as the team laid down suppressive fire. Targets were plentiful but hard to see between shattered trees and smoke that thickened rapidly.

"Set," King and Booker said in unison as they kneeled and fired weapons.

"The *gar'udda* burn too oily to make good firewood," Lo'thar said. "The visibility will only get worse until the ventilation sys—"

Hoffman grabbed him and signaled Max to follow. "Bounding!"

"Covering!" King shouted.

Strike Marine gunfire lashed out at the flare of energy weapons and roaring banshees.

"Can't see through this smoke," Max said. "Lo'thar, stay close."

Additional sirens went off loud enough to activate

the sound-dampening properties in Hoffman's helmet. Fire bloomed in the treetops. Smoke gave the sight an ominous glow that seemed to expand moment by moment as spray nozzles in the ceiling proved minimally effective.

"Button up," King said. "Since being attacked by alien cyborgs isn't bad enough, now we're doing it in a forest fire."

"Way ahead of you," Adams said. "Why have anything that can burn on a ship? Some long-term planning on the Dotari's part."

"Stay close to your partners. Don't want to lose anyone in this smoke," Hoffman said. "Push to the doors. Kill anything that tries to stop us. Lo'thar, is that fire alarm going to shut off anytime soon?"

"That second siren isn't a fire alarm. It's a decompression alarm. The air is going to be sucked into reclamation tanks to starve the fire of oxygen," Lo'thar said.

"Great. Just what we need. Moving," Garrison panted. "Come on, little sister."

King and Booker bounded forward next.

Banshees slowed their rate of fire and pulled back as the flames spread.

"Duke, check in," Hoffman said.

Garrison grunted over the comlink. "Oh look, a door. And it's closed."

"Duke," Hoffman repeated.

"I'm coming. Trying not to get shot or burned alive. Or sneeze myself to death."

"Get that door open, Garrison," Hoffman ordered as he sandwiched Lo'thar between himself and Max and sprinted the final distance.

"Can't," Garrison said.

"What the hell do you mean you can't?" Adams snorted.

"Look at it. This monster is thick as Booker's backside," Garrison said.

Booker smacked his helmet.

"I can't find hinges. Looks like a slider. Complicated. If I do something wrong, it gets derailed and we get cooked in a Dotari nut farm," Garrison said.

"Orchard," Duke said as he joined them.

"Whatever."

"Everyone get on that door and force it open. Opal, we need to get out of here."

"Opal open door." The doughboy slung his rifle and threw all his weight and strength on the crossbar handle to slide the door sideways. Nothing happened. "Opal needs help!"

"Duke, maintain security. Everyone else, help Opal." Hoffman slung his rifle and started pushing. Inch by inch, they moved the door, slipping inside and grabbing the handles on the other side.

"Duke, move," Hoffman grunted.

The sniper rushed into the outer hallway, knelt, and scanned the dark intersection with his rifle.

"Stand clear," Hoffman said.

Everyone jumped away from the industrial-grade hatch and the door slammed shut, shaking the deck beneath their feet. Hoffman winced at the sound of metal shearing and supports breaking inside the door mechanism.

"For the record, I didn't break that by myself," Garrison said.

Lo'thar fell onto the deck and the bag with the banshee limb tumbled out. He stared at the gruesome body part as though he'd forgotten what it was or why he needed it. He stared through Hoffman and the others without trying to stand up as banshees howled from a corner at the end of a dark hallway.

"Move out," Hoffman ordered as he pulled Lo'thar to his feet and shook him. "Get it together, Lo'thar. We need you. Your daughter needs you."

Lo'thar stared at him with wide, unfocussed eyes.

Hoffman wanted to shake him again but resisted the urge. He leaned his helmet visor inches from Lo'thar's and spoke in a low, sincere tone. "Get us out of here, Lo'thar."

Lo'thar lifted the banshee farmer's hand and pointed down a hallway leading away from the sounds of the banshee swarm. "Should be a hangar bay that direction." The fingers on the severed hand twitched and Lo'thar shivered as the Dotari tried to hold the body part farther away from himself.

Hoffman took it and jammed it unceremoniously into Lo'thar's backpack.

****

Hoffman measured the hallway with his helmet optics, tagging each opening he detected, whether it be a hallway or a hatch, in his combat computer, then motioned King over.

"I know what you're thinking," King said. "A tactical retreat in a straight hallway relies on speed, prayer, and cover fire."

"Options?" Hoffman asked.

King faced the sound of banshees at the far end of

one hallway, then the silent hallway leading to the hangar.

"We should split Garrison from Adams and team him with Duke," King said. "They can give our pursuers the improvised device-sniper combo. Garrison sets traps, Duke shoots the bastards as they try to avoid them or—better yet—flop around on the deck with massive injuries inciting chaos within the enemy ranks. Buy us time to get some distance."

Hoffman nodded. "Good. What else?"

"Put Lo'thar with Booker. He's our principal and having our medic close probably isn't a bad idea. You need Max when we try to contact Bradford or the *Barca*, I'll move up to the point position with Adams."

"Works," Hoffman said, then opened a link to the rest of the team. "Garrison, switch to rearguard with Duke and start dropping some toe poppers for the banshees."

"It's always the right time for explosions," Garrison said as he moved.

Hoffman chuckled with the rest of the team. "Adams, I hate to do this to you, but King's your new partner on point. Booker, you're with Lo'thar in position two. Max, you're with me. Aside from staying alive, I want you thinking about how we're going to contact Bradford and gold squad. Opal, you're with me."

King paused before moving to his new position. Hoffman faced the gunnery sergeant and waited.

"I remember the banshees from that god-awful *Last Stand at Takeni* movie," King said over the team channel. "They're a hell of a lot worse in person. Move it, team. Contrary to what Hale and the others said in that movie, today is not a good day to die."

Garrison opened his helmet visor after he passed Hoffman and Max, scratched his nascent sideburns, then dropped the visor. Moving toward the banshee screams, he unbuckled his pack and dropped it to the deck. Duke covered him.

Hoffman checked the position of each Strike Marine. "Team move." Moments later, they arrived at an intersection of thick bulkheads. Using the reinforced corners for protection, they aimed their weapons to cover Garrison and Duke when they came running.

Garrison shaped a charge of plastic explosives, packed it with Dotari nuts and bolts, then wrapped detonating cord around it twice.

"You're going to blow your wad on the first trap," Duke muttered.

"Do I tell you how to handle your boom stick? No, I don't. A little professional courtesy if you please. Move and set, I'll cover," Garrison said. With reverent hands, he lifted his latest creation, examined it, and reached up to place it eye level to a banshee. "My baby's so beautiful I can barely bring myself to leave her to these monsters."

"That you have all ten fingers is why I believe in you." Duke popped to his feet and sprinted back to Hoffman and the others. He took a knee at the corner and aimed his weapon down the passageway. "Set. Covering!"

Banshees entered the longest part of the hallway they hadn't yet traversed and broke into a loping charge that ate up distance like a pack of wild animals.

"Moving!" Garrison yelled, barely ahead of the enemy advance.

Banshees smashed over each other, claws raking the air. High-pitched shrieks from half the banshees cut through the deep roars of the others. Their feet pounded the floor of the hallway as they stampeded forward, brandishing weapons fused directly to their forearms. In some places, the energy blasters had replaced hands. Some looked like cutting torches or mechanical saws, others like they'd been stolen from the ship's armory and grafted to flesh.

Hoffman and the rest of the team bounded away to the next intersection. Duke fired a steady rhythm that took banshees out at the knees, toppling them forward and tripping up the aliens behind them. The scrum of banshees snarled and swiped at each other like a pack of wolves fighting over a fresh kill. The wounded banshees seemed no less deterred in reaching the Strike Marines.

Inaccurate but frequent blasts from the banshees' energy weapons scorched everything from floor to ceiling. A stream of the blinding energy jetted over Duke and Garrison where they knelt and glanced Max's armor. He paused to check his communications gear.

"Good?" Hoffman asked.

Max gave him a worried thumbs-up just before a bolt of energy scorched the floor where Hoffman had been a moment earlier.

"Pick up the pace and thank God that only a few of them seem to have ranged weapons. Shorter pauses on each bounding maneuver. Garrison, you better drop your IEDs on the move when you can."

The first IED charge—already buried by the banshee advance—exploded, slamming several of the monsters into the walls and the ceiling. A brief, bloody hole opened in the banshee ranks.

Duke squeezed off rounds at a faster pace.

King moved into the point position with Adams

while Hoffman maintained command of the unit from the center. Booker and Lo'thar followed close behind King and Adams.

Garrison stuck something to the wall near the corner and then followed the team around. He sprinted, then slowed to a shuffle as he assembled a smaller IED, jabbed a sensor into it, and dropped it. He ran to the other side of the hallway and did the same thing.

With the optical enhancement of his armor, Hoffman saw the laser trip wire connecting the two devices. He hoped the banshees couldn't do the same thing.

Each time the passageway took a new direction, Hoffman worried they were lost and heading away from the hangar. "King, report."

"Lo'thar says we're almost there," King replied, breathing heavily as he ran someplace beyond Hoffman's view.

Hoffman and Max came around the corner and saw the first half of the team facing a set of large cargo doors. Explosions and gauss rifle fire boomed behind him in the direction of his rearguard.

"Garrison, give me a sit-rep," Hoffman said.

"We're leaving behind a trail of body parts and destruction, just as we planned. I'm good, but I'll need to resupply before long. At this rate, I won't have much left to blow open doors and whatnot," Garrison said.

Hoffman heard Duke's rifle from down the hallway as well as through Garrison's helmet microphone. He hurried toward the others. "Our rearguard is locked in a hot fight. The banshees won't be far behind."

"This is the hangar," Lo'thar said, indicating the heavy door as everyone looked at the Dotari pilot.

"Anytime now," Max said.

Lo'thar looked at them indignantly. "This is identical to my service bay on the *Canticle of Reason*. What is the human term? Dee-jay voodoo? Day-us vult?"

"Open. It," Adams said.

Lo'thar pried open a control panel and reached inside. "The ships inside may not be assembled," Lo'thar said and the entire team groaned. "And I may not be able to open the bay doors."

"Anything's better than a knife fight in a corridor with the banshees," Max said.

Hoffman listened to their conversation but filtered out the nonessentials. He tracked the progress of his rearguard by the sound of battle moving closer and closer. An energy beam struck a wall he'd just passed at the last corner. With a final glance at the door Lo'thar was working on, Hoffman moved back toward the hallway and crouched against a corner for cover. He leaned out to aim his rifle.

"Duke and Garrison, I have you," Hoffman said. "Get back here. I'll cover."

The breacher and the sniper each pulled a grenade and lobbed it down the hallway before sprinting back to the rest of the team. The double explosion killed the leading edge of the banshee swarm and collapsed the deck plating.

Garrison finished the race slightly ahead of Duke, despite being fifteen pounds heavier.

"Last man," Duke said as he chugged past Hoffman.

Hoffman flipped his ammunition selector to shot and fired marble-sized beads into the advancing mass of banshees. They were bigger and more muscular than a normal Dotari, with pieces of armor, weapons, and technology melded to their form. Most of these were covered with onyx plates and cybernetic vision components hooked cruelly over their yellow eyes. Their scarred, chipped beaks peeked out from the armored wedge of their heads, and they screamed with such force that Hoffman could've sworn that blood and bits of their throats flew ahead of them.

"LT, I got you. Fall back," King said.

One of the lead banshees stumbled and its brethren

stomped it to the deck as they scrambled over it. There were so many they slammed each other against the walls and shoved each other forward. The passage shook with the violence of their advance.

"Lo'thar! How's that door coming?" Hoffman yelled into his helmet mic. He fired one more burst, then turned and ran without looking at the advancing threat, placing his trust in his team, counting on their rounds to slow the banshee advance. Pushing his combat armor to its maximum potential, he set a new personal record for the fifty-yard dash.

"Working on it! Something is weird with the code. Should be universal." Lo'thar cursed in Dotari. "There! Finally!"

By the time Hoffman reached the hangar, Duke, Garrison, and Max were holding positions at the threshold of the giant cargo door, firing on the advancing enemy in a steady rhythm to conserve ammunition.

"Reloading," Duke said.

"Covering fire," Garrison and Max said.

The banshees were so close and so numerous now, the Strike Marines' gunfire barely slowed their progress.

"Reload—" Max yelled, his voice cutting out.

Garrison let loose several three-round bursts at the

small groups of armed banshees, silencing two of the energy weapons. Duke switched from headshots to throat shots for reasons he didn't stop to explain.

"Pull back and let's get these doors shut," Hoffman said, then conducted a head count once the doors slammed together. Garrison whipped out a cutting torch and began welding the door shut.

After so many hours in sewage tunnels and hallways, the hangar felt like a coliseum. There was a broad path down the center with some sort of rail assembly that Hoffman assumed was for launching ships into the void. He identified several workstations and arms lockers in the corners and nonessential areas. What caught his eye were rows of the Dotari shuttles in storage cradles.

"The hangar is clear," Booker announced as she strode into the light from the shadowy recesses of the large space.

"You see anything that looks void-worthy?" Hoffman asked.

"Everything looks packed for storage," Booker said. "Imagine that. Maybe our resident Dotari pilot has some better news."

"Nothing but time," Hoffman said as he jogged toward the medic and the Dotari pilot while still giving orders to the team. "Garrison, door?"

A banshee fist hit the opposite side of the door, beating a small lump in the metal next to Garrison's face.

"Slagged the locks and the hinges," Garrison said, "time to staple her shut." He pulled a cylinder of metal off his belt and unrolled a thirty-centimeter-long sheet shaped like a flat crossbar with flared ends like a big letter I. The crude sheet of metal was thin, a raw material straight out of a ship engineer's workshop.

"I never thought I'd use one of the staples, but here we are, lost in deep space in an ancient ship full of psychotic alien cyborgs with nothing but my skill, imagination, and good looks to save us." He welded the improvised crossbar across the seam of the closed door and gave each bead of the weld a double-hatch cap.

The door rumbled as banshees beat against it.

"Does he always talk like this?" Lo'thar asked.

Adams leaned forward and smiled. "Only when he's concentrating."

Lo'thar shook his head, judging the tactic from a distance. "Why not damage the servo mechanisms in the door? That will almost certainly snap that—"

"Just break it? OK!" Garrison snapped out his breaching hammer and slammed the spike into the servo housing. There was a screech of metal as he wrenched it out and impaled the other servo box.

"Really hope there's a way out of this bay. We keep painting ourselves into a corner, our luck will run out eventually." Adams drew her Ka-Bar from her forearm armor sheath, paused to sigh dramatically, then slammed the blade overhand through the left servo. After cranking the blade back and forth several times, she moved over and took out the right servo as well.

"Never a dull moment in the Strike Marines." Garrison worked the blunt flame across the crossbar. "Which is why we get paid an extra two hundred bucks a month. That money definitely makes experiences like this better than some logistics post on Triton…if I ever see my recruiter on the street…"

"Keep concentrating, Mr. Garrison," Lo'thar said.

Garrison rapped knuckles against the half-welded-on crossbeam.

"Anything else we should break?" he asked Lo'thar.

"Don't…ah…That's quite enough. Can you make her stop?" Lo'thar shifted from foot to foot and gripped his hands together nervously as Adams kicked in a maintenance hatch at the bottom of the door frame. "This ship is a treasured artifact of my people. It is our history and heritage."

Adams examined her work, then sheathed her knife with a wink at Lo'thar. "Every artist has her medium. Marines break stuff."

"Yes, I remember now." Lo'thar breathed the words with little enthusiasm as the emergency lights in the shuttle bay blinked off and the banshee assault on the door petered out.

Each member of the Strike Marine team switched to infrared optics and helmet lamps.

"They think they have us locked inside," Lo'thar said.

Booker finally walked away from the ships in discouragement and joined the rest of the team near the doors that were barricaded against the banshee swarm.

"They do." Hoffman grabbed Lo'thar by the shoulders and spun him toward one of the Dotari shuttles. "Figure out if you can get that ship up and running."

The lieutenant stared at the very large and very shut bay doors at the opposite end of the bay. "Nothing quite like having our backs to the wall at the ass-end of nowhere." He moved toward three of his idle Marines. "Garrison, take Adams and Opal. I want every possible entrance to this place secured against those things."

"For the love of God," Garrison muttered as he walked. Adams and Opal followed him without interrupting his grumbling.

"What was that, Lance Corporal Garrison?" King grunted as the trio passed.

"Happy to be here, Gunney," Garrison said. "Opal, yank the framework of those crates off. I need something to weld."

Opal pulled apart metal crates and interior door frames. Adams carried them by the armload to Garrison, who welded them across any opening large enough for a banshee to smash through as though he was trying to break a speed record. Sparks flew all around him as he worked.

Hoffman signaled King over. "Do an ammunition and equipment count. I want to compare it with what my armor computer is telling me. Booker, inspect the team and advise me of any unreported injuries."

Without the flying sparks of Garrison's welding torch, darkness gave the place the feel of an eerie green cathedral. Hoffman's enhanced optics magnified details on the Dotari ships. They preferred larger wings and more maneuver jets on their shuttles than Terran engineering, which made the alien ships far more graceful in flight, but significantly more difficult to pilot.

Bas-relief sculptures of the ancient Dotari crewmen and symbols scrolled around the most utilitarian archways. What made them truly strange was the shape of the archways—larger at the top like an inverse tetrahedron but not quite. The shuttle doors were ovals that opened on hinges at the top of the frames.

The hangar seemed both mystical and dangerous with Dotari words scrolling across arches of doorways. Relative silence only increased Hoffman's dread.

Instead of using colored lines like those found on most Terran flight decks, this hangar had paths bordered by descriptions, instructions, and warnings he could not read without Lo'thar's frequent and excited explanations. Hoffman thought the ceilings were unnecessarily high and grand. Even the distant ceilings were inscribed with careful detail, as though the creators of this Dotari fleet had intended the ship to last forever.

"Some of what you are seeing is… how do you say it… graffiti of a long voyage. Do you not observe the difference?" Lo'thar said.

Hoffman shook his head, then stepped across the launch railings, staring at the old ships as he formulated a plan. The shuttles appeared to be asleep, covered with a thin layer of frost.

"Lieutenant Hoffman." Lo'thar hustled away from a mothballed shuttle and pointed at large mechanical wheels on the side of the bay doors. "The manual controls are still operational. We can open this to the void."

"Small favors," Hoffman said. "None of us can fly, Lo'thar. These shuttles void-worthy or not?"

"Still assessing." The Dotari bent his head and went back to the shuttle.

"It's like a tomb in here," King said.

Hoffman nodded.

"The Xaros—or the top banshee, if there is such a thing—are smart enough to cut all power to this area. They're either readying an all-out assault or are about to blow the doors and suck us into space. Either option is bad. No time to waste," Hoffman said. "Lo'thar, how we looking?"

Lo'thar paced near the mothballed shuttles. "So old…and they're broken up for deep storage." He stopped near one and opened the cockpit door.

Booker threw up her hands. "Really? I hadn't noticed. Well, except for these here without engines…or wings. Aren't most Dotari shuttles atmosphere-capable like our Mules?" She shook her head, talking to herself in a loud voice. "Don't mind the medic. What could she know about void-capable transports? She's just a girl…" She thrust a finger toward a ship parked near the end of the flight deck. "This one doesn't even have doors!"

Hoffman and the other Strike Marines watched and waited, splitting their attention between Booker's increasingly theatrical tirade and Lo'thar's reverent approach to the ancient shuttles.

Lo'thar played with the controls. "No power source, no wings. Would take me eight hours to make it flight-ready with a Dotari maintenance team."

"No power source?" Booker asked. "None of these even have batteries?"

"It taxes the system." Lo'thar shrugged.

"Fuel?" Hoffman asked.

"Neither are in this bay," Lo'thar said. "Which is different from my experience. In the event of an emergency, having such components in different bays means—"

"I think we can appreciate the situation just fine." Hoffman beat his fist against the handrail and looked at the door Garrison had welded shut, then to the bay doors.

Lo'thar ignored them as he looked at a row of cargo containers along the wall. "And we'd have to find the parts. Hmm…I don't recognize some of these controls."

Hoffman flinched. "It gets worse?"

"The equipment I know has a thousand years of design evolution since all this was manufactured. The capacitor controls are labelled with a colorful euphemism Dotari teenagers use for their genitalia." Lo'thar frowned as he studied the cockpit. "Something of a language shift. This can't be right. Did they really call the brake a…"

Without warning, thunder boomed through the hangar as the entrance shook from an impact.

"I think the banshees just got reinforcements," King said.

Hoffman pointed at the mechanical wheels, called "dogs" on Terran ships, next to the bay doors. "Seal up your suits. We're going for a walk."

"Get on that wheel and heave to," King said, closing his visor and running systems checks on his armor as he hustled to comply with the order. He gripped the wheels and put his back into it. It moved slowly and with a groan like an ancient tree about to fall.

Opal leaned over King pushing higher on the wheel. Hoffman and the others found their own places and put their backs into the effort.

Atmosphere bled out of the hangar as the large doors opened inch by inch. Warnings popped on Hoffman's visor as he looked at Lo'thar, then pulled him away from the work team to fix his helmet seal. Inside the helmet, the Dotari's eyes were wide with alarm.

"What do you mean, 'going for a walk'?" Lo'thar asked.

"The banshees ever operate in a vacuum during the fight on Takeni?" Hoffman asked. He could still feel the vibration of the banshees banging on the door but could no longer hear it without air pressure to carry the sound waves.

"No…we only fought drones ship to ship." Lo'thar leaned over and looked into the widening gap open to the void. "The *noorla* don't have helmets. But we do!"

"Strike Marines improvise, adapt, and overcome," Hoffman said. "This armor comes in handy most days. Team, follow me."

He stepped through the opening and mag-locked his boots to the exterior of the hull. Time wasn't his friend, but he took a moment to look around. The exterior of the *Kid'ran's Gift* remained dark despite the activity inside. The rest of the Dotari fleet floated in absolute silence.

Hoffman shuddered, paused, then activated the comlink in his helmet. "Clear. Bring 'em out, Gunney."

King brought the team out in good order, setting Opal on overwatch with his oversized gauss rifle.

Hoffman sent an alert to Max's helmet. "Get on the comms to the *Barca* ASAP."

"On it," Max said, dropping to one knee as he swung his backpack off and unpacked his communications gear. "Going to be tough without line of sight."

With several quick movements, he unrolled a whip antenna and sealed the base to the hull with a suction clamp. Grav locks and magnets could disrupt certain comm frequencies, so he extended a shorter antenna from his armor, then nodded to Hoffman.

"Do a radio pulse," Hoffman said.

"In the clear? The banshees will know right where we are."

King turned in a circle, weapon ready. "You think those uglies chasing us don't know we're here?"

Max extended an antenna from his backpack, then typed quickly on his left forearm screen with his right hand. "Sending."

"...this is Barca. *We are receiving poorly. Copy?"*

"Strike Marine Crimson Team, we copy. Stand by for message."

"...say again?"

As Max repeated the protocol several times, Hoffman listened in to his conversation with growing dread.

"We're being jammed. *Barca* commo techs should realize that and switch to freq hoping to compensate…come on, you squid amateurs." A few heartbeats later, Max flashed a thumbs-up and an open channel flickered on Hoffman's visor.

"*Barca*, we're on the ventral hull, just above a shuttle bay. How do you copy?"

King pointed over the edge of the Dotari ship hull. "Here she comes now."

"We have you on visual. Relay to the *Breitenfeld* the *Kid'ran's Gift* is compromised. Active enemy presence," Hoffman said.

Max shook his head. "Radio's not getting through. No way those banshees broke our freq crypto this fast. The computing power—"

"Not for the Xaros." Hoffman's mouth went dry. Earth's entire military had shifted from advanced computers to near analog controls before the Ember War as a safeguard from the drone's hacking. Shifting back to networked systems had been slow since the conflict ended. Just how susceptible the *Barca* and the *Breitenfeld* were to the Xaros was a terrifying question.

"Max, go IR line of sight," Hoffman said.

The commo tech pulled a different antenna up from his back and bent it toward the approaching ship. The tip snapped open into a dish.

Staring at the ship that seemed a thousand miles away, Hoffman flinched when his helmet alerted him of an IR channel communication from the *Barca*. A generic avatar for the ship commander popped into his visor.

"Hoffman? We lost all contact with Captain Bradford and his team several minutes after he made entry. What's going on in there?"

Hoffman felt distinct tremors emanating through the hull and looked around for the source. An armored door rolled back to reveal one of the anti-meteor guns unlimbering.

"The ship is compromised—"

One of the *Kid'ran's Gift* counter-asteroid turrets rose behind Hoffman's team, a massive cannon that could shoot a shell the size of a Marine. The armored mechanism swiveled to track the corvette.

"I thought those were as dead as the rest of the ship!" Adams exclaimed.

"What the hell?" Garrison ducked as he turned to look.

Hoffman snatched his rifle off his back and set it to

a high-power shot. "Lo'thar, where do we hit it?"

"It's designed to take more punishment than that." Lo'thar backed away.

"Team, ready anti-tank gren—" Hoffman's order was cut off as a flash of light erupted from the cannon.

Hoffman expected a concussion and recoil, even though he should have known better. With no atmosphere to carry a shock wave, they were relatively safe, even this close to the weapon fire. Several other anti-asteroid cannons launched electromagnetically propelled shells at the same time as the first.

Booker spoke in a low voice Hoffman could not ignore. "Looks like the *Kid'ran's Gift* isn't the only ship with a banshee problem."

Hoffman watched as shells from other Dotari ships converged on the *Barca*. A half-dozen shells designed to pulverize enormous space rocks struck the corvette within a heartbeat. The ship shattered in a brief fireball. Hull fragments and the ship's broken interior scattered across the stars.

Hoffman, King, and the others stared at the expanding wreckage. He thought of all the lives lost…then saw glints of metal hurtling right for them. One piece grew larger at an alarming pace, ready to splatter the Marines against the *Kid'ran's Gif's* hull.

Opal shoved past Hoffman to grab Max and haul him backward as debris from the impact pelted the entire team. Adams was knocked off her feet. Lo'thar staggered sideways with both arms over his head.

King hustled to restore order. "Get down! Spread out!"

Booker shoved Hoffman toward the counter-asteroid turret, tripped him, and covered his body with hers. A second later, Opal piled on.

"Turret not enough cover!" Opal boomed. "Keep Sir safe!"

Time distorted. Hoffman's heart pounded spots into his vision as he tried to see around his medic and the doughboy's thick arms. Glimpses of his team and streaking fragments of the *Barca* overwhelmed his visor filters.

"No! Too heavy, Opie," Booker grunted.

Opal responded by pulling her arms under him so that no part of her or Hoffman protruded from his bulk. "Keep friends safe."

Bits and pieces struck the hull with incredible force, kicking up sparks against a ship made to withstand impacts from space debris during a thousand-year voyage.

Hoffman pushed Booker toward the turret. Her mag

locks unsnapped from the hull and she went void-borne. The medic did a forward roll and used the momentum to carry her into the turret's shadow before reengaging her boots and landing on the hull again.

As the lieutenant turned to search for the rest of his Marines, a hunk of the corvette's bulkhead slapped against the hull and skipped toward him like a stone across a lake. There was a flash of a gauss rifle and the bulkhead broke in half, sending a section as big as Hoffman sailing a few feet over his head. Out of instinct, he ducked and saw a mass of pipes skidding across the hull. The debris hit him in the shins and broke his hold on the Dotari ship. His world went upside down, then snapped to a halt.

"Dutchman, bad!" Opal had Hoffman by the ankle and tossed him toward the turret. Hoffman spun like a discus, slow enough to gauge when he'd pass uncomfortably close to the turret. He'd find out if the doughboy had sent him on a crash course in a few seconds.

He overloaded his mag linings and his boots locked onto the side of the turret. He slid across the hull for a few feet, his arms out to his sides to steady himself. He looked to one side and saw his Strike Marines gawking at him.

Garrison clapped slowly and Hoffman stepped off the turret and onto the hull.

"Rally on me," Hoffman said. "Set up security. We don't know for sure if the banshees can operate out here or not. Better to be safe than sorry." He needed time to think through his latest screw-up and fix it. How? He had no idea. His decisions led them to this unwinnable situation. He looked up to the void where the *Barca* had been just moments ago. The odds of his team surviving had just dropped.

An alert icon flashed on his visor. Looking at his left thigh, he saw a tiny geyser of air leaking out of a breach in his armor. He pulled a tube off his belt and set the tip against the puncture. No matter what this fight threw at him, he was still a lieutenant of Marines.

"Gunney, get me a status report," he said evenly.

King barked orders while Hoffman sealed the hole. He spread a bit of contact tape over the armor caulk and the alert on his visor went amber. The integrity of his armor was secure…for now.

"That was a surprise we could have done without, Lo'thar," Hoffman said.

"We didn't…we removed our point defense cannons centuries ago," the Dotari said. "I forgot. I can't believe I forgot."

"Anything else you need to remember?" Anger

seeped through Hoffman's words. "We have to assume anything on the ship that can be taken over by a Xaros drone has been taken over."

"Shit," Garrison said as he scanned the hull with his rifle. "Shit, shit, shit."

"You have something to report, Marine? If not—stow it," King said. "Watch your zone. If the banshees climb out here, it should be easy enough to knock them off the hull. Doubt they have grav liners in their feet."

Garrison cursed. "What are we gonna do, Gunney? That was our ticket back to the *Breitenfeld*. Now we're stuck on the outside of a ship full of monsters, and no way to signal the *Breit* or—"

King grabbed Garrison and lifted him off the hull. "I will throw you toward the *Breitenfeld* and you can bitch all you like while you're floating a message to them."

Garrison's rant ended and King lowered him to the hull, releasing him as the grav liners in his boots grabbed hold.

Hoffman faced Max. "Can you contact the *Breitenfeld*?"

"Not with this jamming. Could do it with infrared if I had a line of sight and a transmitter strong enough to keep a signal together. My transmitter is at our breach point."

Max pointed toward the partially open bay doors. "And we can't see the *Breit* from this side of the ship."

"Use your imagination. Think of another way," Hoffman said.

Max shook his head. "There is no other way."

"Then we need to get back to your transmitter." Hoffman felt a surge of confidence he didn't trust. Instructors at Officer's Candidate School talked about showing confidence even if you didn't feel it. "Fake it until you make it" had been one instructor's advice. Hoffman didn't know who he was fooling, only that he was a hot mess inside.

Lo'thar fidgeted within his suit. "Through the banshees and sludge tunnels?"

Hoffman shook his head, then checked on the status of each team member with the command and control authority of his armor's computer. Duke's air was significantly lower than the other team members'.

Hoffman froze in place, thinking through the implications.

King noticed. A moment later, he turned Duke around and physically checked his gear. An ugly gash cut across the air tanks on one side of the sniper's armor. Another inch to the left and it would have opened him up like a gutted fish.

Duke's eyes widened as he saw the damage, then he removed his rifle from his back and inspected it.

"Gunney, if we cross-level air tanks, how long can we last out here?" Hoffman asked.

"We sit still and conserve oxygen, three hours. Moving around and fighting, maybe fifty minutes."

Hoffman cursed in his head, then punched Lo'thar on the shoulder to get the Dotari pilot's full attention. "Get us back to our first entry point."

"That's…"

Hoffman glared at him.

Lo'thar pointed over the ship's hull. "Follow me. We have…quite a hike."

"We go EVA to our initial breach point. Get our IR transmitter and signal the *Breitenfeld.* Air's going to be tight. No more talking." Hoffman followed Lo'thar, looking up one last time at where the *Barca* used to be.

Chapter 10

Admiral Valdar stood at the holo tank, drumming his fingers against a railing. *Waiting. Still waiting.* "I've got lots of practice at this," he said to no one in particular. "Thought it would be easier when it wasn't Hale and that bag of ruffians he led around the galaxy. Doing things I told them to do, for the most part."

"I was thinking the same thing, sir," Egan said without looking up from his workstation. "As one of those ruffians, I hoped this one would be a cakewalk. Will the admiral consider sending me on an away mission so I don't have to endure this miserable wait time?"

"Not a chance, XO."

"Colonel Hale always pulled through, even if he did come back battered and bloodied and dragging strange alien artifacts," Egan said.

"You sum that up nicely, XO."

A soft alert dinged twice from the tank. Valdar looked up. An icon for the *Barca* maneuvered around the Dotari flagship and a garbled transmission opened.

Valdar looked toward Egan.

"They're sending on radio, not IR. Odd," Egan said.

The transmission sputtered out.

"Switch to active sensors. Show me what's going on," Valdar said. Data feeds appeared inside the tank and he zoomed in on the *Barca*'s location.

The corvette was nothing more than hunks of debris spreading away from the massive Dotari flagship, some of it recognizable as parts of the corvette.

"I'm not reading any distress signals from life pods," Egan said.

A cluster of small Dotari ships at the edge of the lost fleet suddenly changed course.

"Those ships aren't coming for us, are they?" Valdar said.

"Confirming," Egan said. "Begging the admiral's pardon, but those ships are on an intercept course for the *Breitenfeld*."

Valdar looked around the bridge, gauging the reactions of his crew. The air suddenly felt thick. "Gor'al, contact the ships and learn their intentions."

The Dotari officer began speaking into open channels, repeating greetings and challenges several times, but there was no response. He looked over the data. "The maneuvers are too precise. The ships are still slaves to the flagship. But there's no one at the helm."

"I don't understand why they would fire on us," Valdar said, pointing to the debris field from the corvette on one of the screens.

Egan pulled up the corvette's last transmission.

"XO, you have that look on your face," Valdar said. "Tell me you're onto something."

"I was a commo bunny in the Strike Marines not that long ago. I can piece together some of the telemetry data from the transmissions." He pointed at a code fragment. "That can't be right. They're broadcasting under condition Zeta—imminent threat from known hostile. Zeta…that's—"

"The Xaros," Valdar said, slamming his palm down on a broad button at his workstation. "Battle stations."

As klaxons blared throughout the ship, his heart pounded and his blood raced hot in his veins. He took a deep, calming breath and donned his helmet. He activated his void suit's life support systems as the ambient air on the bridge was sucked into storage tanks. Fighting in a medium that enabled fires and blast wave propagation was a poor tactical choice.

Gor'al's quills straightened like the hair on a scared cat's back. "Not again," the Dotari said. "How is this even possible? I thought all the Xaros were destroyed."

"We killed the Masters," Valdar said. "We hacked the drone's source code and sent self-destruct orders…but the commands were broadcast from the Crucible gates at the speed of light. There are still some dead zones across the galaxy where drones might still be active…looks like we're in one."

"We need to tell Earth there's still a drone out here," Egan said. "Get them to rebroadcast the kill command in the event that—"

"Secondary concern," the admiral said. "This ship beat the Xaros to save the Dotari once. Failure is not an option." On Takeni, he had a ship full of fighters and an armor company. Now he had a crew full of engineers and sailors ready for anything but a fight.

"Sir," Egan said, "for what it's worth, I'm glad we're doing this on the *Breitenfeld*. But I'm also not going to pretend an ice-cold spear of dread didn't just stab through my guts."

"Understood, XO. Understood. Get the Grinder techs up here. We need to dump that cargo if we want to maneuver."

Chapter 11

Years ago in the Virginia forests, Hoffman had marched through the night after being told the maneuver was just a short exercise before evening chow. The event had been far enough into the training cycle of Strike Marine selection that he and his fellow Marines understood the drill. No one dared ask when it would end. They knew it would end, eventually, when they were thoroughly miserable or when they quit.

No tricks existed to make forced marches shorter or less miserable. They were simply a thing to be endured. The trip across the *Kid'ran's Gift* was little different. Hoffman preoccupied himself with thinking up another plan in case their initial entrance was compromised…and hadn't come up with a viable Plan B.

Every fifty steps across the hull, Hoffman checked

the O2 levels of Duke's armor. Minutes felt like days. Their destination might have been a thousand miles away for all the progress they seemed to make. He felt each breath and wondered if Duke was holding his, maybe exercising his sniper breath control to produce a trance-like state of minimal exertion.

He noticed divots in the metal of the hull. The ship had been in the void a long time. Pitted and worn from space, how long had it stayed on course before a lost drone happened upon it carrying the Xaros programing necessary to turn it into a weapon—using whatever resources were available in the endless void?

"Don't forget to check the rest of the team." King sent a text to the lieutenant's visor.

Hoffman ran through each Strike Marine's armor statistics and noticed that Opal didn't use much more air than a regular-sized grunt. His heart rate was normal. Respiration only slightly elevated from the exertion of the space walk. Doughboys didn't feel fear like normal humans, if at all.

Hoffman wondered if the team would ever accept Opal. Booker and some of the others felt sorry for him, but that wasn't the same. Wasn't enough. King and Duke didn't hide their resentment of the doughboy. He realized that was most likely the source of King's frustration. The gunnery sergeant probably thought the doughboy was a distraction from the mission.

Opal was a monster in any fight; he was designed that way. So long as he had a thinking human to give him instructions, he was a valuable asset. But none of that changed his hidden flaw. The doughboys were biological constructs, all with a shelf life. Most of the doughboys had been "retired" from service after the Ember War, their internal processors shut down, some taking longer than others.

Sadness latched on to Hoffman's heart. Losing his doughboys to the Xaros had been hard enough. Watching them slowly break down over a series of days had been almost more than he could bear. Sometimes they'd shut off out of the blue, stopping whatever task they were in the middle of doing and resting their chin to their chest, never to reactivate.

Other doughboy platoon leaders likened the loss to a family dog that passed away. Hoffman never could separate his charges like that, never think of them as just tools or animals. His doughboys were his soldiers, and Opal had been by his side for years. He continued to function while all the rest shut down within a few months of each other. According to the biomechanical engineers, there was no way to know when Opal would degrade. It could come anytime, but it would come with some warning—failure to carryout simple commands, confusion, erratic behavior. There was a way to shut Opal down prematurely, a series of verbal commands Marc Ibarra taught him when his first doughboy degraded.

Hoffman shivered at the memory. Being around Ibarra had been…difficult.

Everyone knew Opal could fall apart without warning, despite his stalwart appearance. Sudden death was a battlefield hazard for all Strike Marines, human and doughboy. That Opal had lasted so long with no ill effects proved enough for the brass to keep him in the field, though over the years, more than one person had expressed concern to Hoffman about Opal's inherent flaw. Still, even if Opal could comprehend his situation, he would never waver from his duty beside Hoffman.

An alert chimed in Hoffman's helmet. He checked his team. Duke's oxygen levels were in the red.

He pulled his auxiliary tank free and his own O2 levels dropped precipitously. He quietly handed it to the sniper, who accepted it with a nod. The grizzled old veteran looked ashamed as he hooked it up.

Another chime sounded in Hoffman's helmet. "We're not going to make it to the transmitter," King sent in a text.

Hoffman typed on his arm screen as he walked slowly and steadily behind Lo'thar. "Suggestions?"

"Pit stop. Recharge tanks."

Hoffman touched Lo'thar's shoulder, and the Dotari pilot stopped, his eyes looking worried even through his visor.

"We need to get back inside," Hoffman tapped out.

"What?" the Dotari said, wasting valuable air. "You'll note the lack of *noorla* out here."

Rolling his eyes, Hoffman grabbed Lo'thar by the gauntlet and held the screen up to the alien's helmet.

"No choice," Hoffman typed. "Even if we called for x-fil, the *Breit* won't get here in time."

Lo'thar looked around, then pointed to an oval-shaped opening not far away. "Maneuver thruster port. Oops, talking." Lo'thar tapped on his gauntlet. "We can get back inside through there."

Booker's text came up on Hoffman's visor. "And if this ship makes a course correction while we're inside?"

"All our problems will be over," Lo'thar said. "Stop giving me the stinky eyeballs, Sergeant King. I have plenty of air.

"I see no residual heat from the port in the IR spectrum," Lo'thar continued. "I doubt it has been used in years. Still, I suggest we hurry."

"Adams, in you go," King said.

Hoffman put a hand on her slim shoulder to stop her. "Belay that. I'll go first."

King stared at him, his expression unreadable.

Hoffman formed an explanation but stopped himself. He knew better than to countermand his top NCO. It was a sin second only to reversing an order or hesitating. Thoughts of his hesitation on New Bastion threatened to intrude. He squashed the memory.

"Opal volunteers to go first," Opal said.

"You're too big, tough guy," Booker said almost under her breath as she held him back with a light touch of her fingers.

Hoffman did a handstand in the zero gravity and pulled himself through the dark hole. He activated the full spectrum of his helmet optics and could see more than he needed to. The slightly melted walls of the tube felt warm through his gauntlets and he understood this was a mind trick. Knowing and feeling were as far apart as they could be at this point.

The thruster nozzle, large as it was, widened the farther he went until he was able to stand and activate the grav liners in his boots. "King, bring the team down."

One by one, the Strike Marines came headfirst into the small room and reoriented themselves to the floor. Opal squeezed out of the opening and moved away from the nozzle, staring at it with narrow-eyed suspicion. "Opal didn't like that."

"Well, I thought it was a nice break from being shot at by aliens," Adams said.

Garrison patted her on the shoulder. "If it makes you feel better, you look good going face-first into a Dotari ship thruster hole."

"Cover your zones. Three hundred and sixty degrees of sharp-eyed Strike Marine security," King said.

"This room is like ten feet across," Max said.

"Then it should be easy to cover." King stepped closer to Hoffman and Lo'thar but said nothing.

Hoffman pointed at Lo'thar, then at the main doors to the chamber. "Any reason those should be welded shut?"

"Certainly not…that's funny," Lo'thar said.

"Can we get in?"

Lo'thar shot a covert look toward Garrison and Adams. "Not without blowing the door clean off the frame.

The bulkhead servos have been spiked." He walked toward a smaller set of utility doors, pausing to examine a slash mark bisecting the elegant Dotari sign labeling the door.

When Lo'thar touched one of two large buttons on the frame and the door opened, he smiled at Hoffman. "It might be easier to break open the doors and go through the fuel stores… but the foundry sections will work."

Duke, shifting from one foot to the other with un-sniper-like impatience, tapped his helmet. "Air's getting a might thin in here."

Hoffman pulled Lo'thar back. "Opal, now you can go first."

Opal lumbered through the air lock, staying just within view as he aimed his rifle left to right, then right to left in the new room. "Clear."

"Team, move," Hoffman said.

Moments later, Max called out, "Last man." He shut the door and atmosphere flooded into the air lock.

Duke removed his helmet and took a deep breath, wiping sweat off his forehead and blinking hard several times. Hoffman noted his skin was a faint shade of blue.

Adams, Garrison, Max, and Booker all laughed at the old sniper.

"Your lips are a lovely shade of teal, old man. You

ought to dye your hair to match," Adams said.

"Keep flapping your gums. See what happens," Duke managed.

"LT, recommend we take a break," King said.

Hoffman nodded.

"Check your gear. Take in some calories and rehydrate," King said.

Lo'thar and Booker moved off to one side and removed the banshee hand from the plastic bag.

"Can you analyze it?" Lo'thar asked. "I would like to know if it has what my daughter needs. If we can at least get this…part…back to the *Breitenfeld*, this mission will be a success. It won't matter if we're ripped apart by banshees after that," Lo'thar said.

"Dotari always this sunny, Lo'thar? Give me a minute." Booker pulled a flexible roll of tools from her kit and spread it out. She jabbed a needle into the banshee flesh and it entered the bone with a crack. Withdrawing a sample of dark fluid, she snapped the vial into her gauntlet. "Let's see what we've got here…"

Hoffman watched from a distance and said a silent prayer.

"Are these readings correct?" Lo'thar leaned over Booker's shoulder, uncomfortably close to the Marine.

"You have to let it finish," Booker said. Long moments passed. She furrowed her brow and worked her fingertips over a touchscreen on the back of her hand.

Lo'thar held his quills down, murmuring a dismayed sound. "What is wrong with it? There is something wrong, isn't there?"

Booker sat back on her haunches and wiped sweat from her forehead. "The blood has no antibodies, no immune system at all. Which, of course, fits with what the *Breitenfeld* encountered on Takeni. They had a…specimen they tried to free from Xaros control. The subject died on the operating table. She didn't have an immune system either. The doctor—I don't remember his name—"

"Acorso," Lo'thar said.

"How do you…doesn't matter. He thought the Xaros replaced the banshee's immune systems with Xaros tech, made them immune to chemical and biological attacks. Didn't find an immune system in the turned humans recovered on Pluto either," Booker said.

Lo'thar snapped a curse in Dotari and kicked the banshee arm away, then retreated to a corner, one of the only semiprivate spaces in the small area. Lo'thar crossed his arms tight across his stomach and hunched his shoulders.

Booker got up and made for the Dotari, but Max stopped her with a shake of his head.

King nudged Hoffman's elbow. "It will take an hour to recharge our tanks."

Hoffman shook his head. "Still can't get that far if Duke's carrying a quarter of his air."

"Get me a Dotty air tank. I can rig something up for him," Booker said.

From his corner, Lo'thar responded almost absently. "There are emergency kits on every deck and in every compartment. Or there were when all the fleets left Dotari a thousand years ago. But what do I know? I go charging across the galaxy on a sliver of a chance and have nothing to show for it. My daughter wakes up every morning with hope, and if I ever return, it will be as a fool."

Hoffman held up a finger to King and traced a circle in the air, signaling for him to get the team ready to move out, then he went to the Dotari and squared off in front of him.

"Who are you?" Hoffman asked.

Lo'thar's quills twitched. "Lieutenant, did your air tanks fail, causing brain damage?"

"I thought a hero of the Ember War was on this mission. Aren't you the Lo'thar that flew with Gall and the

103rd squadron off the *Breitenfeld*? Didn't you fight and beat the Toth? The Naroosha? The Xaros at the Apex? Didn't you save Saint Kallen on Nibiru?"

"That was a long time ago." Lo'thar looked away. "I traded my wings for a family."

"And you volunteered for this mission to save that family," Hoffman said. "And is there anyone else on this ship that knows it better than you do?"

Lo'thar hissed quietly.

"You are invaluable. Irreplaceable. Vital. Not to just this team but to your daughter. Every Dotari on your home world. You get that?"

"My brother Man'fred would be so jealous right now," Lo'thar said. "You know he's a fleet First on—"

Hoffman grabbed the pilot by the shoulder, confident that the alien was focused again. "You said the foundries are here. What could they make?"

Lo'thar looked from Hoffman to the team. "If they're online, and we could find the raw materials, and—"

"Just find us some air tanks," King said.

Quills ruffling, Lo'thar stared at the gunnery sergeant. He pulled on his helmet and closed the visor. "Fine. We must continue into the ship to find them. This area is without them, unless you Strike Marines see something a mere Void Superiority Fighter pilot cannot."

"Garrison and Adams, up front on point. Lead the way," Hoffman said.

"Right away, boss," Garrison and Adams said.

"My sister is a Ranger. She'd always say that…Rangers lead the way. Well, look who's doing it now," Adams said.

"We're doing it," Garrison said. "Doing it on an alien starship overrun with monsters. Bet this won't make it into any recruiting slogans."

King, Booker, and Lo'thar went next, with Hoffman bringing the rest through the air lock. Duke shouted "last man" and closed the door by slapping his hand on an oversized button several times.

"This isn't dusty," he said. "Those things might be in here."

"Yeah, they look like they know how to use buttons," King said. "Maintain security. Keep your head on a swivel and watch your partner's back."

Garrison and Adams moved around a corner in the hallway.

"You better see this, LT," Garrison said.

King and the others arrived before Hoffman and stood transfixed by the sight of a door that had been barricaded with steel bars welded to the bulkhead.

"Well that's…different," Max said.

"Opal hears footsteps," Opal said.

"Look sharp," King said, aiming his gauss rifle down one of the connecting corridors.

"Light footsteps," Opal said.

A second later, Hoffman heard the running feet just before an elderly Dotari burst around the corner. Thin as a refugee, clothed in rags, the old alien hefted a spear tipped with battery packs on prongs.

"Dotok'ka'ma!" he screamed.

Opal grabbed the spear by the haft, stopping it dead in its path. The oldster locked eyes with the towering doughboy and froze for a heartbeat, then he backpedaled while screaming and ran back the way he came, leaving the spear in Opal's hand.

"We are friends, noble Dotari," Lo'thar shouted. "Wait!"

"You think he speaks English?" Max asked.

Lo'thar mumbled what Hoffman was sure was a series of obscenities, then shouted in his own language.

King and Max sprinted after the stranger and tackled him in the adjoining corridor, pinning him to the deck as he struggled and squirmed. Max covered his mouth with his right gauntlet.

"Hey! He's biting me!" Max shouted. "Tell this Dotty no biting!"

Lo'thar pulled off his helmet and bent next to the old Dotari, showing his face, and began speaking rapid-fire Dotari.

The team alternated their attention between the empty hallways and the unfolding scene on the floor as the rail-thin alien kept struggling.

"He doesn't seem reassured," Adams said.

"Opal can help," Opal said as he bent over the struggling mass of Strike Marines and the Dotari survivor. Opal smiled, displaying big teeth that resembled grindstones. The old Dotari squealed.

Max removed his translation earpiece from his helmet and shoved it into the oldie's ear. "We're not going to hurt you. You understand the words coming out of my mouth?"

The old Dotari's brow furrowed. His quills rustled.

"He understands," Lo'thar said.

"I'm going to take my hand off your mouth. You start yelling again, you'll get my whole fist down your throat."

Adams whistled. "Look at Max. He's all grown-up

and acting like a badass now."

Max pulled his hand back.

As the Dotari looked furtively from Lo'thar, to the humans, then to Opal, Adams and Max released their hold on him.

Max held up his middle finger to Adams. Two of the armored fingers had dents. "Old bastard almost bit through."

The ragged old Dotari scrambled back to the bulkhead, his eyes wide with fright.

"What…" the alien's voice croaked through Hoffman's earpiece, "what in the golden depths are you?"

"I'm from the *Canticle of Reason*," Lo'thar said. "This ship's nestling. You know it?"

The Dotari pulled his knees to his chest and shook his head in disbelief. He pointed a craggy finger at Hoffman. "Lies," he said. "The air scrubbers are broken again. I am having another delusion. Go! Go and tell the cricklaishk I don't want to see you ever again!"

Lo'thar moved between the Dotari and Hoffman's team. "We are true, old father." He grabbed the Dotari's wrist and moved the Dotari's hand to feel his face.

The old Dotari pushed Lo'thar's face to one side, then ran his fingertips through Lo'thar's quills. A heartbeat later, he laughed.

"What happened here?" Hoffman asked as he removed his helmet.

The old Dotari jerked his hand back, holding his fists close to his chest. "What are they? They have mouths of children and no hair. How can they live? We didn't put anything like that on the *Canticle of Reason*!"

"Humans, friends," Lo'thar said. "They're here to help us."

The old Dotari hesitated. "Ambassador…Ambassador Pa'lon spoke of other races. I never thought I'd see one." He looked around at the others, seeming especially suspicious of Max and Opal. "Were you followed? Do the *noorla* know you're aboard?"

Garrison bobbed his head. "Oh, they know we're here all right."

"Come, come. Shouldn't stay here," the Dotari said. "*Noorla* won't go through vacuum, but today's been full of surprises. Isn't that right, Moz'in?" He limped away, favoring the leg King hadn't pinned to the ground.

Lo'thar hurried to walk beside him.

King made eye contact with Hoffman. "What are you thinking, sir?"

"Some answers, at last. I can't tell how long that

Dotari's been here, but he doesn't seem like he's all there," Hoffman said.

King looked to be sure each member of the team was moving well and paying attention, then picked up the Dotari battery spear, looking over the business end of the weapon. "Maybe he knows something about fighting the banshees we don't."

****

"My name is Moz'in," the bent-back old Dotari said over his shoulder. "Hurry. You must move faster. Can you not do it? Do they not teach human soldiers to move their posterior attachments?"

"Nice translation," Garrison said as he and Adams moved ahead of Moz'in.

"The software may have a few problems," Lo'thar said.

"Let us go first, Mozy old buddy," Adams said. "We're here to protect you."

"Lance Corporal Adams is known to have the best posterior attachment in the Strike Marines," Garrison said.

Moz'in looked questioningly at Lo'thar.

"Earth humor," Lo'thar said.

"We are safe. *Noorla* cannot, must not, find my home. That would be the end! Follow me. Move aside, you brute," Moz'in squeezed past Opal and hurried down a spiral staircase so tight it resembled a ladder.

Garrison and Adams led Hoffman's Strike Marines in pursuit.

"Tactical nightmare," King grunted.

Moz'in hustled through narrow hallways that seemed better suited to automated rail drones than a grown Dotari. Poorly lit and cold, the maze had the feel of between decks.

"Right turn, left turn, right turn," Garrison said. "You logging all this, little sister?"

Adams showed him her middle finger.

"Here are the stairs. What can it hurt to show my survival secret to my imaginary friends? Who would they tell?" Moz'in laughed. "I must check the air filters. This seems so real."

Hoffman and the others emerged inside a storage bay. Three hammocks hung limp between open crates. One held tattered clothing and blankets while the other two were stiff and dusty. Wires ran haphazardly between several computer monitors on a workbench.

"King," Hoffman said, then nodded toward the back

of the room.

The gunnery sergeant motioned for Booker and Max. "Garrison and Adams have been on point for a while. They need a break. We're going to clear this room and secure any exits."

"On it, Gunney," Max said.

Hoffman watched Lo'thar and Moz'in, but also took a closer look at the Dotari's living space. Beside one of the monitors was a stack of freeze-dried food packets and what was either a blender or an upside-down servo mechanism full of green liquid.

"Huh." Adams nudged Garrison with an elbow and motioned to the odd device. "Looks like some kind of still. I've heard good things about Dotari booze."

Hoffman watched water drip from a spigot on the device.

Moz'in brushed a space near the hammocks clean. "Welcome home! Ha ha. Moz'in didn't tidy up. Never had visitors before, didn't expect any today."

He jumped onto a crate and pulled the sack of food packs up with him, then flung them one at a time at Hoffman and his Strike Marines. Garrison was so focused on the liquid that he barely noticed when a pack bounced off the side of his helmet.

Hoffman took his helmet off and hooked it on his belt.

King, Booker, and Max returned from their security sweep. The gunnery sergeant tossed Duke a Dotari air tank.

King looked over the team. "Max, you're rated on suit repairs."

"So's Duke, but can't have him drop armor, can we?" Max said. "Should take me a bit to have him up to snuff."

"Speaking of…" Duke fished out a small tin of chewing tobacco and jabbed a wad between his gums and cheek.

Hoffman rubbed the fatigue out of his neck with one hand and tried not to think. How long had it been since they entered *Kid'ran's Gift*? It felt like forever.

"Here, here. This is for you," Moz'in said as he handed Hoffman a food pack.

"Thanks. I…uh…haven't eaten since we got here." Hoffman felt fuzzy, tired from physical exertion and stress.

Moz'in spread food packets on a workbench near the computers. "Mixed-spice carbohydrate-protein-vitamin supplement number eight. I had some number-three packs that were oh, so savory. You could mix them with warm water and make broth." He clicked his beak. "The best."

Lo'thar tore open the food pack Moz'in had thrown at him, then paused to look at Hoffman.

"Does he have enough to spare?" Hoffman asked.

Lo'thar turned away from their host and whispered, "You must try it."

Hoffman carefully tore open the pack, unsure of the consistency of the contents. "Smells like hay mulch."

Garrison gagged. "That's being generous. Mine smells like motor oil mixed with toe jam…"

"Garrison, please. We're guests," Adams said, grimacing as the aroma of her meal wafted into her face.

Moz'in studied each of their reactions with interest. "These are soft rations. Good for baby teeth like yours." Abruptly, he turned to the empty hammock. "I know that, Moz'in! I'm sure they have their own toddler mush."

Hoffman raised an eyebrow to King, who was supervising the repairs to Duke's armor. The lieutenant plucked a sticky cube out of the pouch, popped it into his mouth, and chewed. His eyes watered, the muscles in his jaw and neck clenched, but he swallowed his first bite of Dotari rations.

Adams sat near the door, feet dangling from a crate as she sampled Moz'in's gift. "Tastes worse than it smells."

"There's an aftertaste," Hoffman said through a

frown. "Like old blood." He handed the food pouch to Lo'thar, who was nearly done with his meal.

"There's a spice combination I've never had before," Lo'thar said.

Hoffman addressed Moz'in. "How long have you been here?"

"I've been on the ship since the grand launch. I don't…exactly know how long that's been. Nine Golden Fleets set off across the stars before the Xaros could reach Dotari." He faced Lo'thar. "You were on the *Canticle of Reason*?"

"I was born on Takeni, the world settled by the *Canticle*'s ships." Lo'thar shook his empty ration bag, then raised an eyebrow at Hoffman, who thrust his bag to the pilot so fast some of the sauce sprinkled Lo'thar's armor.

"The passage of time is a mystery. How long has it been since the Grand Fleet set off? Moz'in and his nestlings were in stasis most of the trip. We were in stasis until our emergency repair team was woken up to deal with the asteroid strike. Such an event should have been impossible. What kind of asteroid could get through the fleet's point defense systems? No amount of floating space debris should have been able to hit so near to the bridge of the *Kid'ran's Gift*."

Hoffman, Lo'thar, and the others listened.

"Moz'in's people should have viewed the event as a warning." His eyes glazed over as he stared at nothing for several seconds, then snapped into focus. "My repair team found a single Xaros drone that took up residence on the bridge. Lost half the team when it noticed us."

King sat to eat his Dotari ration as Garrison rose to his feet.

Moz'in ignored the changing of the guard and moaned softly. "Ah, Moz'in. We did what we could. I ordered a retreat when the drone began co-opting the ship's systems. All the way to the foundry. Moz'in got cut off from the bridge. But the drone was so fast. Knew our systems better than we did. Lost three more when it cut off a deck and flooded it with carbon dioxide."

"You're still alive, Moz'in," Booker said. "That isn't easy against a Xaros drone. Nearly impossible most times."

The old Dotari narrowed his gaze, shifting his weight away from Booker. "We managed to set up a firewall the drone couldn't get through. Got a few decks under control. Tried scouting around for another way to the bridge or some way to reach the other ships when the *noorla* appeared."

"How long ago?" Hoffman asked.

"Hard to tell. Last clock I had broke a while back. What, Moz'in? It has not been twenty years. It must be at least twenty-five. No, you're the one that got old!"

Hofmann leaned toward Moz'in. "Do you think they turned all the passengers?"

Moz'in slapped at an empty food packet. "Not enough food aboard to feed everyone for more than a year."

Lo'thar's quills rustled with excitement. "We came through a working hydroponics bay."

Moz'in shook his head, then leaned forward, grabbing the edge of a crate. "Did you bring anything to eat?"

"We were in a bit of a rush," Lo'thar said.

Moz'in seemed to think for a while, then looked at Hoffman. "Moz'in says the hydro bays were for seedlings, couldn't feed more than a thousand people a year."

"So the Xaros may not have turned everyone aboard. Making them all into banshees just to have them starve doesn't fit their programming," Hoffman said.

"Why bother changing us like that? The Xaros kill every intelligent species they find. Had some long talks about that. Moz'in say the Xaros might be assimilators instead of eradicators. But he's an idiot. You heard what I called you!" Moz'in shook his fist toward one of the hammocks.

"The colony on Takeni...encountered a Golden Fleet the Xaros found. They turned every last Dotari in the fleet against us," Lo'thar said. "We would have lost the planet had the humans not rescued us."

Moz'in considered Lo'thar's words. "Not enough mass to convert into drones. So they use us as their cannon fodder. Efficient. The Xaros...have they found all the other fleets?"

Lo'thar shook his head sadly. "We don't know. This is the only fleet we've found in deep space."

"You've never seen another drone?" Hoffman asked.

Moz'in shook his head.

Hoffman watched the refugee for signs of deception or insanity. "Then how are they controlling the other ships?"

Moz'in snorted as though talking to a particularly dumb child. "There is a master station on the bridge of the *Kid'ran's Gift*. All other ships are slaved to it."

Hoffman felt two short vibrations in the sleeve of his armor, an alert from King. He looked over at the gunnery sergeant.

"Sir, come see this," King said, waving him over to a bank of computer screens.

****

Lo'thar carefully drew blood from Moz'in's arm, then handed the small vial to Booker, who plugged it into her gauntlet.

"Dotari is ours again?" Moz'in asked. "You say the Xaros were all but destroyed. Why is there still a drone on my ship?"

"The self-destruct order went out from the Crucible gates across the galaxy at the speed of light," Lo'thar said. "The Xaros kept small garrisons around their gates and sent armadas against the unconquered worlds. It takes time for the message to reach the drones. The last swarm charged into a star ten years ago. Some theorized that there might be a stray drone in deep space that has encountered the order…looks like they were right."

"But we've gone home? Through those Crucibles you spoke of? I miss the seasons…"

Lo'thar clicked his beak at the sample readings Booker shared. "Going home is one thing, being able to stay is another. Your sample has a number of antibodies…but the count is so low." He tried to touch Booker's control screen, but she swatted his hand away.

"Why do you look at me that way?" Moz'in asked. "Why do you click your beak?"

"You've been in a sterile environment for so long. None of the environmental stressors that cause the phage exist here. We may need someone that is still in stasis, fresh from walking on Dotari before the Golden Fleets set off. Perhaps a deeper sample…" Lo'thar touched his pouch with the long needles and looked at Moz'in's thin frame.

"No rush," Booker said.

Lo'thar's hand went to another pouch and he pulled out a shrink-wrapped bundle of wine-colored berries still on the branch.

Moz'in's eyes lit up. "What is…what is that?"

Lo'thar leaned closer. Whispering in a conspiratorial tone, he hunched over and clutched the pouch to his chest. "When we lived on the human's planet, Earth, we discovered a plant."

"They named their home world after dirt?"

"They've begun calling it Terra now, which also means dirt. They aren't the most imaginative species. But this plant, a coffee bush, had the most amazing fruit." Lo'thar opened a pouch, selected a bean, then pressed it into the old Dotari's hand. "Eat. Eat."

Moz'in stared as Lo'thar snuck one into his own mouth and bit down on it, closing his eyes to enjoy the sensation.

Moz'in sniffed the bean, then tossed it into his mouth and chewed slowly. A moment later, his eyes glazed over and the tension ran out of his muscles.

"That is…incredible," Moz'in said.

"The euphoria lasts just a few minutes. Don't eat too many at once. The gastrointestinal distress is rather strong."

Moz'in scratched at Lo'thar's bean pouch and Lo'thar gave him another.

Moz'in's head lolled to one side as he savored the second bean. "The humans don't want you to have this because it makes them feel the same?"

Lo'thar shrugged and ruffled his quills. "They get a mild stimulus from coffee, but they don't eat it raw. They scorch the nuts, crush them into powder, then torture it with scalding water, dextrose additives, and bovine secretions."

"What is wrong with them? Are you sure they're on our side?" Moz'in asked.

"Sometimes they remove the stimulant, creating 'decaffeinated' coffee, which the Strike Marines call 'bitch water.' Don't drink it."

"Will this grow on the home world?" Moz'in took a third bean, sniffed it, and worked it into his mouth like Duke did with his chewing tobacco.

"It will, and the humans are so stupid. They didn't even try to stop us when we brought the bushes back to Dotari. We've had the most success growing them in orbital gardens. Tishara beetles love the berries more than we do. Different soils give the coffee other flavors. The humans like Kona. I prefer the Blue Mountain strain from a place called Jicama. Jammies-Ka. Their language is impossible. Most of the time, they use something called English, which is several languages melded together. Then they'll just use a different language for some places. Or mottos. Very inefficient."

Moz'in snorted. "Damn tisharas ruined my morning-dew flowers back home." He stood abruptly and pointed at Garrison. "Hey, you!"

Garrison stood in front of the still, a small beaten metal cup in one hand, his lips held tightly together, eyes wide with innocence.

"You drink my reprocessed urine, you better piss it back into the still!"

Garrison spat a cloud of the greenish fluid into the

air.

Moz'in shook his head at Garrison and looked back to Lo'thar. "They beat the Xaros?"

"Had I not seen it with my own eyes…humans are tenacious, clever. And these Strike Marines are some of their best. Plus, we have the *Breitenfeld*, the ship that saved us all on Takeni."

Moz'in's quills fluttered. "Seven overgrown children and one ship…best thing that's happened to me in years."

Chapter 12

"Looks like the first real break we've had," Hoffman said as he studied several grainy video feeds. Several of the video boxes showed long hallways like those they had recently traversed. Pairs of banshees patrolled them.

"They look even bigger when they're not charging at us." King kept his voice low. "Not all have weapons. Most have armor, but some of it looks better fabricated than others. I'm not sure if this is a factor of resources or time."

The rest of the team gathered closer as they cleaned and repaired weapons and armor. No one spoke, but they wall watched and listened.

Hoffman nodded. "Moz'in has been evading these things for a while, so I'm not sure time is a factor."

Moz'in pushed King out of the way. "Don't touch anything. She's temperamental."

Hoffman stared at the crazy old Dotari. "How are you getting this?"

"We had access to the air ducts for a while, before the *noorla* showed up, and managed to shunt life-support systems away from the bridge's control. We put cameras up to know where the *noorla* were about to attack. Took us a while to realize vacuum was the only thing that kept them away."

"Can you see the bridge?" Hoffman asked.

"Never got close," Moz'in said, pointing to another screen displaying a cryo chamber. "The stasis pods are under a—what do you call it?—hard lock and have many layers of backup. The drone can't cut power or life support to those still sleeping. But Moz'in can't wake them up to prevent them from becoming *noorla*. Stalemate."

Booker shouldered her way in to point at a screen, a half-assembled rifle in one hand. "Is that engineering?"

Moz'in shook his head violently. "The *noorla* are always there. At least a dozen of them."

"Can you get us there?" Hoffman asked.

"Did you hear me?" Moz'in squeaked as he tapped his earpiece. "A dozen *noorla*, many more ready to come running when they smell a target."

Hoffman held his gaze. "Yes or no?"

Moz'in made a low noise in his throat. "Come all this way just to get ripped to pieces? Fine! What do I know? I've just been on this ship so long my nest has grown into a *gar'udda* tree."

Lo'thar raised a hand to explain, hesitated, then lowered it.

"Moz'in can get you to engineering. If he can find my old vac suit," Moz'in said.

King clenched his jaw as he thought through the changing events. "One, are we sure this is the guide we're looking for? Two, we take engineering, then what?"

"The Xaros drone has the rest of the fleet slaved to it from the bridge. What happens when we destroy it?" Hoffman asked.

Moz'in huffed, almost bored now. "The other ships revert to their own control and awaken their emergency crews."

"And we can control this ship from engineering, correct?"

Moz'in nodded at the lieutenant. "The trip isn't pleasant. We have to go through the sewage sumps, which have been worse since the *noorla* showed up."

Garrison threw up his hands. "Oh good. Another shit show."

King slowly turned his narrowed gaze on Garrison and held it. Garrison sat down and turned his attention to cleaning his rifle.

"Not a problem," Hoffman said, crossing his arms over his chest and putting a finger across the side of his face. "What is a problem is our teams—Captain Bradford and the rest."

"You think they secured the bridge?" King asked.

"No. The fleet wouldn't have fired on the *Barca* if they had. The drone will be alert, ready for another attack. We move on the bridge first, we'll have one hell of a fight."

"Divide and conquer," King said.

Hoffman nodded. "Divide and conquer. We hit engineering, draw defenders away from the bridge. A second team hits the drone while it's exposed."

Moz'in shifted his gaze from Hoffman to King, following their conversation with wide eyes.

"Let me get this straight, Moz'in," Hoffman said. "The banshees, ah…*noorla*, won't move through vacuum. They've been here awhile, so they must be set in their positions. We can expect them to dominate certain areas but not move to others, right?"

"No, no. The ship's tube shuttles are still active. They can move the *noorla* around the ship in a few minutes."

Hoffman smiled. "Then we shut it down while they're in transit. That'll keep the assault element at engineering from being overwhelmed, and keep them from going back to the bridge when they realize what we're doing."

"Most bang for our buck," King said. "But you're talking three different things that have to happen almost simultaneously across this giant ship, and we don't have any way to communicate if something goes wrong."

"You think we can pull it off?"

"We can do it, sir. We just need to have our shit wired tight."

Moz'in raised his hand, his face inquisitive, his quills quaking and eyes narrowed.

Lo'thar put his hand on the oldster's wrist and pushed his arm down. He shook his head. "Don't ask."

"Moz'in definitely needs to check the air scrubbers on this deck and stop hallucinating," Moz'in said.

"Do Dotari believe in miracles?" Adams muttered.

****

Hoffman checked his air tanks and ran a systems check on his armor. Glancing at the ammo counter on his rifle, he felt the weight of full magazines locked to his armor. He had enough bullets and charge packs to end several dozen banshees, but not much more.

Lo'thar rushed his own equipment check and started working on Moz'in's environmental suit. Ill-sized, patched in three places, and faded from a chemical burn, the gear looked like it would provide as much protection as threadbare pajamas compared to the Strike Marines' armor.

Hoffman moved food boxes and small storage crates around on the worktable, stepped back, eyed his work, and held his chin with one hand.

"Not bad, sir." King said. "You've created a generic ship layout."

"Not in front of the kids, Gunney," Hoffman said.

"Yes, sir."

"Finish your inspection and bring it in." Hoffman adjusted his crude mockup of the *Kid'ran's Gift* interior. The doors to engineering were made from a cut-up food packet. A chipped plate rested on top of the cardboard "ship" to represent the bridge.

"Ammo and power cross-leveled," King said.

"Good to go as we can be."

Hoffman aimed a laser pointer from his gauntlet at the engineering section. "Gunney King will take Duke, Opal, Booker, Adams, and Moz'in to engineering. You'll launch your attack and secure engineering forty-five minutes after we step off. Opal, try not to break anything in engineering. We need it intact to get control of the ship."

"Go with you," Opal said, tapping the butt of his rifle against the deck.

"Gunney needs your firepower, Opal. I don't."

When Opal ground his teeth and growled low in his throat, Adams, Garrison, and Max backed away from the doughboy.

Hoffman continued. "Garrison, Max, and Lo'thar will come with me. We'll set a denethrite charge on a power coupling on deck seventeen—"

"Nineteen!"

Hoffman stared at Moz'in as tension filled the room. "You told me it was seventeen."

"Moz'in got confused. His memory isn't what it used to be. Deck seventeen next to the tertiary stasis pods. That could be right. But nineteen keeps flashing in Moz'in's memory."

Lo'thar raised a hand just high enough to draw

Hoffman's attention. "The coupling in the *Canticle* was on deck seventeen. I can find it."

Hoffman nodded, then met the gaze of each member in the team. "We will make an EVA to the deck, set the charge to blow five minutes after the attack on engineering. Any reinforcements the banshees send to engineering should be in the tubes by then."

"I've got three breach charges left, sir. Resupply is very far away," Garrison said.

"Should only need one for the power coupling. The next we'll need to get into the bridge. Captain Bradford had a primary and secondary breach point. We'll use the one he didn't. Soon as we destroy the bridge and the drone, Moz'in can take control of the ship from engineering and signal the *Breitenfeld*." Hoffman smiled at his cardboard-box and food-wrapper mock-up, then nodded.

Duke spat a stream of tobacco juice into a floor drain. "Sir, the enemy gets a vote in all this. What if you can't disable the tubes? Or we're in danger of being overrun in engineering?"

"Gunney King will abort if necessary. You'll fall back here and we'll come up with a new plan. The chain of command is clear if I don't return. It's a long shot. I know it. You know it. We don't have the luxury of time and perfect knowledge of the enemy. What we have is a mission."

The ship groaned from unseen stress on the hull. Hoffman ignored it, despite hearing the echoes of banshee war cries and remembering the swarm of monstrosities that had almost wiped out his team.

"We didn't quit when everything went to hell on New Bastion. There's one Xaros drone on this ship, a drone that doesn't know what a mistake it made when it attacked us and the Dotari. If this really is the last one in the galaxy, then Strike Marines should be the ones to destroy it. We are Strike Marines. In the absence of orders, we attack."

"Oorah, sir," Max said as other members of the team nodded.

King stepped forward. "LT's team needs all your spare air tanks for the EVA. Hand them over."

"We're not going to be on internal air when we go through the sewers?" Booker asked.

Garrison gathered the air tanks. "I'll take banshees ready to rip me limb from limb over that stink pit any day."

Adams sauntered toward Garrison and then stopped, one hand on her hip, to observe his efforts. Long and lean, her form was stunning despite the circumstances. She smirked at him, then started to turn away. "You're a decent

Strike Marine, Garrison. I suppose you'll probably live without me."

He looked up. "I might need my posterior attachment wiped later if you're available. Keep an eye on Opal. He doesn't seem happy about leaving the lieutenant."

Hoffman was done with his gear but watched everything his team was doing. He made a show of double-checking his rifle as he eavesdropped.

"I didn't think you liked the doughboy," Adams said.

"There's nothing wrong with Opie. Well, maybe there is. Hell, I don't know. Just keep an eye on him."

King grunted. "Don't get soft on me, Garrison."

Moz'in looked around nervously as he weaved his way between the Strike Marines, going wide of Opal as the giant, mottle-faced doughboy glowered at the floor. Garrison bumped him accidentally. Duke stared at him until he sidestepped, muttering Dotari apologies. He stopped in front of Hoffman and looked up. "You want me to leave my room? You want me to go to where the *noorla* are waiting for me?"

"We need you to run the ship. Lock down the banshees—the *noorla*—and keep them from damaging anything else," Hoffman said.

The faded and tattered quills on Moz'in's head trembled and his eyes went wide.

Hoffman put one hand on the Dotari's shoulder. "I'm not sure how they'll react once we destroy the drone."

Moz'in pointed at Max. "That one knows enough Dotari. I'll write up the code inputs for him and stay here."

Hoffman squeezed the shoulder he was already holding and pulled Moz'in close to stare into his eyes. "The ship woke you up because it needed you to save it, to save everyone on board. You must have that skill set."

Moz'in tried to pull away but wasn't strong enough. He gazed around the room. Second by second, he slowed his breathing and calmed himself. "Dotari is real? We have our home again?"

Lo'thar stepped forward and handed Moz'in the repaired vac suit, which looked too big for the old creature. "I've walked Cashava city. I've seen the sun rise over the Princess' Brow Mountains, dipped my feet in Reach Bay where Yiir reached the sea. Our people, on this ship and our home, need you."

Moz'in looked at his feet and shook his head several times. He started speaking, even as he raised his gaze to meet Hoffman's and then Lo'thar's. "Moz'in is ready to go. I won't let that braggart say I shirked when there was work to be done."

"Strike Marines, we fight for the *Breitenfeld*. She is the ship of miracles, of victory against impossible odds. *Gott Mit Uns*. Move out."

Chapter 13

Lieutenant Hoffman faced forward in the air lock, grateful that the helmet visors offered a certain degree of privacy. The plan was as complete as he could make it. His team was thoroughly briefed and competent, if a bit tired and broken down from the long mission. He tried not to think about the implications of failure. The *Kid'ran's Gift* was packed full of monsters and their ride back to the *Breitenfeld* had been destroyed. If this plan failed, they ran a good chance of becoming Moz'in's roommates…or dead.

Garrison, Max, and Lo'thar stood behind him, waiting for the air lock to finish pressurizing. A series of dark amber—not green—lights came on above the doorway. Hoffman looked over his shoulder at Lo'thar, who nodded.

"There's no time like the present," Hoffman said.

When nothing happened, he again looked at the Dotari pilot. "Open the door. Let's get this done."

"Oh, that's what you meant. No time like the present," Lo'thar said.

Hoffman moved through the door as soon as it opened, then stepped to the left with his rifle up and ready. His shooting stance reflected years of practice—knees flexible and slightly bent, his center of gravity balanced above the middle of his feet. He looked through his rifle's sights as he swept it left to right, then right to left.

Garrison mirrored his movements on the right and Max came up the middle with Lo'thar beside him.

"Clear, nothing seen," Garrison said.

"Clear, nothing seen," Hoffman said. He signaled Garrison forward and fell in on his left. "Staggered column. Max, you have rearguard."

They moved forward to the next door, then paused for a security check. Hoffman and each member of his team scanned for threats. Quiet, empty-looking hallways could hide nasty surprises.

"This is my favorite hallway so far," Garrison said. "I think we're actually leaving footprints in the dust."

"There shouldn't be dust," Lo'thar said. He moved to a control panel and started to work on it. "It looks like the bridge lacks control of this area. Whatever Moz'in did seems to be working. Still working."

"How would you know if these mysterious countermeasures stop working?" Max asked.

"That's easy," Garrison said. "We can just ask the banshees while they're ripping us limb from limb."

Max looked at Hoffman, alarmed. Hoffman shrugged.

"I have a high degree of confidence the *noorla* don't know we're here," Lo'thar said. "Once we go through this door, we will be in the pod bay. Things can change very rapidly."

"Story of my life," Garrison said.

"All right, let's move." Hoffman took the lead. In a team this small, the idea of a point man was very fluid. He went to the door, up the catwalk, and reposted at the top, rifle ready. Garrison and Lo'thar came up next, followed by Max. They spread out, trying not to make noise. He wanted to curse each time the boots of his armor touched the metal deck. Soft, impact-resistant soles still made ten times the amount of noise he was comfortable with.

Hoffman held up one fist for everybody to stop moving, then opened his hand and lowered his palm toward the floor, kneeling as he gave the signal.

"Right out of a horror movie," Garrison whispered.

"I always hated horror movies," Max said. "What's wrong with a little action adventure? All I wanted when I joined up was to save the princess and steal back the plans to the enemy's secret super weapon."

Hoffman held up one finger for silence but agreed with Max's assessment. Below them were hundreds of banshee pods. Four or five opened at a time, the lids slowly lifting as they depressurized and the cryo sleep wore off the altered Dotari.

Two dozen brutes trembled on the floor, naked except for the torn remnants of silver body gloves. Slick from their recent hibernation, their bodies had grown unnatural muscle mass.

"Those are not my people," Lo'thar said. "The drone has made them abominations."

Not all the new banshees had the weapons and armor of the horde they had faced outside the shuttle bay. Some wielded tools with the precision only their Xaros drone master could have given them. One banshee, quills missing on one side of his head, pushed himself into a shaky stance and looked at his hands. He shook his head, slowly at first, then with violence that looked painful. A scream grew from his throat that sent a chill up Hoffman's spine.

One of the senior banshees strode up to the newly aware creature, summoning a rough-handed crew of monsters to assist him. Together, they forced the protesting banshee onto his back and screwed goggles over his eyes. Without hesitation or sedation, they began bolting on armor and weapons.

"Busy little worker bees, aren't they?" Garrison said. "Reminds me of in-processing at MEPS. Granted, only my beautifully long hair was mutilated."

Hoffman, Max, and Lo'thar stared at the breacher.

"Right," he said. "This is horrible. We need to stop it."

Another banshee was dragged from a tube and beaten until he was motionless. This one received only goggles, brain cables, and a spinning blade in place of her left hand.

"That is from the workshop on the other side of this level. Emergency saw," Lo'thar said, his voice as flat as his gaze. "The drone has been pumping growth hormones into the cryo pods while they sleep. Look closely at the other tubes. The occupants are awake but still trapped inside. They are suffering in a living tomb until the drone pulls them out. They are already in the throes of insanity."

Another group of new banshees were beaten into submission and slaved to the drone with Xaros technology. Cables ran to the backs of their necks, plugging in just below the skull.

Hoffman felt bad for the Dotari war hero as they watched banshees remake Dotari into more banshees. He watched a new group shaking violently as the drone's commands overrode their broken minds. One by one, they looked at their weapons, aiming them or practicing swinging the blades, saws, and modified hammers.

"They're prepping for an attack," Hoffman said.

Lo'thar pulled back his head in surprise. "Not all the tubes have begun the process. There are unaltered Dotari in that far bank of tubes!"

"Oh, shit," Garrison said. "Time to be heroes?"

"I thought only officers were supposed to get visited by the 'good idea' fairy," Max said.

"Everyone they turn is lost to us. We have to hurry," Lo'thar said.

"King is going to launch his attack in…" Hoffman looked at the digital readout on his gauntlet. "Nineteen minutes."

"These banshees are too close. They won't take the tubes, so we can't stop them that way. Can Gunney King kill that many?" Lo'thar asked.

"Gunney'd beat them to death with his fists one by one if he had to," Max said. "They all show up at once, the situation will…be in doubt."

"We must save all my unchanged Dotari people while we can," Lo'thar said.

"Mission first," Hoffman said. "We sabotage the tube system, none of them will reach engineering. Don't forget why we're here."

No one spoke as, below them, a new banshee let loose a mournful wail that turned into confused rage.

Lo'thar pointed to a door adjacent to the catwalk. "There is the power coupling."

Hoffman stood, looked around, then chopped his hand twice in the air toward their objective. "Light feet, Marines." He led the way, with Lo'thar close behind. "Keep an eye on those pods for as long as you can, Max," Hoffman said.

"No problem, sir. Can't really look away. Creepy."

One slow step at a time, Hoffman and Lo'thar crept to the door. Lo'thar activated the pad and read something on the small screen several times.

"Problem?" Hoffman asked.

"No. Why would there be a problem?" Lo'thar

shifted his weight side to side. "Don't rush me. Something is different."

He punched in a code and answered several prompts that came up on the screen in abbreviated Dotari words. The door slid open to reveal an armored plate around the coupling. Lo'thar and Hoffman bent forward to look through a small viewport.

"That's new," Lo'thar said.

"Garrison?" Hoffman asked.

The breacher examined the plate, cleared his throat, and spat into the corner. "If I cut through with burn cord, they'll notice. The composition of this alloy is different from our hulls. I don't know if I can set up a shaped charge to cut through it all…but if I use all our denethrite, it'll do the job for sure. Aren't many problems that can't be solved with enough explosives."

"And kill all the Dotari still in the tubes," Lo'thar said.

"Depends on the overpressure and several other factors. Fine, I will work my magic and save your people. Why don't you all just stand around while I pull another miracle out of my pocket?" Garrison ran his hands along the edges of the plate. "Hinges and screws. Didn't see that with the frost. Hmm. Here we go." He snapped his wrist, extending a multitool from his left gauntlet. Before long, he had the first screw twisted out.

He held it up for Hoffman and the others to examine. "About as long as this glorious finger and twice as thick." He started on the second screw, which was unexpectedly shorter. It fell free before he could catch it and rolled across the catwalk.

Hoffman watched in helpless horror as it wiggled through the grate and plummeted downward before anyone could react. It rotated as it fell through the air, then struck a banshee on the shoulder.

The banshee looked up.

Hoffman met its yellow-eyed gaze through the metal-framed goggles it wore.

"Well, shit," Garrison said.

"Set the charge!" Hoffman ordered.

As banshees raced up the tiered levels toward the stairs leading up to the catwalk, Hoffman and Max opened fire.

"I'll take the big ones on the left," Hoffman said.

"Shooting cyborg monsters on the right," Max said.

Garrison ripped his last block of denethrite from his pack. He pulled detonation cord out and plugged it into the denethrite as he placed the charge. "Skipping some safety protocols."

"Less talking, more exploding." Hoffman fired a shot through a banshee's chest, then dropped the empty magazine out of his rifle. It bounced off the walkway and spun through the air. He pulled a fresh magazine off his armor.

"Should I lay down covering fire while you reload?" Lo'thar asked.

Hoffman slapped ammo into his weapon and began firing as an answer.

"Reloading," Max said.

"Start shooting, Lo'thar," Hoffman grunted as he fired on one target after another.

Lo'thar aimed his pistol and fired into the mass of charging banshees. "I am sorry, brothers."

Max completed his reload, then shifted his full magazines toward the front of his armor for easier access while the expended mags went in a pouch. He picked his shots and fired in a steady cadence.

"How long for the detonator?" Garrison asked.

The catwalk vibrated from the banshees clambering onto the stairs. Hoffman aimed, then squeezed the trigger, sending a burst of rounds into the strut connecting the catwalk to the bulkhead. The entire catwalk shook and wobbled.

"Ninety seconds," Hoffman yelled.

Garrison punched in numbers and a confirmation code. "Set."

"Fall back the way we came," Hoffman ordered.

Garrison slung his demo kit across his back and aimed his rifle. "Covering." He squeezed off several shots.

"Moving," Hoffman said, grabbing Lo'thar and dragging him away. Max ran with them, but fired from the hip at the banshees racing up the stairwells.

"Garrison, catch up!" Max said.

"Moving," Garrison said. He turned and sprinted to catch up with Hoffman and Lo'thar.

Hoffman fired at a heavily armored banshee and froze as the bullet bounced off the onyx metal covering one shoulder. The strike managed to slow the alien to a stop, then it continued its charge, angrier than before.

"Low-power shots won't cut it on the big ones," Hoffman said. He shifted fire to those with the lighter armor where he could—getting kills instead of wasting ammunition.

Banshees scrambled over their dead comrades. When they reached the top catwalk, they ran toward the emplaced bomb instead of the Strike Marines. One ripped the bomb off the capacitor.

"No you don't!" Garrison shouted as he aimed and fired.

The gauss shell struck the bomb and it exploded in the banshee's hands, the catwalk twisting and bucking from the ensuing blast. Banshees were thrown over the edge, smashing into cryo tubes.

The catwalk beneath Hoffman and his team fell, swinging by the hinges still attached to the exit.

Hoffman grabbed the floor and bent it with the augmented strength of his suit, slapping his rifle onto the mag locks on his back just as the catwalk struck the wall. Lo'thar gave off a plaintive wail and fell free. Hoffman caught the Dotari by the wrist and dangled him over the long drop to the cryo chamber below.

Lo'thar clutched at Hoffman's arm, feet kicking as he swore—or prayed—in Dotari.

The lights in the chamber flickered out. Banshees screamed and howled. Far below, the pods remained illuminated.

Hoffman attempted to pull Lo'thar up with one arm but didn't have sufficient leverage. "Lo'thar, a little help?" Hoffman asked. The Dotari pilot climbed up the Marine's arm and wrapped his arms around Hoffman's neck.

Hoffman flexed the pseudo muscles of his armor to resist strangulation and climbed faster.

Garrison and Max dangled from a section of the swinging catwalk, but managed to climb higher, leaving bent metal handholds for Hoffman to use.

Hoffman gasped for air, driving his suit hard to get high enough that Garrison and Max could also escape. Looking down, he saw chaos and destruction. Fires spread. Banshees flung themselves from the stairs toward the disconnected catwalk. Many of them missed and fell, only to crawl back and try again. Some of the jumpers were already wreathed in flames, their skin charring.

"I think some of the stasis pods are still working," Lo'thar wheezed.

Hoffman grunted as Lo'thar squeezed with both arms. There were three more rungs to reach the top of the platform turned into a ladder. Something shook the entire structure. He flicked his gaze down, his mobility limited by the load he carried.

More banshees jumped up, grabbing the bottom of the broken platform.

Garrison and Max stopped. In unison, they gripped the metal grating with their feet and thighs, leaned out slightly, and fired down into the banshees.

Hoffman reached the top and chucked Lo'thar to safety. "Move! I'll cover." He lay on the platform, leaning over the edge as he pulled his rifle into position and stroked the trigger simultaneously with seeing banshees through the sights.

As Garrison and Max scrambled upward, the catwalk groaned. Hoffman thought he could feel it getting ready to snap.

More banshees jumped on and climbed.

Hoffman fired, hitting one target after another despite the awkward firing position.

"I'm up," Max panted just before the catwalk broke free.

Garrison jumped, his feet thrusting the metal grating down more than it propelled him up. Hoffman lunged forward and grabbed Garrison's free hand, their combined weight pulling him farther over the edge. Lo'thar and Max fell on his legs and held on.

"Pull, LT!" Garrison yelled.

"I thought I'd…drop you as a distraction," Hoffman grunted. The pseudo muscles of his suit augmented his strength, but progress only came inch by inch.

Max grabbed Hoffman around the waist and pulled with his legs, back, and arms until Garrison rolled onto the landing and gripped it with both hands, his chest heaving, his voice higher than normal. "Okay, shooting the bomb was not the best idea."

"You found a solution to a tactical problem, and none of us died. Good job," Hoffman said, rolling up to one knee as he caught his breath.

Garrison gave him a thumbs-up.

Max stood with his hands on his hips, shaking his head and gathering his senses while Lo'thar stared in horror at the monsters below. "We should leave now, yes?"

"To the air lock. Double time," Hoffman said, thinking how the plan had just gone sideways.

Chapter 14

King moved through the air duct, muttering under his breath with his IR and radio mics off. The primary benefit to wearing Strike Marine armor was the ability to talk to himself without looking crazy. No one could see or hear him rant. It was a guilty pleasure.

"Is this dust?" Adams asked as she crawled behind King.

"In the right circumstances, dust can be highly explosive," Duke said from the rear of their crawling team. "So shut up and pay attention."

"Can the cross talk," King said. "Booker, how's our principal?"

"Mister Moz'in is doing just as good as ever," Booker said.

"Not reassuring." King came to a grate and looked

at the room below them, where banshees milled around. One stabbed another for no reason and the victim of the stabbing barely reacted. "Crossing a grate. Maintain noise discipline and go slow. Bunch of beasties down there."

He moved ahead, pushing the carcasses of small, long-dead creatures aside. One came apart and smeared his glove and the wall he wiped it on. One of the supposedly dead rodent-bugs scurried out of sight. "Opal. Status report."

"Opal fits through ventilation duct."

"Not well," Booker added.

"Another grate. I think this is the one," King said. "Looks like about three squads' worth of banshees milling outside the door to engineering."

Vibrations rippled through the thin metal King and the others were crawling on. An ominous droning sound followed as power—invisible, unseen, and unheard until now—cut out. The dark space around them became pitch-black for a second. His helmet visor compensated a second behind both the power fluctuation and flickering light jutting up through the vents.

King checked his mission clock. Too soon. Way too soon. "Damn it—shake and bake, go!"

He kicked out the ventilation plate nearest to him,

twisted sideways in the cramped space, and dropped a grenade. Duke, Opal, and Booker did likewise. A combination of fragmentation and flash-bang grenades exploded in the passageway.

Shrapnel cut through the ventilation shaft like it was paper. King felt tugs against his armor as slivers of metal bounced off. His armor was proof against minor shrapnel and the deafening explosions. Feeling the hits instead of the pain of torn flesh was a relief, but he didn't want to make a habit of trusting the lowest-bidding manufacturers. Booker shielded Moz'in with her body armor while the old Dotari pressed his hands to the side of his helmet, trying to cover the ears within.

"Now I know how the fish in a barrel feel," Adams said, dropping into the fray. King, Duke, and Booker scrambled through the small openings and fell into a tangle of stricken banshees.

King came to his feet as he fired a stream of bullets into a banshee twice his size. Haphazardly placed armor plates deflected some of the bullets. Flesh fountained from other bullets as they impacted at close range. Expanding gas from his rifle barrel stapled the forehead of the monster.

He kicked it hard, driving himself back from his

dying attacker. He turned, looked for his team, and fired on a new target. "Circle up. Watch the cross fire!"

Booker and Adams backed up to him.

"Reloading!" Adams yelled. "Hell, yeah! Die, you ugly…"

King heard Booker fire one quick shot at a time.

Duke, ten strides away, jumped on a banshee and stabbed it three times through the eye slits of its armor as it tumbled backward. Standing on its chest as it struck the ground, he swirled on the balls of his feet, shooting one target after another in the throat. A second later, he moved farther away from King, Booker, and Adams.

King switched to shot and blew out the knees of two charging banshees with a tight group of metal beads. "Duke! Rally!"

"Working on it! Can't get there from here. Doing my own thing for a minute," Duke said as he fought his way closer to the door to engineering.

"Let's go to him, best speed," King said. "Move closer to the wall. Eliminate at least one of their angles of attack."

"Shit!" Booker yelled. "He can't shoot that thing one-handed."

King transitioned to his pistol and emptied it on a

banshee about to take Adams out as she reloaded. He holstered and finished his reload as Adams killed things with bullets and profanity. Her face was pale, her lips and cheeks flushed red through her translucent visor.

King saw blood and banshee bits splattered across her visor just as he realized he could barely see through his own visor. "Move! I'll cover. Link up with Duke."

"Gunney…" Adams yelled.

"Do it now!" Booker grunted, shooting as she moved.

Focused on shooting banshees as they went down flailing, King was vaguely aware of their progress.

"Throat shots! They never have armor on their throats!" Duke's over amplified voice echoed in King's helmet speaker.

King aimed and fired, striking banshees in their necks, shoulders, chests, and faces as Booker bounded back to cover and Duke dropped one after another with precision marksmanship.

"We're set! Come on, Gunney!" Booker yelled.

King spun around and sprinted, not trying to shoot or reload. As Duke, Booker, and Adams formed a firing line and went full auto on the remaining banshees, King dove and slid on his stomach. He stood in time to join the killing frenzy, but the rest of the fight was short.

"Where's Opal?" Adams asked.

King looked up. The doughboy was rocking back and forth in the air duct, threatening to bring the entire structure down.

"Opal wants down!" he grumbled just before his huge fist punched through the side of the duct and ripped open a hole.

The doughboy fell.

King and the others winced when the better part of three hundred pounds of muscle hit the deck.

"Like a sack of potatoes but dumber," Duke said. Opal's big gun fell on him with a heavy thud.

King looked up. "Where's Moz'in?"

"I'm up here. Still here. Fine up here. Yes. Moz'in and I will just watch," Moz'in said.

"We need you to open this door. Get your ass down here before I send Opal back up there to get you."

Slowly, with all the enthusiasm of creeping fungus, the old Dotari climbed out and hung from the grate. He swung for a while as the Strike Marines stared in mute exhaustion and fascination, then dropped.

"Oh, oh! I got him," Adams said, running forward like a baseball outfielder. She caught him easily with the enhanced strength of her armor's pseudo muscles.

Banshees screamed from several connecting hallways.

Moz'in hurried to the door and opened the control panel, typing fast. "That's not it…"

King cursed under his breath, turned away from the fumbling Dotari, and shot a banshee in the face as it came out of a hallway.

"Was it five?" Moz'in said on the second try.

Duke ran to a hallway opening and kneeled to aim. "Sooner is better than later!" He fired several times, then reloaded as Adams stood over him and provided covering fire.

"Ah, nine? Are you sure?" Moz'in said. He shrugged and entered the code. The doors opened. "Thank you, Moz'in," Moz'in said, then stage-whispered, "I knew it was nine the whole time."

A banshee reached through the door as it came open and grabbed Moz'in, but Opal snatched the banshee by the side of its face and bashed its skull against the slowly opening door. He picked Moz'in up with one hand, then set him out of the way before aiming his gauss rifle into the room and shooting several times.

King hurried to his side and saw a mass of banshees

inside the engineering area.

Opal stepped forward and swung his rifle like a club, crushing a half-helmeted banshee's head. Roaring like a beast, Opal shoved the wounded thing backward. Two more replaced the first, both big and grotesquely over muscled.

Opal head-butted one hard. King looked for a shot, but Opal filled the doorway, following the head-butt with a vicious elbow cross that slammed his victim out of view.

Three more crowded forward.

Opal drew his block-shaped sidearm and emptied the magazine into one's face. A second later, he front-kicked another just below the waist, then drove his knee into its face. Gripping the rifle with two hands, he slammed the butt of it into another, snapping its neck.

A banshee climbed over its fallen comrades to stab sharp, elongated fingers through Opal's chest armor. Opal grabbed his attacker's wrist and severed it from the hand. Twisting to one side, Opal yanked the banshee aside and struck it in the head with his knee. The doughboy brought his oversized rifle up as he stomped the banshee lying at his feet. Opal's weapon boomed as he shot up the rest of the banshees in the corridor.

Backing up, Opal continued to fire as more

banshees charged. His weapon clicked empty and he swung it like a club into the first alien to enter range, crushing it against the bulkhead in a splatter of dark blood.

Opal dropped his rifle and howled at the banshees. With God as King's witness, the sergeant swore the aliens hesitated. The doughboy shoulder-charged into the lead banshee and knocked it up and into the air ducts. He slapped his hands against the head of the next enemy and crushed it with a grunt.

Duke and Adams watched the fight, jaws slack.

"Let's help the dummy out," King said.

All three of them opened fire on targets outside the reach of Opal's wrath. The doughboy ripped an arm off an alien and used it to club another to the ground. When that one stopped moving, he whirled around and stomped the one-armed banshee to death. The construct picked up another corpse by the chest, then flung it to one side. He looked down the corridor and growled.

"Opal…stand down," King said. The doughboy looked at the banshee hand still embedded in his chest and pulled it free. Blood ran from the punctures as he picked up his rifle and swapped out the magazines.

Duke lowered his weapon abruptly. "And…we're done. Good work, Opie. Scary, but good."

"Opal, how bad are your injuries?" King asked.

"Unit suffering compromised lung function," Opal said. "Armor integrity compromised."

"Booker, patch him up," King said.

"Any pain, big guy?" the medic asked. She held her medical gauntlet perpendicular to his chest and three surgical probes popped out.

"No pain," Opal said. "No fear. Opal fights."

"So weird when you go from computer to lummox," she said. The probes pressed into the holes in his armor and blood spurted out. "Can't do this with a human…the puncture almost nicked one of your hearts. I can stop the bleeding easily enough. Time for self-repair?"

Opal stared into the distance.

"Opal? Time for self-repair?"

"Unit will reknit tissue in nine hours," Opal said as Booker pulled her gauntlet away. The probes vibrated, shedding blood onto the deck. Antibacterial mist rose from the device as it reset.

"Nine hours is longer than usual," Booker said.

"System degradation detected," Opal said.

"How degrad—" She looked over her shoulder at King, who was speaking with Moz'in at the engineering command center. "Can you fight?"

"Opal fights." He hefted his rifle up.

"We'll tell the lieutenant about this later, OK?" Booker asked.

"Sir needs Opal."

"We all need you, Opie. Stay strong."

"Booker! Opal!" King pointed to a door on the other side of the command center. "Secure that entrance."

King felt time ticking by as Moz'in went from workstation to workstation, mumbling to himself. The Dotari fell to bony knees, opened an access panel, and reached inside. There was a snap of electricity. He yanked his hand out and shook it against his thigh.

"Serves Moz'in right. Obvious that was a live wire." He looked up at King. "The bridge still has control. I can't access any systems yet."

Silence filled the room as the sound of approaching banshees echoed down the outer corridors.

"Then we wait for the LT to deliver," King said. *Come on, sir. We're counting on you.*

A new chorus of banshee howls rose from the far end of the engineering chamber. Shadows flickered against huge reactors at the far end of the long, wide, high-ceilinged room. The clear walls surrounding the engineering room had been designed for visibility and oversight of a colossal power center. King didn't think it looked defensible. The doorways were all too wide, and the blast door, heavier even than decompression doors in other parts of the ship, hadn't fallen during the recent battle, which probably meant it couldn't be lowered without full control of the engineering workstations.

Moz'in looked up from his work, alarm contorting his features.

"Do you need any of that crap?" King asked, pointing at a dense row of computer banks.

Moz'in patted the computer in front of him. "Just this station."

King quickly surveyed the area between his team and the new swarm of banshees. An energy bolt arched toward them in slow motion, missing, but sending a chill up his spine nonetheless. "We need barricades. Opal! Break stuff!"

"LT said no break stuff."

"He did, Opal 6-1-9. But I'm giving you a new order. Break up those workstations and stack them across the doorway facing the reactors," King said.

Opal hesitated.

"They're not shiny, Opal." King rolled his eyes.

"Opal break!"

Chapter 15

Sweat ran down the back of Valdar's neck as he studied the holo display, the slow trace of the *Breitenfeld* toward the oncoming Dotari ships. These were the moments naval officers trained for, the long bouts of time that could fill with indecision and doubt.

"Estimated time of contact?" Valdar asked.

"Nearly three hours, sir," Egan said.

"Any other threats trying to sneak up on us? Maybe a Toth battle cruiser or a Vishrakath stealther? Why not? That's how things happen this far out in the void."

"None, sir."

"Well, there's that, at least."

Gor'al and Egan leaned over a workstation, examining data.

"The smaller ships have pulled into a tighter formation, blocking our line of sight with the *Kid'ran's*

Gift," Valdar said as he studied the main holo and drummed his fingers on a railing. "How are the Xaros controlling those ships?"

"Laser relays," Gor'al answered. "Direct line-of-sight communication, not as secure as your infrared, but longer range."

"So there will be some communication lag between whatever's controlling the ships, the farther they are from the *Kid'ran*. Won't be much, but the slower they react to us, the better chance we'll have when they get closer. Helm, bring us on a parallel course to the Dotari fleet, then edge us away at ten degrees to starboard."

The *Breitenfeld* lurched sideways.

"She's sluggish," Valdar said, thinking the mass of the gate in his hold was weighing his ship down. "What's on those vessels moving to intercept us?"

"Sleeper ships," Gor'al said. "Each with ten thousand Dotari."

Valdar punched the side of the holo tank, then faced Egan. "Give me a sensor sweep on those ships. Tell me if there's any life signs."

"Aye aye, sir."

Valdar pointed at Gor'al. "What happens if we break the laser link with the flagship?"

Gor'al twitched his quills as he made calculations. "Should send the ship back to local control. Onboard computers are programmed to preserve the crew at all costs and maintain formation with the fleet."

"How do we break that link?"

"Destroy the ship's antennae." Gor'al zoomed in on the approaching ships, highlighting commo arrays on four sides of each ship.

"Backups for backups," Valdar said.

Gor'al shrugged. "It's a long trip."

"If we had fighters knocking out those antennae, this wouldn't be difficult," Valdar said. "Instead, all I've got are my rail cannons and the ship's point defense guns."

"These aren't warships, Admiral. If you hit those ships with your rail cannons, you'll rip them to pieces," Gor'al said.

The three-dimensional icons in the holo tank changed slightly and silence held the bridge. Valdar almost wished someone would crack a joke. "We came out here to save the Dotari, not kill them in their sleep."

"Admiral, those ships are packed with life signs," Egan said.

Gor'al looked at Egan, then back to his own work. "The engines…they could be temperamental and were designed to be ejected at the first sign of malfunction. The strongest armor on the ships is between the engines and the rest of the ship."

"We can hit the engines without risking the passengers?" Valdar asked.

"There is still some danger, but if there's one place we can damage them…" Gor'al tapped the screen where it indicated the engine blocks of the ships.

"To get a clean shot will take some maneuvering. And we're as nimble as a doughboy tap-dancing team," Valdar said.

Egan shook his head. "Sir, you can't be thinking…"

Valdar took a small step forward. "Time to jettison the dead weight. Have the Grinder dumped into space and have the crews begin assembling the device. We need to get word back to Earth and Dotari that there's a Xaros-controlled fleet out in the void. Then run firing solutions to target those ships' engines."

Gor'al's eyes were wide and his words came slowly. "This is a strike carrier, Admiral Valdar, not a destroyer. What are you planning?"

"We want a clean shot that doesn't kill the civilians on those ships? We need to get into a knife fight."

Chapter 16

Hoffman stayed close to Lo'thar as they moved from room to room looking for a hallway that would take them around the banshee infestation. He pulled the magazine from his rifle, looked at it, and slammed it back in.

"You have plenty of ammunition?" Lo'thar asked.

"Sure, as long as there's only one lightly armored banshee in our way."

Lo'thar dropped his chin to his chest, staggering slightly as he forced himself to continue walking. "We will die and my daughter will never be cured of the phage."

Hoffman put a hand on his shoulder. "I have ammo. Less than I like, but some. Strike Marines are resourceful. We'll get a viable blood sample back to Dotari."

Lo'thar nodded, eyes downcast. "Thank you,

Lieutenant Hoffman."

Hoffman touched the side of his helmet to activate his IR link. "Max, how are we doing up front? Have you found a way to the bridge that doesn't involve a frontal assault of the entire banshee horde?"

"Not exactly. You better come up."

Hoffman reached Max and Garrison, who were staring at a blast door thicker than any other he had seen. At first, he didn't understand what was wrong with it.

"That is a decompression barrier. Once it drops into place, it cannot be raised until the ship dry-docks for repairs," Lo'thar said. "We have reached a dead end. Unless you are ready to go outside now."

"Not in the plan," Hoffman said. "But I guess there is no time like the present."

"There certainly is not," Lo'thar said.

"Garrison and I have been talking. Lo'thar can correct us if we're wrong, but I think we should be near Bradford's breach point," Max said.

"He is right," Lo'thar said. "I saw this barrier in the ship diagram during the mission brief. It does not bode well that something caused it to lock down."

"Get us outside. Time for our spacewalk," Hoffman said.

"There is a maintenance air lock. Follow me," Lo'thar said.

Hoffman stayed close to the Dotari war hero, weapons ready. "Garrison and Max, use a stim patch. We've been going nonstop for hours."

"Yes, sir," Garrison and Max said.

Hoffman told his armor computer to do the same for him. Inside the shoulder section of his bodysuit, something sticky adhered to his skin and grew warm as he walked.

"This is the air lock," Lo'thar said.

Hoffman examined the small chamber. "Check your EVA buddy's suit, then we're going out." He checked Duke's suit, half-watching as Garrison did the same to Lo'thar.

"Your suit looks very good, Hoff," Lo'thar said, brushing away dust and ice crystals—which wasn't part of the standard check.

Hoffman tensed, one eye twitching.

Lo'thar's quills rustled inside his helmet visor. "Is that not the right thing to call you? Your Strike Marines call you that."

"We don't call him the Hoff," Garrison said through gritted teeth as he ran his hands along the ring of Lo'thar's helmet.

"I distinctly heard you and Booker—" Lo'thar kept talking, but his words didn't transmit over the IR.

"Had to reset his transmitter," Garrison said quickly

"—beloved in a place called Germany. Didn't know he could sing," Lo'thar said.

"He's good." Garrison slapped Lo'thar on the rear end.

Hoffman slapped the air-lock controls and waited as air was sucked out and the doors opened. He stepped out onto the ship's hull. The void was as empty as ever.

"Focus, Marines. Focus."

He led the way across the hull, checking the grav liners in his boots every ten or fifteen steps—unnecessary but hard to avoid with hard vacuum in every direction. "Approaching the bridge," he said to his team.

"Ugliest bridge I've ever seen," Max said. "Looks like a flattened cow patty."

"Is it necessary to insult the ship of my people?" Lo'thar asked. "Wait until you see the elegance of Dotari style on the inside."

Hoffman and the others faced the Dotari pilot and stared at him as the blackness of space loomed above them. The utilitarian exterior of the bridge looked cold and uninviting.

"It is not beautiful," Lo'thar admitted.

Button-shaped, the flattened mound of metal was covered with dents and scrapes from thousands of years of debris strikes. Point defense systems couldn't stop every grain of dust during the thousand-year voyage. The speed of impact made every speck a dangerous accumulation of kinetic energy.

"Max, I see where Bradford took his team inside. They have a commo array. Tap into it," Hoffman said.

"Yes, sir." Max removed tools and cables from his backpack and went to work. Time passed. "Can't get the *Breit*…they must be outside the IR cone. Why would the ship move?"

A number of answers came to Hoffman, none of them good.

"If I switch to radio, the Xaros will know we're here." Max stepped away from the IR transmitter.

Hoffman gazed across the hull and the black void beyond it. "Load up a situation report into the buffer and have the transmitter do a sector scan. It can dump the message if—when—it makes contact. As for us, the clock's ticking and air doesn't come cheap around here. Drop the message and let's move."

It took Max less than a minute to transfer the

message from his gauntlet to the transmitter. The dish moved a few degrees to one side, paused, then moved again. Max flashed a thumbs-up.

Hoffman set a brisk but steady pace, forcing himself to relax and his heart rate to slow. Garrison met him at Bradford's secondary breach point and unrolled a denethrite cord without a word from Hoffman.

"I'm really going to be out after this," Garrison said.

"You have breaching charges after the coupling?" Hoffman asked.

"Trying to work, sir. One moment and I can inventory my kit. Didn't have time to disassemble any of my premade stuff—or disassemble grenades, which is against regulations, sir—to add to that last epic blast. Just please remember I have limits and only carry so much cool stuff." Garrison burned a circle in the door and Hoffman and Max helped him pull it free, tossing it away. Air vented from the opening, setting them all off-balance for a second.

"Max," Hoffman said.

The communication specialist gripped his gauss rifle and slipped inside. Hoffman, Lo'thar, and Garrison followed.

"Hold on. There's an escape pod. Can't get around

it," Max said.

The team converged on the problem.

"Options?" Hoffman asked.

"Get rid of it?" Garrison asked.

Lo'thar traced the nose of the simple craft, then looked over his shoulder the way they had come. "We can open the door from the inside and push it out. I doubt it will fit through Garrison's tiny hole."

Garrison shook his head. "Ha, ha, ha." He grabbed the pod and started to pull. It moved slightly.

"Lo'thar, open the escape pod bay door. Max, stand guard while Garrison and I manhandle this thing," Hoffman said.

"Keep it on the rails or you will never be able to move it. The gravity is good here," Lo'thar said. "And be warned the interior doors will start to close. Please do not take too long moving that thing out of the way."

Hoffman was sweating down his back by the time they introduced the escape pod to space. As it tumbled into the void, lights appeared over the door to the interior, disappearing one by one.

"Hurry!" Lo'thar said.

Hoffman and Max jumped through, then threw their weight ineffectively against the sliding doors.

"Outta my way!" Garrison sprinted to the door and shoved a pry bar between the closing panels. Holding it in place with one hand, he grabbed Lo'thar with the other and dragged, then pushed him unceremoniously through the narrowing gap. At the last second, he slid through and kicked the tool. It quivered under the force of the closing doors.

"What are you doing?" Max yelled.

The pry tool snapped and shot outward, tumbling through the escape pod tube and into space.

"That was my favorite breach tool," Garrison said, staring after it through a small view port.

"Are those tears?" Max asked. "Dude, it's a pry bar."

Garrison shouldered past the communications specialist. "Had that one since I started. I should have let it explode into your face, Max."

Hoffman swept the room for threats. "Looks like gauss bullet marks on the walls."

Garrison composed himself, cinching down his backpack and raising his weapon. "And bloodstains."

"Captain Bradford was here. Look sharp," Hoffman said. "I'll take point for a while."

"One of us can do it, sir," Max said.

"We need to rotate. Just watch my back. You'll get your turn." He moved forward and slowed as he turned a corner and found a body in Strike Marine armor.

"Looks like one of Bradford and Fallon's men," Hoffman said.

The corpse lay on its back, limbs in an unnatural contortion that only the dead could manage. Dried blood covered the torso and visor, and a tear in the armor extended along the collarbone. Hoffman knelt and removed an identity chip from the corpse's chest armor along with two gauss magazines.

"Let's keep moving. Max, log the locations of anyone we find so we can recover them later for full honors," Hoffman said.

"Yes, sir."

Hoffman used combat breathing—in for two seconds, hold for two, and exhale for two—to relax and focus as he worked his way through the aftermath of a deadly confrontation. Lights flickered and sparks sputtered from damaged wiring around doors and mini-workstations throughout the ship.

He came to an enormous doorway that marked the section. "Moving to the next section of the ship. Should be getting close to the bridge."

A wide catwalk stretched out ahead of him. Steam rose from both sides as he moved across and his team followed. Lights flickered in the roiling mass of atmosphere below and above them.

Directly ahead, a shape loomed toward the high ceiling. "We've reached the elevator shaft to the bridge."

Garrison joined him and looked down into the steam. The elevator shaft extended even farther down than it did up. "You hear something, sir?"

Hundreds of soft clicking sounds penetrated the gloom. Hoffman heard metal renting as it was torn by something moving up the outside of the elevator shaft. Banshees grunted and snorted as they climbed up the walls.

"We don't have that many bullets," Garrison said.

"We must hurry," Lo'thar said.

Hoffman sprinted toward the elevator doors as a pair of banshees swung up from the bottom of the catwalk and roared, teeth flashing as saliva sprayed into the air.

Hoffman's gauss rifle came up in a well-practiced motion as he picked his targets through the sights of the weapon and squeezed the trigger. The first round struck the nearest banshee in its left eye and yellow and gray slime exploded out the back of its head. Remembering Duke's suggestion, he shot the next banshee in the throat where the armor was thin.

"On your left, LT," Garrison said.

"Moving," Max said.

Hoffman heard both Strike Marines firing rapidly but did not track their exact positions. He pressed forward and snapped his left wrist twice, extending his Ka-Bar and stabbing a banshee in the face, making time so he could reload.

More banshees climbed over the railing. One stepped on another and sent its comrade hurtling into the abyss.

"I've got more of these things coming up the other side," Garrison said.

Hoffman killed two more with his rifle, then slung it and moved forward in a fighting crouch with his bayonet. Two banshees charged. He waited until the last second and sidestepped to the left, thrusting the blade into the temple of his adversary. Without hesitation, he clambered over the falling body and jammed the bayonet into the eye slit of the second banshee.

"These things aren't wearing much armor. So that's nice," Hoffman said.

"You're full of good news today, boss," Garrison said.

A thin bolt of energy shot between them, then Max let off a pained curse. Hoffman turned and saw the commo Marine's arm hanging limp at his side, blood seeping out of a rent just beneath the shoulder. The armor compressed the wound automatically and Max lifted and flexed his arm amidst a slew of profanity.

"Grenades free," Hoffman said.

Garrison and Max hurled frag grenades into the growing mass of banshees blocking their progress toward the elevator shaft. Hoffman pulled a grenade and bounced it off the ceiling and into the back ranks of charging aliens. Explosions rippled through the banshees, blasting them into an ugly carpet of corpses.

Hoffman kicked a mostly intact banshee to make sure it was dead. Blood seeped around his boots, and he was grateful that his armor filtered out the smell that must have permeated the air.

"That's the way it's done, boss," Garrison said just before something grabbed Hoffman's ankle. He looked down and realized two things: the banshee was ready to rip his leg off, and he was very close to the edge of a long drop.

Lo'thar fired at Hoffman's attacker, striking it directly in its temple. The banshee rolled away but didn't let go.

Hoffman's feet whipped out from under him as he was dragged over the edge. On the way down, he bounced against walls and pipes. He saw the bottom of the shaft a split second before it came up hard and fast.

Chapter 17

Valdar gripped the railing with both hands. "Combat stations, full alert. Brace for impact."

He watched the Dotari ships racing straight for the *Breitenfeld*. "I think we're right about the Xaros controlling those ships. They're fearsome in a fight when they have the numbers, but not much in the way of imagination."

Egan kept his eyes on his own workstation. "Thank the Saint for that. At this distance, our scans have much better resolution."

"How many ships are we up to?" Valdar asked.

"Looks like nineteen ships, twenty if we are counting the *Kid'ran's Gift*," Gor'al said. "The drone must be pushing their engines hard. My study of the old ships in preparation for this mission suggested they don't normally move this fast."

Valdar nodded, watching the holo display as he listened to his officers. In the back of his mind, he thought about how far behind he had left the crucible gate. "Jamison, status report on the beacon links."

The junior ensign had spent the last several hours staring at his terminal as though the entire mission depended on his vigilance. "The Grinder gate, sir, is under construction. Crews are reporting delays as half the labor force is still aboard ship. Timeline for completion is several days."

"Good to know, Ensign. You can relax. They're not going anywhere. Just keep an eye on them for me," Valdar said. "Egan, take us around the Dotari ships. You know the plan."

"Maneuvering now," Egan said.

Several of the Dotari ships opened fire with counter-asteroid batteries. The first several salvos missed, then peppered the side of the *Breitenfeld*. Valdar swayed on his feet but remained standing, with both hands on the tactical railing around his bridge station. "Not bad for some asteroid busters. I think the *Breit* can take heavier hits than that."

Nervous laughter spread through the bridge crew.

"We're coming around their formation," Egan said.

"It is my duty to inform the admiral that, from this position, they are able to aim a lot more of those guns at us."

Valdar grunted. "Hold on, everyone. We're about to take a broadside." He moved his gaze around the room to judge the morale of his crew. Some were veterans; others were not. If they were shaking in fear, he didn't see it, which meant they were all excellent actors. "XO, I wouldn't say no to evasive maneuvers."

"Always wanted to be a fighter jock," Egan said.

The Dotari ships continued to fire, striking more often than Valdar would've liked. "Damage report."

"We've suffered two hull breaches, but they've been contained. No casualties," Jamison said.

"Sir, we have a problem," Egan said rapidly.

Valdar saw the problem. One of the Dotari ships was too close to miss. Every counter-asteroid cannon on the port side of the Dotari ship aimed at the *Breitenfeld*. "Lieutenant Clark, weapons free."

"Firing rail batteries two, three, and four," the weapons officer said in a dry voice. "All hits, sir. I assumed you preferred I take out the engines before killing the civilian sections of the ship."

"Well done, Lieutenant," Valdar said.

"Brace for evasive maneuvers," Egan said. "I mean

really brace."

Egan's hands flew across the controls, and then he grabbed the manual joystick to finish the maneuver. The ship rolled, and Valdar was suddenly glad he was wearing armor and had pumped the atmosphere into storage tanks. He locked his eyes on the holo tank and spread his feet for stability. From what he was seeing, the *Breitenfeld* looked like it had already been rammed. He'd never seen such a close call without a collision.

Egan spoke through clenched teeth as he fought to override the ship's safety protocol. "Just keep rolling. Just keep rolling. Just keep…rolling."

Something massive struck the *Breitenfeld*. It felt like they'd run into a moon. Valdar was thrown sideways, saved by his safety harness linked to the railing and the pseudo-muscle strength of his armor. "Did we actually get rammed? Damage report."

"They tried, but it was a glancing blow," said Egan's relief officer, Lieutenant Morgaine-Phillips.

"Nice flying, Egan," Valdar said.

Several of the Dotari ships fired at once, spraying the *Breitenfeld* with kinetic projectiles that blasted holes in the armor. If Valdar hadn't decided to fight in void conditions, the atmosphere would be spraying into space and fires would be sweeping through hallways.

"That was a bad one," Morgaine-Phillips said. "Engineering is reporting substantial damage. We have serious casualties on decks four through eight."

"Understood. Egan, are you all right?"

His XO nodded. "Just catching my breath. Thanks." She nodded.

"Guns, hit those engines. We need to even the odds," Valdar said.

Another series of impacts rocked the ship. The icons in the holo tank turned to encircle the *Breitenfeld*. It was a basic Xaros mob attack. The only thing that saved the *Breitenfeld* thus far was how slow the Dotari ships were compared to a Xaros drone. Valdar felt the comforting thump of his ship's rail cannons. Clark, his weapons officer, lined up his shots with precision and fired only when he was ready.

"You're doing good work, guns. Just do it faster. Don't give me perfection—just give me a victory," Valdar said.

"Aye aye, sir," Clark said.

Gor'al shook his head side to side, quills whipping this way and that. "No, no, no. More ships are peeling off from the main fleet and heading our way."

Lieutenant Clark and his weapons team fired rapidly, soundless explosions marking their success. Several of the Dotari ships drifted out of control.

"Gor'al," Valdar said.

The Dotari officer faced him.

"We're on the *Breitenfeld*. Crewed by the best men and women the Terran Alliance has to offer. The only reason we've suffered this much damage is because we're playing nice."

"Yes, Admiral."

"Guns, show me something amazing."

"Aye aye, sir!" Clark said.

"Egan," Valdar said, "do you see what I see?"

"They're moving in a perfect triangle. We can fly straight down the middle. Every time they miss, they'll hit each other. And we can use all our guns."

"Guns, ready all your gunners. Gor'al, what kind of damage will their asteroid busters do to the civilian sections of those ships?" Valdar asked.

Gor'al hesitated. "I believe they are aiming at the bridge. Our closing speed will be…fast. My concern is that they'll ram us, or each other, depending on Egan's skill."

Valdar studied the holo tank. "It's a risk, but it's the only way we can put all our guns to work. XO, make it happen."

"This is going to be ugly," Egan said as he plotted a head-on collision course with one of the ships, with a last second run down the middle.

"Firing solutions are programed for all rail cannons. Faster than human reflexes, sir."

"Very good. Brace for combat," Valdar said.

The Dotari ship grew large in the holo tank. Valdar held his breath, standing motionless at his station. His gauntlets gripped the railing. The grav liners in his boots held the floor.

Egan let out a whoop a second before the *Breitenfeld* slipped through the gauntlet. Dozens of gauss point defense turrets fired almost simultaneously. The holo view spun to watch the destruction behind them.

Three Dotari ships veered away from each other at random angles and made no effort to correct course. Debris clouds expanded where each of the ships once had engines.

"XO," Valdar said, "bring us around. Let's have a look at our work. Should be a lot easier to avoid their teeth now. Good work, crew."

Cheers erupted on every deck of the ship.

Valdar gave them some time before quietly gathering casualty and damage reports.

Chapter 18

Opal grabbed a computer tower near the back of the room.

"That's bolted to the wall, Opie," Booker said.

Duke shook his head. "Dummy."

Opal heaved backward, driving with his legs and straightening his back as he pulled higher and higher with his hands. The mainframe computer tore free of the wall and rose into the air. Opal turned and carried it overhead to the doorway. He dropped it with a loud smash.

"I bet you were all thinking he couldn't do that," King said. "Don't just stand there. Help him build the barricade—except for you, Duke. Find a position and start shooting."

An energy beam glanced off King's shoulder. He dropped to the floor out of reflex even though it had already touched his armor. Rolling to one side, he came to his feet and moved to Duke's side to return fire. "Hop to it!" he yelled over his shoulder.

Duke locked his sniper rifle to his back and drew his combat carbine. He fired the smaller gauss weapon in single-fire mode, but he did it so quickly it almost seemed like an automatic weapon. Every shot struck a target, either chest or throat. The first two ranks of banshees wore heavier armor than the others, shrugging off rounds that hit their piecework armor.

King fired at the banshees Duke had only wounded, finishing them off. "Get to it, Opal!"

"Break stuff!" Opal said as he grabbed two benches at a time and flung them into the stack of debris at the doorway. Booker and Adams rearranged it to make it more efficient and to create firing holes.

"That's as good as it gets. Everybody online. Weapons free!" King shouted.

****

The hiss of a sliding door woke Hoffman. He opened his eyes a crack, wincing as light seemed to slice his brain in half. He was being dragged across the deck by the carry handle on the back of his armor. He couldn't turn his head, but he saw legs in Strike Marine armor next to him. He blinked, waiting for the fuzzy display on his visor to clear up.

"Garrison…where's Lo'thar?" he asked. An error icon popped up on his visor, alerting him that no one was in range of his IR. He tried to twist out of the grasp on his body, but the hold only got stronger.

"Max? Why are our comms—" He was dropped to the deck and a boot stomped onto his upper back, pinning him down. His helmet came off with a violent snap and was thrown against the bulkhead hard enough to shatter the visor. Hoffman twisted his head to one side and looked into the white eyes of Captain Bradford. If his commanding officer could show emotion, it didn't penetrate the metal discs bolted to his face, head, and neck. Wires ran under the plates and through the Marine's skin.

Bradford slapped a hand on Hoffman's throat, cutting off the blood flow to his head. Hoffman fought through the near panic of being strangled and the knowledge that his commanding officer had been corrupted like the banshees.

Strike Marines had encountered twisted humans during the war and dubbed them wights. The Xaros' thralls were deadly, vicious, and utterly without mercy.

Hoffman struck Bradford's wrist and broke the hold. He drove his knee up, aiming for the groin, unsure if it would do any good given the state of his former commander, and struck home.

Bradford grunted, but it was almost mechanical—completely devoid of emotion. Hoffman kicked Bradford in the chest, driving him back.

Bradford rushed forward, feinting with a left jab, then swinging a vicious right hook. Hoffman executed an upward and outward left block with his forearm, which was more of a strike than a defensive movement. The captain seemed slow but just as skilled as he ever was.

Hoffman retreated, looking right and left for other threats. The scene at the bottom of the shaft was a nightmare. He suddenly remembered where he was and where he needed to be. The captain came at him and Hoffman retreated again.

"Captain? Can you hear me? Fight the Xaros, not me!"

Bradford opened his mouth to release a soundless shriek as he charged. Hoffman waited until the last second and sidestepped the advance, driving his palm into the captain's chin and twisting his head up. Hoffman bumped his right hip into Bradford's and used his arm as a lever as he twisted around, slamming the captain's upper back against the floor as his feet flew into the air.

The captain pulled his knees back almost to his chin and kicked forward and onto his feet. He charged at Hoffman and snapped a kick at the other Marine's knee, faster than Hoffman was prepared for. Bradford's foot glanced off Hoffman's shin and knocked the lieutenant off-balance. The follow-on punch thumped into Hoffman's chest so hard Hoffman felt like he'd been shot. Hoffman ducked under the captain's hook and rammed an elbow into the changed man's sternum, then he shoved the captain against the bulkhead and pinned his arms to the metal.

"Talk to me, sir."

Bradford tried to head-butt him but was too slow.

Hoffman chopped against the back of the captain's neck and sent him stumbling to his knees. There, locked to his lower back, was a holstered gauss pistol. Hoffman tore it away and kicked the captain in the hip, sending him tumbling away. Hoffman activated the weapon and braced himself, the muzzle aimed at Bradford's head.

"Stop, captain." Hoffman put his finger on the trigger.

Bradford's head snapped toward him, and light ran

through the wires embedded in his skin. The wight charged and Hoffman changed his point of aim to the captain's midsection. He fired three shots into the seam of armor joints over the stomach, a point Hoffman knew the underpowered pistol might break through. Bradford stumbled forward, blood spurting from his side. He raised his arms up and launched forward, tackling Hoffman, and the two went down.

Hoffman rolled and landed on top of his commander. He jammed the muzzle beneath Bradford's chin and looked into the man's eyes. The Marine Hoffman knew wasn't there.

Hoffman pulled the trigger and blew a hole out the top of the captain's skull. Bradford twitched for a moment, then went slack.

"I'm sorry, sir." Hoffman got up as the image of his dead commander and the smell of blood and the ozone wafting from the muzzle etched themselves into his memory forever.

Behind him, an elevator door opened to reveal a pair of altered Marines in full armor.

Hoffman raised his pistol and pulled the trigger. The weapon vibrated, alerting him that it was empty. He tossed it aside and charged forward, popping his Ka-Bar from the forearm housing and launching himself through the door. His shoulder caught the first turned-Marine and drove him off his feet. The other, Lieutenant Fallon, jumped on Hoffman's back.

The elevator lurched into motion and rose.

Hoffman rolled to one side and dislodged both his attackers. Coming to his feet, he realized there was no place to run and no room to fight. He stepped even closer to the first Strike Marine and drove his Ka-Bar under his chin with all the strength he had left, forcing the blade into the armor's seams. Before he could twist the blade, the other turned-Marine hammered him with a gauntleted fist.

Hoffman got an arm up to deflect the blow from his bare head. The blow struck hard and sent a spike of pain down through his hand. Hoffman twisted at the waist and drove the palm of his right hand against his attacker's collarbone, just hard enough to move him back a few inches. At the same time, he cycled his left arm back with the bayonet, reversed the motion, and thrust up under the armpit. He leaned into the upward lunge and pushed his opponent to the other side of the elevator. Slamming into him with all his weight, he felt the blade slide home and used the rebound from the collision to yank the blade free. A glut of blood spilled onto the floor and the wounded wight swiped a fist at Hoffman.

The stabbed Marine fell against his companion, moving with grace of a drunk. The bright red blood running down his armor told Hoffman he'd severed the artery. Fallon pushed the dying Marine against Hoffman hard enough to bounce the back of his head against the wall.

Hoffman saw a punch hurtling toward his face. He got a forearm up and took the blow square against his gauntlet. Fallon pushed his punch farther and Hoffman cocked his head to one side a split second before Fallon's Ka-Bar snapped out. The blade sliced Hoffman's cheek open.

The lieutenant twisted his gauntlet up and jabbed a punch beneath Fallon's arm against his helmet. He anticipated Fallon's next knife strike and deflected the blade into the wall, where it tore through the thin metal and jammed against the elevator's frame. Fallon tried to tug his weapon out, but he was stuck.

The wight hissed just as Hoffman slammed his fist against the visor, sending a spider web of cracks through the ballistic glass. Hoffman punched again, driving deep cracks across Fallon's faceplate. With his third blow, Hoffman popped his own Ka-Bar and pierced the wight's visor. Blood painted the inside of Fallon's helmet and he went slack, one arm still pinned to the elevator wall.

Hoffman pulled his weapon free, his body singing with adrenaline, and he took a few seconds to stare at the turned Strike Marines. It was hard to accept that he'd just killed men who had been fellow Marines a few hours ago.

The Marine that bled to death still had his gauss rifle mag-locked to the back of his armor. Hoffman took it and set it to high-power shot. Fallon had a single anti-armor grenade on his belt. He took a grenade from the dead Marine's pouch and tapped the grenade against Fallon's helmet in thanks.

The anti-armor grenade would explode and turn a cone of depleted uranium into a shaped charge of metal. Hoffman didn't care for the underlying physics, but he knew from experience during the Ember War that the white-hot lance of metal from the grenade could crack a drone's shell.

The elevator stopped with a chime and the door opened.

Kid'ran's Gift's bridge was no longer Dotari. A substance roughly the texture of iron pyrite lined the walls, floors, and most of the ceiling and was thicker along the corners and edges of workstations. Hoffman felt like he was walking into a giant geode.

Marines hung on the walls, bound by their wrists and ankles with the same crystalline material. Wires and tubes ran into their ears, eyes, and down their gaping mouths. Some moved; others did not. The flickering lights within the crystals gave Hoffman a headache.

Hoffman studied the ceiling and saw an oblong shape longer than he was tall embedded in the crystal. Fractal patterns pulsed across the surface. The Xaros drone. Eight stalks radiated out from the drone across the ceiling. As motes of light snapped down the drone's limbs, an atavistic fear coursed through Hoffman's body.

He remembered the skies of Earth full of thousands on top of thousands of drones as he fought them in the mountain fortresses of Utah. Machines like this had driven humanity to the very brink of extinction, had wiped out sentient life across the galaxy in a reign of terror that lasted for millennia. Now he was so close to one that he could almost touch it.

One stalk broke loose of the metallic geode moorings and pointed directly at Hoffman. The tip glowed red.

Hoffman aimed at the arm stalk without thinking and fired, severing the stalk halfway across the ceiling. Crystals fell to the ground like shattered glass. The stalk writhed against the deck like a wounded snake, then disintegrated, burning away from within.

Hoffman held up the grenade so the drone could see it.

The drone's surface rippled with fractals.

"You know what we are?" Hoffman slowly moved his thumb toward the grenade's activation switch. "You know what happened? We beat you. We found your Masters beyond the galaxy's edge and killed them. Destroyed every last drone in the galaxy…except you. They program you with fear?"

During the war against these machines, from the first scouring of Earth to the final battle aboard the Xaros Master's Dyson sphere, the drones had never communicated with their victims. Hoffman didn't expect an answer now.

The patterns on the drone's surface changed and he felt the deck shift beneath his feet. More stalks snapped away from the ceiling and a crimson beam struck the deck and traced a line straight toward Hoffman. He jumped to one side and threw the grenade.

Another stalk broke free of the metal latticework and knocked the grenade aside just before it exploded. The molten lance clipped the drone's side, leaving a glowing furrow against the shell. The blast wave slapped Hoffman onto his back.

The drone fell from the ceiling, landing in the center of the bridge. It pushed itself up with its stalks as hunks of pyrite fell from the damaged shell like it was bleeding. The drone lifted a stalk and pointed the tip at Hoffman. It struck toward him like a shot arrow.

Hoffman swung his rifle butt around and knocked the stalk aside, then he flipped his rifle over and fired point-blank into the drone's shell. The drone staggered sideways, cracks spreading across its surface. The Strike Marine dropped the spent battery from the rifle and slapped a new one home. He rolled forward and dodged another stalk as it scythed through the air where his neck had been a moment earlier.

He grabbed the base of a stalk and jumped up, using his handhold to swing up and land on top of the drone. He fired and blew a crater out of the shell.

"That's for my captain!"

A squeal sounded from the drone as Hoffman fired again. The shell shot clean through the drone and it fell flat against the floor. The shell glowed red-hot and Hoffman felt his feet scorch through his boots.

Hoffman jumped aside as the drone disintegrated,

crumbling to ash that seemed to evaporate away into nothing.

Hoffman waited, rifle ready. The bridge was eerily silent; the only trace of the drone was the gap in the crystals on the ceiling. Tiny cracks formed in the geode, spreading with the creaks and groans of an ice floe. He went to one of the Marines bound to the wall. The woman had her chin against her chest. He felt for a pulse and found none.

Hoffman took her identity tag off her armor and repeated the process for the rest of the captured Marines. None had survived the drone's destruction.

At the end, he held a fistful of dog tags as the geodes encasing the bridge crumbled to dust.

"Semper Fi, Marines." Hoffman went back to the elevator.

****

"I hate the ones with laser beams," Adams said. She knelt behind an overturned workbench and reloaded with smooth efficiency.

"Laser beams?" Moz'in asked. He stood without thinking as he pondered his own question and the possible answer. "I think you use the term without precision."

King grabbed him and shoved him back behind the workstation. "Stay low and keep working."

King rushed back to the barricades, leaned around the edge of the doorframe, and fired three short bursts at the banshees. Several energy beams converged on his position from the roiling mass of mutated and cybernetically enhanced Dotari. He shoved himself backwards and rolled sideways as a shower of splintered alloys and sparks covered the entire team of Strike Marines.

King came to his feet and ran in a low crouch to utilize the smashed and rearranged computer stations as concealment. At this point, he wasn't sure if they were good cover, but they did hide his movements. He reached the end of the pile of broken things, ducked around the corner, and shot a banshee who had been creeping around the flank. His rounds took it directly in the face and flipped it onto its back on the catwalk just outside the doorway.

"The really great thing about the situation," Booker said, "is that we can't go back the way we came."

King stared at the reactors in the distance, not bothering to estimate the number of enemies assaulting his position. "We still have a mission."

"Kill enemies!" Opal roared as he fired his oversized gauss rifle.

"I'm so glad we brought that guy," Adams said.

"It's on!" Moz'in shouted. "It's working!"

"Then *do* something!" King yelled.

"I know what to do. You tell him that I don't like his attitude." Moz'in snapped his beak.

The team looked toward King.

"Step back and be ready if they come over the barricade. I think I know what he's going to do," King said.

Moz'in typed furiously on the dusty keyboard. The ship shuddered and the blast door fell, obliterating the barricade. Banshees charged, slamming into the barrier.

"One more thing. Ah, that should do it," Moz'in said. An alarm sounded and a warning in an ancient dialect of the Dotari language repeated several times.

Air vented from the power station outside the engineering room. The banshees didn't react at first, but moments later, they started to fall to their knees and gasp for air. Dozens fell from catwalks and other places they had been climbing to attack the Strike Marines. In the distance, reactors fired online.

King sat down near the transparent wall to watch the banshees suffocating.

Adams went to Moz'in and gave him a big hug. "You're the best crazy old Dotari I've ever met."

"Good work, team. Check your gear and check your buddy for injuries," King said.

Moz'in extricated himself from Adams' hug and typed furiously on the computer station.

Chapter 19

"Hit that ship now!" Valdar touched a Dotari ship in the tank that was heading straight for the *Breitenfeld*. Point defense turrets on his ship slewed toward the target and opened fire. Valdar watched as the oncoming ship closed in, and he realized the math was not in his favor.

"XO, we need—"

The ship lurched forward as the engines went into overdrive. Valdar winced as the sudden acceleration threw off the aim of the defense turrets and hits peppered the Dotari ship. A flash burst from the alien's engine banks and the port thrusters spun off the ship.

"Approaching the *Kid'ran*. Dotari small ships moving to intercept," Egan said

"Gor'al, what types of ships are those?"

"Maintenance and transport, lightly crewed," Gor'al

said. "But they are crewed."

"Understood. Guns, aim for the engines. Do not allow them to ram us."

Lieutenant Clark and his team used programed firing solutions in conjunction with manual controls. Valdar kept his mouth shut and let them work. The chatter of their voices on the commo band soothed him, not like the half-crazy cross talk of his Strike Marines in other types of engagements.

Valdar thought of his godsons, Ken and Jared Hale, wondering if their lives on Terra Nova were a good deal less exciting than what he was going through right now.

The new Dotari tracks suddenly slowed and banked away.

"Gor'al, what is this?" Valdar asked.

"Strange," the old officer said. "They're returning to their fleet positions."

"Active guns, hold fire," Valdar said.

"Sir, we're about to get clear shots on their engines," Egan said.

"Hold…something's off." Valdar tapped fingers against the edge of his tank.

"It appears they are establishing a holding pattern near the *Kid'ran*," Egan said. "All point defense, cease-fire."

"XO, maintain our momentum. I don't want to be caught flat-footed if this is a trick," Valdar said.

"Aye aye, sir. We're picking up transmissions from the *Kid'ran*. A text message, sir?" Gor'al said. "It's from the emergency override channels…recalling all ships. Waking up the emergency crews. There's something else here."

"On display," Valdar said.

Letters typed across the holo tank. C-O-D-M-I-T-T-E-N-S.

"Cod mittens?" Egan asked.

Valdar smirked. "Dotari."

In the holo tank, the letters blinked off and were replaced with G O T T - M I T - U-N-S.

A hailing frequency opened on a larger ship near the *Kid'ran's Gift*. Gor'al opened it.

A Dotari, painfully thin, stared into the view screen. Lines marked his face. Tubes were still connected to his forehead and throat, like he'd just come out of cryo sleep. He warbled something in Dotari, eyes wide with shock.

"Gor'al, I will let you explain. Egan, get me a damage report. The sooner we can recover and build the gate, the sooner we can get home."

Chapter 20

Valdar sniffed a cup of coffee and took a sip. Sneering at the oily black liquid, he made a mental note to figure out who made this pot and relieve them of the additional duty. Though after so many hours on his feet, any manner of caffeinated liquid was appreciated.

Gor'al held his cup of coffee awkwardly. He wafted the steam toward his face and clicked his beak.

"Egan, let's clear the bridge of nonessential personnel for a conference," Valdar said.

"Aye aye, sir. Does that include the Strike Marines?"

"I only see one, and he needs to stay for this," Valdar said.

Egan, Gor'al, and Hoffman joined Valdar near the holo tank that showed ships towing parts of the Grinder into place. In one corner of the holo-tank display stood an image of the first Dotari captain to wake up from the Golden Fleet. He watched the construction efforts with interest.

Valdar leaned his head toward Hoffman. "Have you ever seen a Grinder jump gate under construction, Lieutenant Hoffman?"

"No, sir," Hoffman said.

Gor'al stared at the tank, eyes tracking each development in the tediously slow construction process. "Nor have I, Admiral Valdar. My people are proud to be a part of it."

Terran Alliance ships and the recovered Dotari maintenance vessels worked together to tow the pieces closer together.

"Captain Shin'ji, are you receiving?"

The first Dotari captain to awaken from the Golden Fleet came up in the holo tank.

"Yes, Admiral Valdar. I have a superb video and audio links. Your engineers have been most helpful restoring our ships after the *noorlas* damaged them."

"Good," Valdar said. "This is going faster than we planned, but we need to discuss the elephant in the room."

Egan winced as the Dotari discussed Valdar's

words in rapid, back-and-forth Dotari. Valdar rolled his eyes.

"Sir, I believe we have discussed your use of metaphors while in the presence of non-Terrans," Egan said.

"We have, XO."

Gor'al made several soothing gestures and calmed the hologram of the Dotari captain, then faced Valdar. "I explained the difference between an elephant of Earth and the nearest approximation on Dotari—the Yah'var—which is what the translation protocols put into our language. Then I explained there is no elephant/Yah'var and gave him the conversation tables we use to understand how much of the human language we must ignore to communicate properly."

"Ah…thanks," Valdar said, then waited a moment until he had everyone's attention. "There are more ships than we anticipated. The Grinder has enough energy stored in the control unit—what we call the Keystone—to send only a quarter of the ships in the Golden Fleet to a star system with a Crucible gate and then back to Dotari."

"We can move crews and passengers to other ships," said the recently awoken captain. "There will be a strain on life support, but—"

"It won't be enough," Valdar said. "The math isn't in our favor. My engineers insist we can recharge the Grinder with the Dotari ships' power cores so we can open more than one wormhole. But that will take time—time the Dotari dying of the phage don't have."

Valdar opened a file and tossed it into the holo tank. A graph appeared.

The awoken captain peered over the data. "You wish to send a single small ship through almost immediately. Then the rest of the fleet in intervals. We'll be in the void for…almost half a year. If this is the last hardship before we return to Dotari, my fleet will endure. Besides, almost everyone is still asleep in their pods."

"It may well be longer," Valdar said. "The Grinder isn't designed for this much stress, but the *Breitenfeld* will be the last ship through the last wormhole. I'm under strict orders to bring the Keystone back to Earth. As for the first ship back to Dotari…"

"Yes, of course, Admiral Valdar. I will have the doctors awoken right away," the captain said. He turned to Gor'al and spoke excitedly.

Valdar looked at Hoffman. "Hoffman, you're going back on the first ship."

"Sir?"

"There's still a bit of a journey once you're back in a Crucible system. A Strike Marine officer can smooth out any travel difficulties. My crew took some casualties during the fight, and they need treatment that this ship can't provide. Get them to a medical center. Get the Dotari doctors and the cure to the phage back to their home world and send an update to Fleet Command. I'm dead serious about *Breitenfeld* being the last ship out of here. Every civilian on this Golden Fleet will get to safety before we do. No shortcut home for me or the old girl. Besides, what would you and your Marines do for months aboard my ship besides cause trouble?"

"Yes, Admiral. Idle hands."

"Gor'al, I'll leave you with Egan and our new friend to work out the immediate logistics." Valdar stepped away from the holo tank, motioning for Hoffman to follow.

"You did well, son. This ship and I have been through some close calls, but what you and your Marines did was in keeping with this ship's reputation. You saved the mission and a lot of Dotari lives in the process, and you stopped the *Breitenfeld* from taking more of a beating."

"It was my Marines, sir. I'll pass on your compliments," Hoffman said.

Valdar studied the man, glad he hadn't kept the

controversial Hale persona of other doughboy platoon leaders. "The *Breitenfeld* isn't a museum. I've been keeping her safe for far too long. I'll release her back to the line when we return. She'll need a Strike Marine complement. You interested in the job?"

"Serve here? Under your command?"

Valdar chuckled at the combat veteran's wide-eyed expression. "That's how it works."

"Yes, sir. I'd be honored."

"Good," Valdar said. "Prep your team to return home. We'll link up once my mission out here is done." He shook Hoffman's hand and left the man standing in the hallway, still wearing the same stunned expression on his face.

Chapter 21

The halls of the Dotari hospital were quiet, almost mournful as doctors and nurses went about their duties. Acorso stopped to write out a few notes on a data slate. This day was no different from the last. Dotari stricken with the phage continued on the disease's uneven path. The latest round of synthesized antibodies had failed tests…again. The sound of muffled shouts echoed down the hallway through shut doors. The shouts grew louder, and he could've sworn he heard English.

Acorso swiped a finger down one side of his slate and opened a call to Bi'mal. The line pulsed, but she didn't answer as banging echoed down the hallway.

"I can't work like this," Acorso muttered, squaring his shoulders and going to the doors. One burst open just before he reached it and Lo'thar bumped into the doctor, knocking him off his feet and sending his slates everywhere.

The Dotari wore dirty combat armor and clutched vials in one hand.

"Acorso?" Lo'thar looked at him in a near panic. "Where is my daughter?"

"Look at you. You should know better—we have strict decontamina—"

"Where is my little girl!" Lo'thar's cry echoed off the walls.

Acorso pointed down the hallway.

"Room seven."

Lo'thar ran past the doctor, nearly slipping as he made the sharp turn into the doorway.

Hoffman, in even worse-looking armor, helped Acorso off the floor.

"Who the hell are you? What's the meaning of all this?" Acorso smoothed out his white lab coat with as much dignity as he could muster.

"Armor's normally supposed to be the cavalry." Hoffman motioned behind him to a Dotari in red doctor's robes trimmed in gold thread, which Acorso had never seen before. The Dotari moved with a sense of dignity and purpose unlike the medical personnel he normally worked with.

"But as a Strike Marine, I'll fill in," Hoffman said. "Come on. Lo'thar said you'd want to see this."

"See what?" Acorso asked.

"A miracle." Hoffman took the human doctor by the elbow and led him to the room.

Inside, Lo'thar knelt beside a bed. Monitoring equipment beeped around a painfully thin Dotari girl, and air lines ran into her nose and down her throat. Lo'thar clutched her hand in his; the cluster of vials lay atop the blankets.

"How is she?" Hoffman took a post against the wall.

"Stage four," Acorso said quietly. "She lost consciousness days ago. There's nothing I can do but keep her comfortable…but if Lo'thar's here…and you're here. There were rumors about the *Breitenfeld*."

"*Gott Mit Uns*," Hoffman said.

The Dotari doctor with the gold-embroidered robes entered the room. He warbled something in Dotari and touched his fingers to the edge of his beak.

"Trin'a," Lo'thar ran his hand down the side of her face, "Daddy is here now."

The Dotari doctor pressed his shoulder to Acorso's

and looked at him with a glint in his eye.

"Dr. Acorso, I presume?" the Dotari asked with an accent Acorso had never heard before.

"Correct. I don't believe we've met. And I thought I knew every physician on the planet."

"Jin'al." His quills rustled. "I was Dotari's chief healer many years ago. Let's see if I still have my touch." He pulled a sleeve back, revealing an intricate device similar to the gauntlet Hoffman bore. Wan blue light glowed through looped wire.

"What on earth?" Acorso asked. "Why have I never seen—"

Hoffman touched his shoulder, then the Marine put a finger to his own lips.

Jin'al went to the opposite side of the sick girl's bed and hovered his palm over her forehead. He panned his hand slowly over her body as he and Lo'thar spoke to each other in Dotari.

"He's…you found him in the Golden Fleet?" Acorso asked.

"We did. Along with a lot more like him," Hoffman said.

"Admiral Valdar comes through again," Acorso said. "You know I served on that ship."

"The mission went about as easy as you'd expect," Hoffman said with a frown.

Jin'al reached over his patient and picked up the cluster of vials. He plucked one out and snapped it onto his antique device. One hand tapped at holo keys Acorso couldn't see.

"Lo'thar?" came from the doorway. A Dotari woman peeked around the frame. She was panting as if she'd just finished a sprint.

"My love." Lo'thar pulled away slightly from his daughter as his wife rushed into the room and Lo'thar put an arm around her shoulder.

Jin'al spoke to the parents quickly. Acorso tapped the translation bead in his ear.

"Of all the times for this thing to go on the fritz," Acorso said.

"Classical Dotari," Hoffman said. "All the ones we woke up speak it. The Dotari we know can understand it well enough, but our software can't figure it out. I'd guess that Grand Surgeon Jin'al's telling them about the bone-marrow transplant."

"'Grand Surgeon,'" Acorso said. "They explain their cure beyond the transplant?"

"I'm a Strike Marine, not a biologist," Hoffman

said. "Though they mentioned you and your gene-mapping work several times on the way over here."

"Nice to be appreciated." Acorso crossed his arms. "But I want to see her smile again more than I want credit."

Jin'al held his hand over Trin'a's neck and said something to her parents. They put their hands atop his and a small tube snaked out from the doctor's device and pressed against the girl's skin. Dark fluid flowed into her.

The doctor laid the parents' hands on their daughter and went back to the door.

"Prognosis?" Acorso asked him.

"Poor, but it should improve," Jin'al said. "Will you accompany me on my rounds?"

"Certainly." Acorso heard Hoffman sniff and saw him wipe beneath an eye. "Lieutenant, are you…"

"Just go," Hoffman said. "I'll stand watch."

Acorso took one last look at Lo'thar and his wife huddled next to their daughter, and left.

****

Lo'thar woke up as dawn's light cut through the windows. He picked his face up from Trin'a's bed and worked his beak from side to side. His wife clung to him, still sleeping. Lo'thar shrugged his shoulders, wishing the engineers could design armor that wouldn't itch so much. He gave his daughter's hand a quick squeeze…and her tiny fingers squeezed back.

He looked at the head of the bed and found her looking at him, her eyes open and clear.

"I knew you'd be here when I woke up," she said.

Lo'thar nudged his wife and she woke up with a snort.

"Trin'a?" she asked.

"Who's the big hummie?" Trin'a asked. "He's been watching us for so long."

Lo'thar looked back at Hoffman, who nodded with a smile.

Trin'a's skin was still the wrong color and there were bags around her eyes, but she was awake, and Lo'thar couldn't believe it. Lo'thar hugged his daughter gently and she giggled, a sound that almost broke his heart.

He held her for what felt like forever. When he turned back to thank Hoffman, the Marine was gone.

****

Hoffman made his way through the Dotari

spaceport. The facility was alive with energy, video screens full of images of the first small ship from the Golden Fleet. Two more ships had arrived since Hoffman and his team made the jump and the Dotari in the city seemed like they were on the verge of a holiday.

He found his Marines on a landing pad, lounging around a medical transport Mule, the gurneys inside empty of any patients. They'd dropped out of their armor in the hours since he'd left them to take Lo'thar to the hospital. Adams and Booker were wearing sleeveless undershirts with combat fatigues and boots that were untied. Garrison didn't even have a shirt. Duke wore a faded combat uniform, but it was clean if not well pressed. Max relaxed in an improvised hammock.

Opal saw him first and stood from a supply crate he had taken to carrying around for a stool. "Dotty better?"

"She's not out of the woods yet, but she—and the others with the phage—are doing better," Hoffman said.

Duke spat a wad of dip spit into a plastic bottle. "At least this whole thing wasn't for nothing."

Max sat up from the hammock. "We'll be going home soon?"

"Hope so," Hoffman said. "Not that this isn't a nice planet, but I wouldn't mind getting back to Earth."

"Good, the Dotari don't have shit for booze on this planet," Duke said.

Garrison lifted what looked like a milk container. "Is that what this is? I didn't..." he looked around sheepishly, "...I didn't know that."

Booker and Adams laughed at him, moving in unison to bump him and cause him to stagger.

"You want me to draw blood? I suspect Lance Corporal Garrison is in violation," Booker said.

"Who's ready to go home?" Hoffman asked and got a cheer from his Marines.

King, in pressed fatigues, came down the Mule ramp. "Got a priority message from Fleet Command. We're on the next transport back home. And we're still on commo blackout."

Hoffman raised an eyebrow. News of the mission's success and the Golden Fleet's recovery was no secret on Dotari. That they had to remain on blackout struck him as odd.

"Guess I can surprise the kids," Max said with a shrug.

"Pilots are on their way back now," King said. "Get into a full uniform and look pretty. I bet there's a dog-and-pony show waiting for us soon as we get home."

Hoffman thought of the mission debriefings he'd have to give. As the ranking officer that returned from the mission, he had a feeling just about everyone on Earth would want to know why the *Breitenfeld* hadn't retuned yet. At least his team could enjoy some time off.

He ran the back of his knuckles against the stubble on his cheek.

"Anyone got a razor?"

Chapter 22

Moz'in walked through the capital city of Dotari. When he came to a plaza, he stopped in the center, turning in a slow circle to admire the mosaic work that depicted a harvest scene from long ago. The setting sun cast orange rays across the highest of the buildings and backlit an urban skyline he'd never hoped to see again. Flashing lights to warn aircraft blinked on the tallest spires as dusk settled across the city.

The sound of civilization was all around him, a low murmur of people going about their lives. He heard the steady rhythm of vehicles and people talking. Not far away was a Dotari food vendor hawking his wares and the image reminded him of his childhood. He thought about sampling the food but decided against it.

He remembered the annual festival in the square.

His imagination overlaid ancient times on top of this peaceful place. The horrors of his fight against the banshees seemed distant. What was he doing here? All his adult life had been spent training for the great voyage and now he was back where he started.

Nothing could be better. The Xaros drones were a thing of the past, defeated by the Terran Alliance and the Dotari. He was home, but it would take a while for him to really feel like it.

He walked the streets of the city, exchanging pleasant greetings with street vendors as they packed up their wares and headed home. There would be other food carts at night, and restaurants, but the Dotari people were not notorious for late-night revelry. During the voyage back from the Crucible, he'd spoken often with the humans. Duke and Garrison told him stories of human behavior he still did not believe. Why would a soldier fill another soldier's boots with shaving cream? What was shaving cream? Booker cautioned him not to trust their revisionist narratives of their past adventures.

He stopped near a bridge crossing the river bisecting the city and leaned on the railing. Looking up, he remembered watching the sky and trying to see the flagship of the Golden Fleet being built in orbital space docks. All his friends had trained diligently to escape the Xaros invasion and find a new home. Ancient Pa'lon had told him it was the only way.

Now there was a Crucible that could take ships across great distances.

Several families walked along the street, heading for the park, where there was to be an evening concert. He wondered if Duke and Garrison would consider this "nightlife." From what Booker and Adams had told him, he doubted it. All he really knew was that he never thought he would see such a sight again.

As a couple holding the hands of the two young girls passed by him, Moz'in stepped aside and tried not to draw their attention. He was a thousand years old and not sure how they would receive him. The accents of their speech were complicated and interesting.

He sat on a bench and listened to the passing conversations, content to wonder at all the mysteries his home now held for him.

Chapter 23

The Mule circled the Phoenix spaceport three times before it headed for a landing pad. Hoffman was nervous for reasons unknown, but he soaked in the excitement of his team. Max was so happy and anxious, it was giving Hoffman butterflies.

"Hell, yeah," Garrison said. "There's no way they can keep us from our leave time now. Party party." He wore a shockingly floral shirt in all the colors of the rainbow. It stretched across his chest, revealing the muscular build that his armor concealed. Most people looked more buff in their pseudo-armor gear, but not Garrison. He was lean to the point of absurdity despite his extraordinary strength. His pants were slightly baggy and he wore open-toed shoes. On orders from Fleet Command they received the moment after their transport made the jump back to Earth, the entire team wore civilian clothes. His team was officially on leave…but still on commo blackout.

Exactly why his team had to be in civvies perplexed Hoffman, but wearing something other than combat armor was a nice change of pace.

"First order of business is to get you clothing that fits," Booker said to Garrison. Adams laughed hysterically. Since the ordeal on the *Kid'ran's Gift*, the two women had bonded more than they had prior to the mission, even though they remained opposites in almost any dimension of human behavior that could be measured.

Whereas Garrison and Duke appeared ready to drink cheap margaritas at a tacky bar, Max looked like he was dressed for church. He bounced his feet in front of his chair, where he sat against the wall of the Mule.

"Can you stop doing that?" King said.

Max immediately stopped moving his feet but started chewing his fingernails.

Opal wore fatigues and remained seated toward the fore of the small civilian ship that had carried them from Dotari. An addendum to their orders was that Opal remain out of sight. Opal didn't complain, but Hoffman would figure out what was behind all this.

The Mule touched down. The pilot and crew went through several checks before the ramp could be opened to allow them out. As homecomings went, it was underwhelming. There were no marching bands or lines of waiting families. In fact, the entire spaceport seemed almost abandoned, like it was on lockdown.

Hoffman led his team down the ramp and looked around. He was about to go back to the ship and ask if they'd landed in the wrong spot, when Max's wife and three children burst from the terminal and sprinted across the tarmac to jump on him. Somehow, he caught all three of them and managed not to fall. The children talked excitedly as Max nodded and tried to listen to everything they were saying. Tears rolled down his wife's face as Max promised to take them to every amusement park on the planet and buy them about a thousand stuffed animals.

Although Hoffman felt deep satisfaction as he watched each member of his team, the depopulated nature of the spaceport bothered him, so he went on alert without ruining the moment for his Marines. Moments later, a man with a jug head and wispy platinum hair made his way toward them from the same door Max's family had used. He wore civilian clothes, but his gait and bearing marked him out as a military man.

I'm not gonna like this, Hoffman thought.

"Lieutenant Hoffman, I'm Commander Kutcher," the man said. "Your team will drop their gear inside the terminal, then you'll be treated to an all-expense paid trip to the Mauna Loa recreation facility on Hawaii soon as that shuttle arrives. I do need you for a moment. In private." He gestured back up the ramp.

Hoffman signaled for King to take care of their Marines and noticed the gunnery sergeant kept a watchful eye on Kutcher.

Opal stood up as Kutcher and Hoffman came back into the cargo bay.

"Home now?" Opal asked.

"Good lord, he's real," Kutcher said.

"You want a hug from him?" Hoffman asked.

"Sorry," Kutcher said. "I'm a navy man. Never saw many of…those."

"There is no R&R facility on Mauna Loa, sir," Hoffman said.

"Not that we tell people about. I'm with intelligence. We had something of a security incident that we need your team to handle."

"This have something to do with the Dotari?"

"Not a thing with them." Kutcher pulled a picture—

a physical picture, not an image on a data slate—from a pocket and handed it to Hoffman.

Hoffman looked at it, expecting a long-range shot of an enemy facility or super weapon. Instead, it was a picture of the blond woman from the New Bastion incident. "Her? What about her?"

"She's been busy since you've been gone. We've encountered her on three different planets, using a different alias each time. We believe she's part of a rebellion against Earth, a rebellion that has its roots deep inside our military, which is why you're not officially back on Earth. If anyone asks, you're still on the *Breitenfeld*. Unofficially, your team's been reassigned to intelligence for covert action. Mauna Loa's not that bad of a place to cool your heels."

"Rebellion? That's impossible," Hoffman said. "The colonial administration and Terran Union are—"

"Not…all there is. The Ibarras have their claws in everything. I'll explain more to you on Hawaii."

"Ibarras?"

Kutcher nodded slowly. "I understand what you and your team went through was a bit unusual…but we need you on point for this mission. The Ibarras are the single-greatest threat to the Union. I'll explain more once we're on Mauna Loa. The beaches are fantastic. So's the food."

Hoffman looked at Opal. The doughboy grunted.

Hoffman met and held Kutcher's gaze. "We're Strike Marines. We'll be ready when the mission calls."

THE END

The Story continues in **Rage of Winter**, coming Spring 2018!

FROM THE AUTHORS

Hello Dear and Gentle Reader,

Thank you for reading The Dotari Salvation. We hope you enjoyed Lieutenant Hoffman and his team's adventure, much more on the way!

Please leave a review on Amazon and let us know how we've done as storytellers, you're feedback is important to us.

Drop us a line at Richard@richardfoxauthor.com and scottmoonwritesanovel@gmail.com.

Also By Richard Fox:

The Ember War Saga:
1. The Ember War
2. The Ruins of Anthalas
3. Blood of Heroes
4. Earth Defiant
5. The Gardens of Nibiru
6. The Battle of the Void
7. The Siege of Earth
8. The Crucible

9. The Xaros Reckoning

Terran Armor Corps:
1. Iron Dragoons
2. The Ibarra Sanction
3. The True Measure
4. A House Divided (Coming Spring 2018!)

The Exiled Fleet Series:
1. Albion Lost
2. The Long March
3. Their Finest Hour (Coming 2018!)

About Scott Moon

Scott Moon has been writing fantasy and science fiction for over thirty-six years. When not reading, writing, or spending time with his awesome family, he enjoys playing the guitar, Brazilian Jiu Jitsu, and watching movies. Dog guy. Fan of the military. A career law enforcement officer, he served on the SWAT team, Gang Unit, Exploited Missing Child Unit, and helped catch a serial killer. He is also a co-host of the popular Keystroke Medium show (www.KeyStrokeMedium.com)

More Books and Stories by Scott Moon

The Chronicles of Kin Roland

Enemy of Man
Son of Orlan
Weapons of Earth

Read the entire Chronicles of Kin Roland trilogy on Kindle Unlimited!

SMC Marauders

Bayonet Dawn
Burning Sun

Son of a Dragonslayer

Dragon Badge
Dragon Attack

Dragon Land

The Fall of Promisdale

Death by Werewolf

Grendel Uprising

Proof of Death
Blood Royal
Grendel

Darklanding
Episode 1: Assignment Darklanding
Episode 2: Ike Shot the Sheriff
Episode 3: Outlaws
Episode 4: Runaway
(A new episode of Darklanding will be published every 18 days!)

Please visit http://www.ScottMoonWriter.com for more information.

Join the Scott Moon Group on Facebook to talk about books and stuff:
https://www.facebook.com/groups/ScottMoonGroup/

Printed in Great Britain
by Amazon